Arizona Son Rise

George Davis

PublishAmerica
Baltimore

© 2008 by George Davis.
All rights reserved. No part of this book may be reproduced, stored in a retrieval system or transmitted in any form or by any means without the prior written permission of the publishers, except by a reviewer who may quote brief passages in a review to be printed in a newspaper, magazine or journal.

First printing

PublishAmerica has allowed this work to remain exactly as the author intended, verbatim, without editorial input.

All characters in this book are fictitious, and any resemblance to real persons, living or dead, is coincidental.

ISBN: 1-60610-620-1
PUBLISHED BY PUBLISHAMERICA, LLLP
www.publishamerica.com
Baltimore

Printed in the United States of America

DEDICATION

To my wife Betty for her commitment and support that made this book possible and to my daughters, Jennifer and Emily, for their willingness to tell me what I needed to hear.

To all Native Americans whose cultures continue to create inspiration across this land, whose struggles shall never go unnoticed and whose spirits have risen from the ashes.

ACKNOWLEDGMENTS

My heartfelt thanks to

PublishAmerica for taking a chance on me.

My father, George, Sr. for giving me the gift of "storytelling."

My family and friends including Kathleen, Sharon, Dick, Chuck, Mario, Pat, Dave and so many others for having faith in my ability to write this book.

Jenny for making me look good.

Gabby Deering who was my inspiration for Gabriela. Love to you always, Georgie.

CHAPTER 1

In the years before the end of freedom, the Arizee Indians waged wars with other tribes as well as the armies of the United States, Spain, and Mexico, all of whom sought to take God's land as their own. So it was the Arizee Indians were engaged in yet another battle to preserve their way of life. It was not their nature to fight, they were a peace seeking tribe, but when provoked they rose to defend their people and God's land. As is often in battle, to the victor goes the spoils.

Such was the case in eastern Arizona when the Arizee were engaged in an altercation with an isolated Irish settlement. The victory resulted in the capture a young woman named Meara. Meara's capture fulfilled the prophecy by Laspirtia, spiritual leader of the Arizee, that a son of mixed heritage would be born to the Arizee Chief Lone Eagle; and this son would help his people gain the respect of the white man.

Fearing for her life, Meara fought, kicking, clawing, and screaming, as she was captured. She was large in stature, very strong and fought heroically as the battered and exhausted warriors tied her on an Indian pony and began the journey back to their village where she was destined to be Lone Eagle's wife

Much to Meara's surprise, her arrival at the village was heralded with celebration and ceremony. Her treatment by the Arizee people was exceptional, for a woman with red hair and green eyes was thought to be sent from God to produce many brave warriors. Three young Indian women attended to her every need. In return Meara knew she was expected to accept Lone Eagle as her husband. To Meara's surprise, Lone Eagle wisely gave her time to assimilate into Arizee life and appreciate her lofty status before arranging for their marriage ceremony by the holy priest, Laspirtia. Meara found her new husband to be a kind and majestic man who treated her with compassion and respect. Within a year of their marriage a son, whom they named Eagleson, Son of Lone Eagle was born. At his mother's request, he was also named James after his maternal grandfather. He was the first son born to this chief of the Arizee nation. There were four other children born to Meara and Lone Eagle, but none were as revered as their first born.

GEORGE DAVIS

Except for his green eyes and his brown hair, Eagleson resembled his father. Tribe members were in awe of this young boy who at the age of six was physically fit and already five feet tall. He was quite handsome and spoke both Arizee and English, the latter being taught to him by his mother. By his eighth birthday, Eagleson's education and training were the responsibility of Lone Eagle and the elder members of the tribal council. In time Eagleson became a gifted pony rider, accurate marksman with a rifle, as well as bow and arrow. At an age much earlier than other Indian boys, he was well on his way to becoming a brave warrior and leader.

Because of his birthright, Lone Eagle took Eagleson to meet the infamous Apache chief Geronimo. He and Geronimo had formed a strong, long standing alliance, and Lone Eagle wanted to present the future Arizee chief to Geronimo. The young Eagleson made quite a favorable impression on the great Apache chief, who expressed approval of Lone Eagle's son as his successor. Eagleson never forgot meeting with Geronimo. It was that day that he knew that he would never disappoint his father and realized that his father's pride demanded that anything less than being a respected chief of the Arizee Nation was unacceptable.

CHAPTER 2

Eagleson continued his education with the tribal council. He studied under Lone Eagle's most trusted braves who taught him the skills necessary to become a great warrior. Laspirita taught the young man all he knew about the spirit of the great Arizee God and the spiritual passage into eternity. He was an exceptional student who by age 15 had completed his education and mastered the skills necessary to become a great warrior.

Lone Eagle felt his son had come of age to participate in his first hunting trip. Eagleson knew that he was a top marksman when shooting at fixed targets, but wondered how he would perform when faced with a charging bull or herd running wildly to escape certain death. The hunting party of twenty braves readied themselves for a long difficult trip. Since the buffalo had decreased in numbers, they had to travel many miles to find a herd. After traveling several days without seeing buffalo, the hunting party came upon a herd of wild longhorn, remnants of cattle left in this country by the Spanish many years ago.

After careful planning for the hunting party, Lone Eagle signaled to his son, who knew it was now his turn to show bravery and marksmanship. Eagleson's breathing became rapid as he felt his muscles tense and his brain race, trying to remember all he had learned from his father. Although longhorns were large targets, they were fast and difficult to bring down. Eagleson knew that it required much effort and expert skill; but he was willing to approach this difficult challenge and make his father proud.

Lone Eagle pointed to a large bull leading a herd of cows who was trying to maneuver the herd away from the hunters. Lone Eagle sensed a challenge for his son and told Eagleson to approach the bull from his left. With his senses sharpened in readiness, Eagleson moved up on the trotting herd. He knew a well placed shot through the shoulder would explode the bull's lung, killing him instantly. The cattle in the small group picked up speed, alerting the bull that danger was approaching. Still Eagleson stayed up with the bull and cocked his gun to shoot. Suddenly the bull stopped. He was so close that Eagleson could hear the animal's breathing and grunting. He slowly directed his pony to the left of the bull, raised his rifle and took aim. Unfortunately, just as Eagleson pulled the trigger to deliver the lethal blow, his pony stepped in a gofer hole and threw him to the ground. The shot, which did not kill the bull as expected, hit his neck, and only served to enrage him. As Eagleson tried to recover from the fall, he saw the bull directly in front of him. Blood spewed from the wound and the ground shook as the snorting bull pawed, ready to charge.

Eagleson was terrified, as his father approached and shouted, "Stand and shoot, stand and shoot!"

As the bull began to charge, Eagleson heeded his father's words and once again aimed the gun at the bull's shoulder, but the spent cartridge from his previous shot had not been discharged. Quickly he pulled the new bullet into the chamber, knowing it was up to him to kill this bull since his father was out of range. Jim took aim on his victim who charged, spewing thick mucous from his expanded nostrils. Eagleson finally discharged his rifle at point blank range and immediately rolled to the bull's left to avoid the giant beast. The bull tumbled and turned end over end sliding past Eagleson as he expounded an immense bellow.

Lone Eagle arrived and put another piece of lead into the bull. He ran to Eagleson, dropping his rifle so he could help his brave son. The young man was dazed, but regained his composure as his father spoke to him. Thinking the bull was dead, Eagleson smiled proudly at his father.

What happened next was indeed shocking. As father and son stood together, they heard a noise behind them. To their amazement the determined bull was back on his feet and focused on revenge. Lone Eagle had no recall as to the location of this rifle. In his haste to reach his son, he had not planned for the need to defend himself. The bull, bleeding profusely, charged toward his victims. As Lone Eagle lunged to push Eagleson out of the path of the bull, a shot exploded hitting the big bull in his right eye. The bull dropped dead directly in front of them. Lone Eagle wondered if God had possibly interrupted the deadly charge with a bolt of lightning. But then he saw that Eagleson had picked up a rifle and delivered the fatal shot. On his first hunting trip, the young man had not only killed a bull, but saved his father's life. Just then Eagleson saw his pony was not as fortunate and lay dead from his fall.

His father said, "No, my son, your pony did not die from the fall. The pony died from sheer freight." With utmost pride Lone Eagle looked at Eagleson with a smile. "My son, you stood your ground and showed great courage; today you have become a brave warrior."

Lone Eagle proudly shouted to the hunting party that Eagleson had saved their lives. He was pleased and humbled by his father's praise. He demonstrated bravery and courage in the face of adversity and was rewarded with his father's approval. Pleasing his father was of immense importance to Eagleson. It became the motivating force in his life.

That afternoon, two Arizee warriors from different generations came together for a treasured custom. Lone Eagle and his son each took a slice of liver from the very bull that attempted their murder. Both father and son ripped off a mouthful of the raw warm organ and from the depths of their shaken bellies roared out an Arizee conquering scream. As they looked at each other, eyes still wide with lingering fear and hearts still pounding with adrenaline, a sense of unity and family radiated between them.

This was truly a great day in Eagleson's life. He not only killed a longhorn bull to feed his people, but he also saved his father's life, and probably his own from a bull hell bent on killing.

CHAPTER 3

On the trip back to the village, Lone Eagle, as usual, had a small force in front of his hunting party to avoid ambush by anyone looking to steal their bounty as an easy meal. Other Indians usually knew to stay away from the fearless chief, but Lone Eagle took no chances. The Arizee did not tolerate thievery among their own or from other tribes. They were quick to defend their people and possessions and were infamous for punishment of enemies.

As the hunting party approached the crest of a small mountain, they heard yelling and saw Shotomish, one of Lone Eagle's warriors, riding furiously toward them. He brought news that a large force of soldiers was just outside of their village. Lone Eagle raised his hand in a peaceful gesture to calm his warriors as he and Shotomish rode slowly to meet with their leader. In an attempt to avoid any misunderstanding, Lone Eagle spoke in English.

He immediately recognized Col. John Thompson, a man with a reputation as a gritty and thick-skinned soldier. Even though Thompson took a tough stand concerning Indians, he personally never fully understood the reasoning of the government in its antagonistic treatment of them. But being a dutiful soldier, he obeyed orders.

Thompson nodded and was first to speak, "Lone Eagle, our patience with the Arizee is being exhausted with their continued theft of the ranchers' longhorn cattle."

Lone Eagle defended his tribe, "We have made it clear. We only kill the wild cattle left by the Spanish over the past hundred years. Cattle that are branded are not harmed in any way."

With disrespect that made it clear that he had heard this before, Thompson angrily replied, "Indian lies, always lies! Do not lie to me. The ranchers are becoming increasingly angry and impatient with the killings, and the government wants it stopped now."

Realizing that nothing beneficial could come from words exchanged in anger; Lone Eagle accommodatingly apologized to the Colonel for any mistakes that his tribe may have made in unintentionally killing ranchers' branded cattle.

Thompson demanded that Lone Eagle ride with the soldiers to the fort to discuss what action should be taken to stop the unlawful cattle raids by the Arizee. Thompson let it be known that two braves were being held hostage in an attempt to assure that Lone Eagle would comply. Realizing he had no choice but to return to the fort with the soldiers, he sent word to the rest of the hunting party to return to the village. He and Shotomish, accompanied by Colonel Thompson and his soldiers, headed for the fort to negotiate a peaceful solution to the problem.

As they approached the fort it was immediately evident that there were over 100 soldiers with rifles raised prepared for an attack by the Arizee. A loud shot broke the silence just missing Shotomish's head.

From the fort, another errant shot followed, and an officer yelled for a cease fire. "For God's sake hold your fire men before you kill Col. Thompson!"

Lone Eagle shouted, "There is no need for shooting. We come in peace; we do not come to harm you. We only want to find a peaceful solution to the longhorn problem."

His words caused a profound silence to settle over the fort.

Thompson, still unimpressed, ordered Lone Eagle and Shotomish to relinquish all weapons and approach the doors. Since both had discarded their weapons after the initial meeting with the soldiers, they proceeded cautiously and soon found themselves surrounded by soldiers who felt no shame in taunting and shouting obscenities at the two Indians. Lone Eagle remained quiet and focused on the purpose of this meeting. Upon entering the fort, both were ordered to dismount and hold their hands above their heads. Several soldiers had their rifles cocked and ready to fire, while a few others searched for concealed weapons, as all soldiers assumed Indians were devious. Lone Eagle and Shotomish were treated with much disrespect and humiliation.

Once inside a large building, Col. Thompson began the discussion. "It is well known that your people are thieves and want to force the ranchers to leave this territory by killing their herds. And if that doesn't work, then you will burn the homes and kill the ranchers and their families. You mean to take what you feel is yours, no matter the cost. Well, the army is here to stop you. So, you can do it peacefully by ending the raids on cattle or be prepared to fight until there is no trace of the Arizee in this territory."

Several of the soldiers laughed and continued their name calling. Col. Thompson turned to his soldiers and barked orders for them to hold their tongues.

Lone Eagle, who was troubled by these most disgusting lies, bowed his head as if in prayer. After a moment of uneasy silence, he raised his head and stared into Thompson's eyes. In a strong, but calm voice he said, "I am but a humble servant of God. Why do you ridicule and humiliate me? You and I are both leaders of our people. We are both entitled to the respect of our positions. I am a leader of a proud people who just want to live in harmony with nature, which includes both the white and red man. I do not seek to harm you or the ranchers, but we must have meat to survive. With all the many thousands of cattle owned by the ranchers, why do they want the wild cattle too? We need them to feed our families."

Col. Thompson, outwardly portraying the harsh rigidity of an Army officer whose assignment it was to deal with the Indian problem, seemed startled by the respect from Lone Eagle after the humiliating treatment from the soldiers. There was something about Lone Eagle that was beyond any man he had ever met. As Lone Eagle spoke his voice commanded attention, and he presented himself in a forthright manner. The Colonel saw in Lone Eagle a man of honor and peace and knew he was dealing with someone extraordinary. His demeanor changed, and he welcomed Lone Eagle and Shotomish into his private office. The scene turned from one of accusation to one of reasonable men trying to find a solution to a difficult problem. The Colonel expressed his government's discontent with what was perceived as the Arizee's theft of the ranchers' cattle.

"You see, my general is pressured by government officials who are, without exception, influenced by ranchers." In trying to be honest and forthright with Lone Eagle, Thompson said with some emotion, "I must tell you that the days of Indian control of any part of Arizona are numbered and your people will have to adjust to reservation life as provided by the U.S. government. The government and ranchers are using the cattle thief issue to promote reservations as a way to control the Indians." He hesitated a moment to emphasize his point. "Lone Eagle, there are many white men coming, more than you can imagine. It will not stop. They want to take your land and under the banner of Christianity save your souls." Thompson stopped just short of an apology when he said that all of this would come to pass without regard to how the Arizee accepted their fate.

Lone Eagle appealed to Thompson, "Why can we not live together and share the great gifts of life provided by our common God?"

The Colonel shook his head. "The white man does not see God as you do. The Christian God has a white face. Your people are considered heathens who have progressed very little over the ages. The white man must tame the savages and show you the way of the Lord." Thompson leaned back in his chair and heaved a sigh knowing that Lone Eagle could not understand the realities of a Christian nation at war.

Lone Eagle said no more, realizing that he may have found someone in the Army who, at the very least, was honest with him about the possible destiny of his people. Col. Thompson had given him a better understanding of the future. In return Lone Eagle's intellect and sincerity had challenged Thompson's view of the American Indian. This meeting had a dramatic effect on Thompson and materially influenced both men. Lone Eagle and Thompson gained a profound respect each other.

However, none of this made any difference in the immediate cattle problem. In an effort to maintain peace, Lone Eagle agreed that his people would make a better effort to assure that any cattle branded by ranchers would not be shot. In return Thompson said he would speak with ranchers about making an improved effort to brand all stock and maintain better control of their herds.

Before Lone Eagle left the meeting Thompson cautioned, "I will do my best, but I cannot be responsible for reprisals by the ranchers should they not be satisfied with the arrangements we have discussed."

Lone Eagle nodded as if to say he understood. He said that his people would continue to pray to God for future friendship between Indian and the white man.

Thompson, seeing an Indian chief who sounded more like a follower of Christianity rather a heathen, stood and shook Lone Eagle's hand. "I hope your God is listening to your prayers. You will need Him because it is most certain that your people will be wiped out if they do not submit to the white man."

Lone Eagle remained silent for a moment and then said, "God will be with us in life and death."

Col. Thompson expressed his sentiment as he said to the great chief, "Save your people! Go to the reservations now."

CHAPTER 4

As Lone Eagle and Shotomish rode back to their village Shotomish asked, "What will happen to us when the soldiers come to kill us?"

"Don't worry my brother, God is surely with us, and if we should die by the hand of the soldiers, our flesh may rot in the sun and be devoured by the buzzard, but our souls will be with God."

"And our innocent woman and children—will they be slaughtered, too?"

Lone Eagle looked at Shotomish, "My brother, have faith in God that our families will be cared for by our Spiritual Father. Our killers will have to answer to God."

Still Thompson's warning weighed heavy on Lone Eagle. He feared for his people and worried about white men too numerous to count who would come to take God's land.

Aside from Thompson's warning, the hunting trip was a success. Much meat had been gathered for the coming winter months. There was great celebration of thanksgiving, both for the hunt and for a brave son as a successor to Lone Eagle.

The women cooked the meat for the feast as the warriors danced and chanted in high spirits, wearing the skins of the longhorns. The women were careful to save meat for use during the long winter when the earth was quiet and coated in white. But for now the pungent smells of cooking beef saturated the evening air. The meeting with Col. Thompson and the frustration over the accusations by the U.S. Army were replaced with great rejoicing that Lone Eagle and his young son had survived the terrifying ordeal with the bull. As was their ritual, Lone Eagle led his braves on a trip to the nearby mountain to pray to God for the blessings of a bountiful hunt. Eagleson accompanied his father on his first trip to the holy mountain, which had a profound affect on him.

Upon returning to the village, Lone Eagle saw two horses near his tent. The horses were not Indian ponies. They had saddles with blue and yellow tassels attached. Lone Eagle galloped toward his tent and recognized the horses belonged to the U.S. Army. He had just met with Col. Thompson and could think of no reason for soldiers to be in his village. He dismounted and ran into the tent to find two U.S. soldiers dressed in dusty blue uniforms adorned with brass buttons. They were standing over Big Horse shouting. Since Big Horse understood no English, he could only shrug his enormous shoulders in confusion. Lone Eagle moved between the soldiers and Big Horse.

"What business do you have at my village? You should send ahead to request a meeting because few of my people speak English. Your voices have fallen on ears that do not understand."

The soldiers told Lone Eagle the cattle ranchers were complaining of Indians stealing their cattle in night raids.

Lone Eagle was mystified and replied, "This situation was settled at a meeting earlier in the day with Col. Thompson."

The oldest solider who appeared to be in charge began to speak. "Col. Thompson? We know nothing of a meeting with Col. Thompson; we have been sent by Gen. White, the senior officer with the 15th Calvary, who is in charge of the area of residency of the Arizee. He sent us in response to complaints of Indians killing cattle."

Lone Eagle again defended these accusations by saying that the Indians were only hunting wild, unbranded longhorns. As the situation escalated, Meara came from the tent and faced the soldiers in an effort to confirm her husband's words. This only served to inflame the situation with the soldiers accusing Lone Eagle of being a rapist of white virgins and the father of bastard sons. Lone Eagle let these insults go without response, for retaliation served no purpose with these lowly messengers.

As the soldiers turned to leave, the older soldier warned, "The next time we come regarding cattle theft; there will be bullets and death to you ruthless savages. Your people should go and live on reservations like other Indians!"

Lone Eagle knew a response could lead to destruction of his village, as he had heard stories of armies burning Indian villages and killing, men, women, children, and even their dogs. This total disregard for the sanctity of Indian lives had become acceptable to the U.S. Government. Lone Eagle realized that the lack of communication within the Army could lead to tragic consequences. He prayed to God to take care of his people when the evil comes to kill the innocent.

CHAPTER 5

One week passed without further accusations or threats from the Army. Yet, as with all moments of peace, it was is destined to be interrupted in such trying times. Early one morning, an Army messenger rode to the Indian village under a white flag with a request from Gen. White to attend a peace conference at the fort with the ranchers for the purpose of resolving the accusations of thievery. The meeting would be at the fort in three days, and Lone Eagle could bring as many as twenty armed braves for protection.

When Lone Eagle asked if Col. Thompson would be in attendance, a very nervous soldier replied, "My orders say that all relevant representatives of the Army will be included in the meeting."

Although he was uneasy about trusting the Army because of their lack of integrity in breaking treaties for their own benefit, Lone Eagle agreed to the meeting.

He said, "Go tell your leader that Lone Eagle will arrive at the fort in three days when the sun is at its highest in the sky. As we come in peace, my braves will not be armed."

The young soldier was taken back when he heard these words. He knew that for Indians to come to the fort without arms was stupid beyond comprehension. He thought *Who is this naive leader of such a great Indian Nation?* He turned, mounted his horse and rode away.

The night before the meeting the village celebrated with a Feast for Peace. Laspirita lead a religious ceremony to give Lone Eagle knowledge and powers from God to negotiate a peaceful solution and make wise and beneficial decisions.

Laspirtia warned that the soldiers may have lied about their intent, and that Lone Eagle must keep a keen eye for deception. "Beware of those who you want to trust, for they may betray you."

Lone Eagle thanked Laspirita for his concern, but said the possibility of peace was worth the risk. However, he instructed 50 armed warriors to trail his peace party and wait out of sight of the fort in case of treachery by the Army.

The following morning Lone Eagle, Shotomish, and three council elders, and 20 braves prepared for their peace mission. Lone Eagle hoped for a conciliatory meeting with the soldiers and ranchers. Even though Eagleson asked to go with his father, he was told to stay at the village to help protect his mother and those who stayed behind. Also he felt that a young boy accompanying this peace mission may be seen as a weakness by the Army.

The journey to the fort was uneventful. When the peace party approached, they were met by two soldiers and directed through the heavy wooden doors. As they entered, the fort seemed almost deserted. He thought about his 50 warriors who were watching just out of sight with instructions to attack only if they heard gunfire. Lone Eagle, Shotomish and three elders dismounted and were led to the General's office. There were several officers, as well as armed ranchers, in the office, but no sign of Col. Thompson.

Lone Eagle was the first to speak. "We come unarmed in peace to this meeting to address the misunderstanding as to the wild longhorn cattle."

Gen. White replied, "Well now, ya see, that's where we differ. The government does not see this as a misunderstanding. We see it as outright thievery. The ranchers and U.S. government are out of patience with the Arizee."

Lone Eagle was dumbfound at the General's response and repeated the purpose of his visit. His message was not acknowledged by Gen. White, who immediately ordered the arrest of the Indians. At that time, a dozen soldiers entered the office with guns drawn and surrounded the peace delegation.

Lone Eagle pleaded with the General, "Please, I ask you with my pride, do not do this. It will certainly cause bloodshed among all of our people."

The General took great pleasure in telling Lone Eagle that at this very moment his soldiers were attacking his village and arresting his people for relocation to a reservation. The soldiers had orders to kill those who resisted. Suddenly gunfire erupted outside and Lone Eagle realized that this meeting was just a ploy to intimidate his people and force them into reservation life.

Unable to contain his anger Loan Eagle yelled "This army is evil and will be cursed by the great God in heaven for evil injustice to the Arizee people!"

Before Lone Eagle released his last breath from speaking, the General drew his pistol and shot him point center in the head, killing him instantly. The General immediately threatened the same to the rest of unarmed peace delegation. Big Hawk, second in command, did not understand what the General said and threw his arms in the air in what the General viewed as an attack. A nearby officer turned his gun on Big Hawk and killed him with a shot to his chest. The remaining Indians submitted to the soldiers. The Army, along with ranchers, captured or killed the Indians that Lone Eagle had brought with him into the fort along with the braves who were waiting just over the hill. Even though it was much too late, Shotomish realized why there were so few soldiers in the fort.

Gen. White knew that he had to cover this crime. So he decided that all Indians who entered the fort would be executed. So one by one, the remaining members of the peace delegation were senselessly murdered.

Back at the village where the Arizee went about their daily activities, gunfire erupted. Eagleson and his mother thought that the Comanche were attacking. Meara though it was probably only a few braves as the Comanche were no longer counted in large numbers. Then they both realized that the attackers were soldiers along with a few Comanche mercenaries who had been recruited to fight with them so as to make the murder scene appear as a Comanche attack. The few not killed were captured for relocation to a reservation.

Against the fervent pleas of their mother, Eagleson and his oldest brother rose up to save their people and defend the hollowed land. His brother was shot and killed instantly. Eagleson fell to the ground with a bullet wound to his left shoulder. His mother and sisters fell over his body in an attempt to save his life while the brutal, unprovoked attack continued. As his mother and sisters shielded Eagleson, soldiers on horses galloped by, killing both sisters and wounding his mother. Just as a soldier was about to shoot Eagleson, he fell struck by a bullet from Eagleson's nine year old brother trying to save his family. As in battle, he who is standing one second may fall the next, and his brother was then instantly struck and killed by a Comanche. When the attack ended Eagleson realized that his brothers and sisters were dead. His mother, who was unconscious, lay heavily against his wounded body. He sensed she was dying. As he felt her chest rise and fall, his ears became infected with the cracking sound of air desperately trying to fill his mother's lungs. When he tried to move her in an attempt to make her more comfortable, he saw the wounds to her head and stomach, no doubt making for a slow, painful death. He closed his eyes and prayed to God to stop all this death and destruction and allow him to see his family in the Land of God, where they would be together forever. As a sharp pain suddenly exploded in his head, he slipped into unconsciousness.

CHAPTER 6

Eagleson awoke in an enormous tent; its deteriorated condition evidenced by the sunlight that filtered through holes in the top and sides. The tent was filled with the moans of the wounded and dying and the repugnant smell of sulfur and decay infused the stale air. Many white men and a few women, dressed in blood stained clothing, attended to the injured. His wounded shoulder was wrapped with what once had been white cloth. His whole body felt stiff, and he was in tremendous pain. It was a miracle that he was alive. His thoughts turned to his father and mother. *Where is my father; is my mother alive? Will my father come with his braves and rescue me from this hell?* He began to yell his mother's name. Over and over he shouted for his mother without response to his pleas. As he attempted to move, he noticed that his hands and feet were bound by leather straps that confined him to the bed. He recalled that his father told him about the evil land where souls awaited punishment for sins. Realizing this was a possibility, Eagleson closed his eyes and prayed for God to spare him and his family. What Eagleson thought was the evil land was actually an Army field hospital, and he was a prisoner, bound to the bed and considered a dangerous enemy.

He gradually became lucid enough to realize that he was not going to make any progress toward freedom by yelling or tugging at the straps. However, his screams had caught the attention of a soldier, who responded with a slap to his face and a knee to his side.

"You are lucky to be alive, you worthless Redskin. Had it been up to me, I would have skinned you alive and fed you to the coyotes!"

As the soldier cocked his arm to strike again, an officer caught his hand, spun him around and pushed him to the ground.

In a loud voice, he addressed the evil soldier, "This man is a human being, not some piece of shit that you can defile anymore than the army has already done!"

The soldier rose to his feet, saluted the officer and ran from the hospital.

This savior apologized to Eagleson and said, "I promise that soldier's actions will not go unpunished." The officer introduced himself as Col. John Thompson.

Eagleson recognized the man as the officer who had met with his father on the way home from the hunt. Yes, this man was called Col. Thompson. Rage filled his heart and tears his eyes as he tried his best to reach this liar.

Eagleson yelled, "You evil, evil man. You killed my tribe for no reason. I will kill you and feed you to the buzzards to defame your soul and condemn you to hell!"

Thompson sat at the side of his bed for what seemed an eternity, saying nothing as the young Indian cried for revenge. When Eagleson could cry no more, he noticed something very unusual about Col. Thompson. He, too, was weeping.

Thompson spoke to Eagleson, "Please be calm. I want to help you."

Eagleson continued to yell, "Hate you, hate you. You betrayed and killed my people. I hate, I hate your army."

Thompson replied in a quiet voice, "I, too, cry for the loss of your people. Your father was deceived by some bad people who wanted the Arizee to leave their land. By attacking and killing your people, they sent a message that Indians must relocate to a reservation or be killed. The U.S. government sent a well trained group of soldiers to subdue your people without my knowledge. Like your father, I was deceived so as not to interfere with the shameful slaughtering of your tribe."

Eagleson asked, "What did my people do wrong?"

Thompson replied, "Your tribe did nothing wrong; you were in the way of what the white man calls Manifest Destiny."

"What is this Manifest Destiny?"

Thompson responded, "It is the notion that the white man was ordained by God to seize all the land and covert the Indian savages to their religion."

Eagleson said, "There is but one God. We have the same God. Why would He want to have the Arizee people treated so cruelly?"

Trying to help the young man understand Thompson replied, "Our God doesn't want the Arizee killed. Men who commit and justify such murder are not true believers, but are instruments of Hell, craving wealth and possession of the land."

Eagleson looked at Thompson and cried out, "I need my father! Where is my father?"

The Colonel pulled a chair closer to the young brave's bed, for he knew he must tell him of his father's death.

"Eagleson, your father came to the fort on a mission to make peace with the army and ranchers. He was met with deception and killed when he spoke of resistance to being forced onto a reservation. In fact, all of his peace party was killed, including the armed braves who had followed him to the fort."

Although tears came to Eagleson's eyes, Thompson was surprised how he took the news of his father's death. But he was an Arizee, part of a people at peace with God where death was but a passing and not the end of life. Eagleson tried to be brave, but this young boy could not stop the tears that flowed down his face. Thompson touched Eagleson's hand and sat in silence trying to ease his loss.

Eagleson could see that Thompson was not to blame for the murder of his people. But that did not lessen the hatred for the blue uniform with the yellow stripes and brass buttons that Thompson wore. Eagleson looked again at his painful shoulder which continued to bleed through the bandages. Thompson summoned someone to help the young man. Immediately Dr. Smith came to help Eagleson.

Thompson was walking away when Eagleson asked, "Col. Thompson, where is my mother. I know my brothers and sisters were killed in the massacre, but my mother was still alive when she tried to protect me from the murderers."

"Your mother lives, but rest for now. You need to sleep. I will return in a few days, and we can talk about what has happened to your mother."

Eagleson nodded in appreciation of Thompson's kindness.

CHAPTER 7

It was over a week before Col. Thompson returned. He hoped the young man would heal both physically and emotionally before telling him about the grave condition of his mother. Dr. Smith indicated that Eagleson's physical health had improved primarily due to his youth and excellent physical conditioning. The doctor, however, cautioned Thompson against pushing him emotionally. Eagleson had been calling for his mother, asking the nurses if they had seen her. Thompson understood but whatever the case Eagleson deserved to know the truth about his mother.

When Thompson walked into the field hospital, he saw Eagleson sitting in a chair next to his bed. It gave him comfort to see the young man physically stronger. But he could see that the young man was still emotionally fragile. Eagleson tried, but could not hide the tears in his eyes.

Thompson spoke in Arizee, "Eagleson, brave warrior, you look fit and ready to ride a pony."

Eagleson smiled at a friendly face and replied in his native tongue, "Welcome my white friend who hopefully brings me happy news of my mother."

But Eagleson saw the sadness in Thompson's eyes and knew that the news was not good. Thompson had learned that the Arizee were simple, honest people who expected truthfulness. Thompson's manner did not hide the truth, and Eagleson prepared himself for bad news. Using an old barrel for a seat, Col. Thompson, speaking in English, began the sad account of the dreadful day of the massacre.

"Do you remember what I said about the U.S. government's motives for asking your father to a meeting? The ranchers with great influence in the government wanted all the land owned by the Arizee."

Eagleson politely interrupted and speaking in broken English said, "What do you mean Arizee owned land? We do not own the land. It is owned by God and only through His permission are we allowed to live and travel the land. We are only caretakers of the land."

Thompson who had underestimated the simplicity of Arizee life replied. "The ranchers and some soldiers were being paid by the government to round up all the wild cattle and deliver them to the Army as a food source. But the Arizee were in the way. Since the number of buffalo had decreased, they knew the Arizee were hunting the wild cattle. The government gave the army money to pay the Indians for land rights. Reservations were established for Indians displaced by land purchases. Unfortunately, the ranchers and some in the army were thieves. They decided to take the money from the government, but not live up to the agreement. The ranchers and army officials decided to claim the cattle and seize the land, keeping most of the money and paying the Arizee little or nothing. Even the Indian Agency and other government officials whose jobs were to assure fair treatment of the Arizee were paid by the ranchers to look the other way. Those Indians not cooperating were killed in an effort to scare others onto the reservations with appalling conditions and worthless land where homes are rotting army tents and food of poor quality."

Eagleson looked at Thompson in bewilderment. Thompson had gone beyond what Eagleson could understand, but felt it necessary to let him know that this injustice was too against the white man's laws.

He continued hoping the young boy could begin to understand. "Your father was a revered and fearless Arizee chief who could not be manipulated by the ranchers or the army. This caused the rancher and army officials to take desperate measures. When threats failed, lies were concocted saying that Lone Eagle had rejected all offers of money, food and home for his people and had sworn to slaughter all white settlers living in Arizee territory. The next step was a conspiracy to kill your father. The ambush was set up under the pretense of a peace conference at the fort. Gen. White, knowing that I would not agree with the merciless slaughter, sent me away from the fort on a mission the day of the meeting. When I returned the execution was over and all evidence of it was gone. The official statement from the General was that your father had attacked with many warriors, and Lone Eagle was killed in defense of the fort."

Eagleson was enraged. "My father went to the fort unarmed seeking only peace."

Thompson said "Yes, I know that now. I learned it from a sergeant who would not participate in the slayings. He told me to go to your village, and I would find your entire tribe slaughtered. That is when I found you and your mother and brought you both here to the hospital. Sadly the sergeant was later shot by a firing squad for cowardice because he refused to slaughter the Arizee. When I confronted the arrogant General about this, he denied the unjustified attack on your father. He then opened a closet door and proudly produced trophy scalps of the Arizee whom he said had attacked the fort. It was a horrendous, morbid sight."

Thompson saw that tears were once again spilling from Eagleson's eyes. He, no doubt, realized that his father's scalp was among those kept by the malicious general. Thompson embraced him as the young boy grieved for the loss of his father.

Then Eagleson pulled back remembering his heritage. "I have to be brave as I need to lead my people as their chief."

But when he realized there were few if any Arizee to lead, he began weeping. His father was dead, as were his brothers and sisters. All he had left was hope that his mother was still alive. He looked into Thompson's eyes and asked, "Where is my mother, is she alive?"

"Your mother is alive, but very ill. She is in another part of the hospital. In time I will take you to her."

Through his sorrow, Eagleson found hope.

CHAPTER 8

Several weeks passed with Eagleson steadily gaining physical strength, but emotionally haunted by his loneliness and yearning for his mother. Because he was under arrest, he was not allowed to leave the prison section of the hospital, even to visit his mother. He was, however, kept abreast of her health by Thompson who was looking in on her regularly. Eagleson was gradually seeing him as a good friend even though he still strongly hated his blue uniform with the gold buttons. Thompson's information about Meara could not replace her loving embrace. She was the only family Eagleson had left. He tried to control his emotions and anger. If he desired any degree of freedom, even if it were on a reservation, he knew he would have to act like the passive Indian the white man wanted.

During his recuperation Dr. Smith asked a young Arizee girl to give him further instruction in the English language. Even though his mother taught him English, he graciously accepted the instruction, and he enjoyed the company of an Arizee, even though she was not from his tribe. Through this young girl he became more versed in the white man's language. Eagleson realized that the English language was so well developed it allowed for communication on any subject. And from what he saw all the white man's tribes spoke the same language, unlike his brothers from other Indian nations. Such common language probably went a long way in preventing misunderstandings and conflicts. He came to believe if his tribe and his chiefs had spoken and better understood English; the massacre that killed most of his tribe may have been avoided. However, Eagleson did not blame his father because lying and deception from the army in any language were evil. Eagleson knew that he needed to better understand the English language and other ways of the white man if he were going to make a life for himself in the white man's civilization.

When Col. Thompson again visited Eagleson he brought his young son, Joey. The boy was but three years old and innocent of the hatred that existed between the white man and the Indian. Joey ran to Eagleson and gave him a giant hug. "Me love you, my friend."

Eagleson did not know what to say or do other than to return the hug. He felt love and joy that he once had with his family. Joey was a happy little boy and being with him brought back fond memories of Eagleson's lost childhood. He looked at Eagleson with unconditional love. The harshness that was etched upon Eagleson's face softened to reveal peacefulness that had long been missing. The bond between Eagleson and Joey began that day and continued for decades to come.

After Joey left with Thompson's aide, there was yet another surprise for Eagleson.

Col. Thompson told him that he would be able to see his mother. For the visit, Eagleson was given some used clothes the hospital was discarding. Although the clothes were foreign to Eagleson, he thought they were a definite improvement over his current outfit, which was a sheet with holes for his head and arms. In the front of the pants was some kind of metal strip that he had no idea how to use. Thompson saw that Jim was confused and offered an explanation.

"That's called a zipper and you use it use it when you have to urinate."

Eagleson replied, "Urinate? What's that?"

"You know—relieve yourself."

Eagleson looked confused and then suddenly understood. "Oh, you mean go pee!"

Thompson laughed. "That's right," and felt somewhat relieved that he did not have to go further into an explanation.

Thompson called a guard to remove the shackles, and together they proceeded to an adjoining tent, where Eagleson was immediately overwhelmed by the conditions that were blatantly pathetic and heartbreaking. There hundreds of Indians lay sick and dying. A smoky fog hovered in the tent almost blocking the light from the dim glow of the oil lanterns, which flickered in and out just like the life of the people that lay helpless in this crowded tent. Indians were lying on the ground tightly packed in this small tent, many of them pleading desperately for help, though Eagleson was sure nothing of the sort would ever come. He hoped deep within his soul that this was not real, perhaps a nightmare. He prayed that he would wake up. His hopes were quickly swept away by the harsh bite of reality gnawing at his heart. It was real. This was happening, and even when he closed his eyes he could still hear the voices of injustice. The tent was filthy and the stench of death hung in the air, hovering over the patients, reaching out with ghastly arms just waiting to snatch the life to which they so tentatively clung. His stomach rolled from the foul odor, and he prayed that his mother was not in this dirty place. His gut told him otherwise but was quickly relieved when Thompson explained that his mother had been moved to another building with considerably improved conditions. Somehow, though, it did not make him feel much better; the fact that she had once been here was heartbreaking.

Eagleson was glad when they left this tent and entered the one housing his mother. It was a brighter place where the air was fresher and filth was not apparent. There were many women attending to the wounded who were lying in clean beds with clean bandages. They walked toward the end of the tent to his mother's bed.

Thompson approached Meara and said softly, "Are you awake? I have brought your son to see you."

They both heard a soft murmur, not distinguishable as any specific word. Thompson, who had visited Meara several times, hesitated a few moments and warned Eagleson that his mother was not as he may have remembered.

"She has lost a lot of blood and is not able to speak or understand very well."

"It does not matter, she is my mother, and she is all that is left in my life."

Thompson looked at Eagleson and said with earnest, "Young man, you show great bravery. Your father would be very proud of you."

Eagleson walked to his mother's bedside. Her aged face and frail, thin body made her look much older than her years, and he was momentarily taken back. It seemed not so long ago that he remembered a much younger spirited mother.

Thompson placed a hand on the young man's shoulder and said "You have to realize that your mother was very near death when we found her. She asked that I save her son who was hurt badly. She has fought hard to live and see you once more. Most of the time she stares straight ahead and calls for you and your father. I believe her love for you is what has kept her alive." Thompson paused and told Eagleson the sad news that the doctors did not expect her to live much longer.

Eagleson nodded in a gesture that said he understood. But he could not hide the tears that spilled from his eyes. As a brave Arizee warrior, he wiped his tears and went to his mother. Her eyes were open but without expression. He called her name. She blinked and a slight smile graced her face. However so slight, it meant the world to Eagleson. He hugged his mother's wilting body and told her how much he loved and missed her. Meara continued to smile while salty tears fell from her left eye, making it apparent that she was partially paralyzed on the right side of her face. As best she could, Meara began softly chanting a lullaby in Arizee, occasionally calling out, "My loving little Eagle."

Thompson drew back from the bedside, as he too shed tears. He was angry at what his army had done to such decent people and wished the murderers could see these people as human beings, instead of savages lacking in emotions. He stepped outside the tent and vomited from his sickened stomach. Thompson realized that he could no longer serve in this unfair and inhumane army. On that day, at that moment, he made his decision to resign. He hated himself for being part of the horror and a contributor to so many deaths.

When Thompson stepped back into the hospital tent, he saw that Meara's spirit had brightened after hearing her son's voice, and even though her vision was indeed blurred, she could see the boy in her mind just as she had seen him before the massacre.

She leaned shakily on her left elbow speaking softly to Thompson, "You have given the joy of God to this lonely old crippled woman by bringing my son who I feared was dead. May God bring health and as much happiness to you and your family as you have brought to me." She gripped Eagleson's hand and looked into his eyes saying, "My brave warrior son, always remember that Thompson cares enough for you, me and our people to make sure we had this meeting. He saw in us what he sees in his own family without regard to the color of our skin. He is truly a man like your father, whom I hope to be with soon. Always remember my words. And to you Thompson, as I go to be with my husband, I plead with you to help my son become a chief so his people will know him as they knew his father, Lone Eagle. I have lived to see and embrace the son I love. I am ready to go to my husband and rest."

She embraced her son with tears spilling aimlessly down her cheek. No one within hearing distance, soldiers, doctors and patients alike was without tears as Meara lowered herself on the bed and slipped into a peaceful sleep. She was still alive, but very weak. Her face was drained of color, but Thompson and Eagleson noticed a subtle calm radiating about her. Perhaps she had seen her husband ready to welcome her into the afterlife.

The next day Meara died from her wounds. She was ready to pass as she had seen her son and knew he had a friend to help him through life. Even though it was against Army regulations, Thompson had Meara's body removed from the hospital and returned to the lonesome tribal burial ground. There, as Indian custom dictated, an Arizee holy man gave her the burial rites before cremating her spiritless body. A few unfamiliar Arizee faces, along with Col. Thompson and Eagleson, who had been released in Thompson's custody, attended. They chanted the prayers of celebration that assured Meara and Lone Eagle were reunited.

As the two friends returned to the hospital, Thompson talked about how difficult it would be for Eagleson to make his way in the white man's world while trying to keep the dignity of his birthright. Thompson told him that he thought a white man's name would be helpful. So Eagleson decided to use his maternal grandfather's first name, James. And to honor his friend, he added Thompson to his name. James Thompson Eagleson, still son of the great Arizee chief, but tied forever to his kind loving friend.

Col. Thompson promised Meara that he would look after her son. He told Jim, as he now preferred to be called, that while he wished to make him a son, he had five children which consumed his meager officer's pay. However, he was hoping that as a civilian he would be making more money and in a better position to help Jim. Thompson, who had grown to love Jim, told him something that he would never forget. He promised Jim that he and his family would someday make up for all the terrible injustice that had befallen him at the hands of the government.

"I do not know when, and I surely do not know how, but I will try to help you attain the level of respect in the white man's world as your father, Lone Eagle had in the Indian world. I pledge this to you."

Jim felt blessed to know this fine human being and held this promise in his heart.

CHAPTER 9

When Jim was released from the hospital, he was sent to a nearby reservation. This captivity clearly brought a difficult change in his young life. He found that reservation life was crippling and oppressive. The Indians were poverty stricken and many were in poor health. They lived in cramped quarters on worthless land. He saw many unfamiliar Indian faces and was startled when he attempted to communicate to strangers, who were confused by his language. This created a barrier that was noticeable in attitude and friendliness. He found that his English was often more useful than his native tongue. Most of the inhabitants were Crow, Pawnee and Cheyenne who were at times bitter enemies of the Arizee. Serious conflict fueled by long standing ethnic differences exploded daily. This situation made transition into reservation life very tumultuous, and challenged Jim as he matured into his destiny.

Jim's first days were spent trying to overcome the communication problems. So when he saw an older man sitting outside of a hut smoking a pipe chanting familiar Arizee words, he was naturally curious.

He spoke in Arizee. "Hello, old wise man. I am called Jim, and I want to know your name."

The man stopped chanting, opened his eyes and look at Jim. The old man thinking that Jim was an odd name for an Indian said, "Jim, no understand."

Jim realized that he needed to use his Arizee name, Eagleson, Son of Lone Eagle.

When he heard this, the old Indian's eyes widened and a smile came on his face, "Son of Lone Eagle!"

This brought great pride to Jim, knowing that someone on the reservation remembered his great father. The old man led Eagleson into his hut and offered him water and jerky.

He said, "My name is Manso, and I was once a spiritual chief of the Sachewo Arizee. I knew of Lone Eagle, and he was much respected by all Arizee for his wisdom and bravery. I heard that your tribe was massacred by soldiers in a vicious attack."

Jim recounted the details of the attack telling Manso that most of his family had been killed instantly, but his mother later died of her wounds. Manso told Jim that he had been captured by a Comanche, who told him that dead or alive he was worth $10 from the U.S. government.

"I chose to live so I surrendered peacefully. I now know that death would have been better than suffering here on the reservation. I saw that Comanche on the reservation not long after I arrived. When he went to collect his reward, the army wanted to give him only $5. When he objected, he was arrested and brought to the same reservation."

Manso, having difficulty seeing at a distance, brought Jim closer and said, "You speak like an Arizee, you act like an Arizee, but your hair and eyes are not so dark. Your hair is brown like the white man and your eyes are green like trees in the spring."

Jim told him that his mother was a white woman who had been captured by the Arizee.

Manso warned, "You tell no one else about your mix or you may be killed as a white man sent to spy on Indians. When you meet other Indians, first talk about your father and then it will not matter what you look like."

For the remainder of the day, the two new friends talked about the days of freedom with Manso having the best and longest stories. As the day ended, Jim realized that he had to find a place to live and inquired of Manso how to do so. The old man directed him to a building where he could take care of the matter.

"There is a soldier named Johnson. Tell him I will need help with my business so ask for a place next to me. Be sure to tell him of our friendship or you get worthless supplies and a poor location."

"What business do you have?"

"I make spirits, whiskey, and I will need your help. Now, do as I tell you."

"Show me the way, old man."

Manso pointed the way to Jim. As he walked to the building, he noticed more deplorable conditions including stagnant water teeming with mosquitoes and green scum. There was no specific place for human waste except large holes scattered around the reservation. The stench was repulsive as the soldiers who guarded the perimeter of the community gave limited amounts of lye to cover the waste. Also, there were many filthy, naked children running around in groups trying to steal what they could to feed themselves and their families. The pathetic conditions brought pain to Jim's heart. He felt he was seeing the death of Indian civilization, where various tribes' identities were meshed together as irrelevant characteristics. Sadness swelled inside this son of Lone Eagle. He realized that in a matter of months, his tribe had been disseminated into a mixture of Indians with little respect at all for tribal culture, religion or self pride. When he reached the building, he took a few moments to remember who he was. He stood with his arms at his side and his posture as straight as his father's arrow.

He opened the door and stepped into the gray building. A most unimpressive building from the outside was an atmosphere of richness on the inside. There were bottles of medicines, food, clothing, building material, and even weapons throughout the building.

Jim had taken no more than a few steps inside the building when a large soldier called out, "Hey Injun boy, why ya coming into this building without being invited?"

Jim, still recovering from the shock of what he saw, mumbled in English, "I am Jim Eagleson. Manso sent me to get some supplies. Are you Johnson?"

The big man yelled, "Speak up boy so I can understand ya!"

Jim repeated himself as the big man approached.

"That's my name. Now did you say you are a friend of Manso?"

Jim nodded in the affirmative.

The big soldier then shouted at him, "Ain't ya the lucky one cause I was ready to kick your red butt out of here."

Although Jim first felt anger, he knew that he had to choose his response carefully so he simply nodded his head in the affirmative because, as he saw it, there was no other choice.

He then yelled again right in Jim's face, "What ya want boy?"

Jim said he was new to the reservation, and Manso sent him for supplies. Jim also told Johnson that Manso said that he should ask for the piece of land next to him.

The big man had a puzzled look on his face and blurted out, "Why in the world did Manso tell you all this stuff? What made you so special? Did you know Manso before he came to this reservation or what?"

Jim found his nervousness and his lack of fluency with the English language was causing him to have trouble keeping up with Johnson's questions.

Gathering his courage, Jim said, "Manso knew my father, Lone Eagle and because of their friendship he is trying to help me."

"Who the hell is Lone Eagle?" the solider blurted.

Johnson's response startled Jim because he was sure everybody knew of his father.

But before any more was said Johnson yelled, "Heck it don't matter no way who Lone Eagle was—all you Injuns are the same to me; just a pain in the backside, if ya know what I mean."

Jim was quite happy when the discussion of his bloodline ended because it seemed only his relationship with Manso was important to Johnson.

Johnson seemed to soften a bit as he talked of his relationship with Manso. "I've done a lot for that old man. Ya see when I first got to this place a ways back; he saved me from some savage Injuns who were trying to scalp me. I owe him."

Then quickly turning back to his ornery ways, Johnson abruptly asked Jim to step out of the building through the doorway. He told Jim that he was never to come into the building again without permission.

"Even Manso asks permission to get in here."

Jim yielded to the big man's orders, and Johnson went on to say, "The reason you can't come in is cause this stuff is top secret and only big shot generals and politicians can come in without my permission. That stuff you saw is for some white folks and not for your savage butt. Ya got that straight boy?"

Jim nodded his head in agreement once more. Johnson stepped back into the building to get Jim's supplies. No more than a minute passed before the door opened and Johnson appeared holding an old army blanket, a piece of canvas and a bag of what looked like hard bread. He handed these to Jim reminding him again never to come into the store without permission. Jim was discouraged by the old supplies particularly after seeing the better looking supplies on the shelves. He was being given another dose of the status of Indians—low class supplies go to low class people. With that look of not giving a damn what Jim thought, Johnson, who was close enough for Jim to smell his liquored breath, turned to walk away and the door closed with a loud bang.

Then Johnson opened the door again and said, "Don't say nothing about what ya seen. If ya do, I'll tar and feather ya little red butt like we do back home in Texas."

Jim started to ask a questions when the door slammed in his face. He got the courage to yell, "Johnson, can I put my tent next to Manso?"

From behind the door, he heard, "I don't give a rat's ass where ya park ya red butt. Just don't tell nobody what ya saw in this store else ya die the same day ya tell."

Jim did not reply, but walked quickly away from the building, glad that his encounter with Johnson was over.

The canvas was dry rotted, easily torn; but based on what he had seen of the other Indians' tents, it was pretty good. Jim gathered the material and food into a big bundle and walked toward Manso's hut.

Jim thought the stuff he had seen in the store was probably for the Indians, but would end up being used by some important white men. Yes in Jim's mind, he had seen in that room yet another example of lying and cheating by the Army—just like they had done when they killed his father and his people while pretending to want peace.

As he approached his piece of land, Jim noticed that the entire wood frame of his hut was in place. Manso was sitting next to three Arizee men, one sporting a giant toothless smile. Manso introduced Jim to his grandsons Mansolin, Noteto, and Nabeto, the toothless one.

Amazed at how much work these men had completed, Jim thanked them for their kindness.

Mansolin spoke for his brothers. "We are happy to help the son of Lone Eagle."

Jim nodded and turned to Manso. "Old wise one, where did you get the wood?"

Manso said, "I have big connections and can get anything Lone Eagle's son wants!" But he added a warning. "Eagleson must follow Manso's orders and do what he says. Don't ever go in white mans' building without storekeeper permission. If you do, he will kill you. The stuff in the building is no business of the Indian. The way I get what I want is to protect the store from Indians who meddle in white man's business. Manso will not be there for you if you try to challenge the white man!"

This seemingly friendly old man turned very serious when it came to the white man. Jim wished Manso had given him this warning before he went to the store and wondered how Manso found out so quickly about this confrontation with Johnson. Jim later discovered that Manso had connections all over the reservation and was usually the first to know any news.

Then the old man's stern face immediately turned serene. "I should have told you this sooner. I am sorry. You see, Johnson has had many troubles with bad Indians so he is always mad at every Indian. When he lived in Texas many years back, some Comanche tortured and killed his wife and children. Johnson was away and found what was left of them when he returned home. So he hates all Indians, except a few harmless old ones like me. But, understand he would no doubt kill me over most anything if he got mad enough."

Jim responded, "Johnson told me that you had saved him from being scalped, and he is beholding to you."

Manso responded, "That is true. Johnson made some Crow braves mad when he cheated them out of supplies. Three Crow held the big man down ready to scalp him. I stopped them by offering each one a bottle of spirits. So, Johnson was lucky that day. The best thing for you is to stay away from him!"

While daylight remained, Jim and Manso's grandsons completed his home while Manso told more stories about Johnson and protocol for reservation life.

Life on the reservation brought many new trials for Jim. He found that adjusting to the latrine area would be among the most difficult. Jim was obviously use to disposing of bodily waste outdoors, but he wasn't use to the embarrassment of doing it in front of others and in a ditch that was filled with days, if not months of human waste. Jim tried to take his new life in stride while he dreamed of leaving the reservation some day. His body adjusted, but his mind was another thing all together.

CHAPTER 10

Jim was maturing into an impressive young man. His brown hair and vivid green eyes made him unique among the Indians on the reservation. He was taller than most Arizee, who were as a rule, somewhat short in statute. His unusual characteristics were definitely of his mother's heritage. He had a muscular build and stood out among all the younger Indian men. Most of Jim's peers paid no attention to his unique appearance and respected him for his ancestry and his tolerance. Jim's specific characteristics were certainly of no significance to the soldiers and guards on the reservation. As far as most of them were concerned, all Indians were the same, nothing more than a short step up from the primitive.

Ten years passed with little change in living conditions on the reservation. Misery defined daily life. Older people died much faster than babies were born. Jim feared one day that there would be no Indians, which seemed to be the white man's plan. Had it not been for the friendship and promise of John Thompson, Jim would have lost faith in everything.

His relationship with the now retired Thompson and his son Joey continued. Jim thought of himself as the boy's older brother and Joey was particularly appreciative of their relationship since his siblings were all older girls. He also liked being friends with the son of an Arizee chief. John encouraged their relationship so that Joey would not grow up thinking that Indians were savages, as was too often reflected in books at his school.

Jim introduced Joey to a sport that he had learned from his mother. She taught him and his brothers and sisters a game similar to baseball. They would use round pieces of wood or rocks wrapped in layers of rawhide forming a ball that they would throw to each other as well as hit it with a stick at a target. The young boy loved the game and played every time he visited the reservation. Their relationship flourished through Joey's childhood, but they gradually lost touch as Joey grew older and eventually the Thompsons' moved back east.

Jim stayed in contact with John Thompson for many years after his family moved. Jim felt that John may have stayed in the army and been promoted to

General had he not publicly defended the Indian race against mistreatment. John sent Jim money each month, and he proudly saved it to use when he left the reservation, which would take much longer than Jim ever imagined.

CHAPTER 11

Manso and his grandson Mansolin were constant companions of Jim. They shared a tragic past that they tried to erase with their new friendship.

Manso was 60 years old as best as anyone could guess. He spent most of his time sitting outside his tent praying, chanting or offering counsel to his fellow Indians. His charisma and respect were such that he counseled members of all tribes and on occasion even white men. Jim later found out that Manso's sitting had very little to do with his physical needs, but instead his height. Mansolin told Jim that his grandfather was part Cheyenne therefore taller than most Arizee, except for Jim. He did not want a focus on his height. He wanted to disguise his Cheyenne heritage lest he would fall out of favor with his Arizee brothers. So Manso remained seated most of the time claiming his aging body prohibited him from standing or walking distances. It was decided that this should remain a secret among friends.

Manso's favorable relationships with many of the soldiers were bolstered by the operations of his business. Even though it was illegal, he was heavily into making whiskey for anyone who could pay the price. Most of the time the soldiers were paid off to look the other way. Because of the demand for the spirits, Manso gladly welcomed Jim as one of his assistants. Manso's experience as a spiritual leader gave him the knowledge to distill juice of green cactus into a very potent and much coveted brew. It was said when the once powerful chiefs would contemplate the future of the Indian, they found Manso's brew helpful to their meditation. The army soldiers were, without a doubt, the best customers particularly since the Indians had little or no money. Manso, with his solitary knowledge of making whiskey, was increasing his personal wealth, as well as his value and influence on the reservation. Jim realized why Manso always seemed to have access to the best.

On the night before the Christian Sabbath, better known as Saturday, the white men would get a load of fresh brew and go to the hills to drink. On occasion, the soldiers would get drunk and look for merriment within the walls of the reservation. There had been a number of recorded attacks on Indian women during those times; but as usual army officials blamed offensive acts on the Indians. So often these attacks were not even reported. Such conflicts between the white man and the Indian were prevalent on the reservations and were further aggravated by alcohol consumption both by the white man and the Indian. It was on the reservation that Jim acquired his taste for alcohol—a taste that was a curse for the rest of his life.

As their friendship grew, Mansolin and Jim often talked late into the evenings sharing memories and what they knew of the white man's world. Jim found out that Mansolin also knew of the game of baseball. He received his knowledge of baseball from Jesuit priests on a mission to Christianize his tribe. They presented the Indian boys with baseballs and bats hoping a game respected by civilized white people would be a bridge to making the Indians more acceptable. Jim's interest and participation in this All American sport would be a great equalizer in his future.

Word spread through the reservation about the game. It did not take very long for the Indian men to start playing. The young men and boys played often; but as with beginners, they were undisciplined and had only elementary knowledge of the game. That was true until Jim first pitched and hit the baseball. Jim's immense physical talents, as well as the instruction from Mansolin, allowed him to excel at baseball and teach it to others. It was this game that helped define Jim's life and provided a sport to help the men of the reservation pass the time. Because baseball was an accepted sport of the white man, it seemed to help ease the racial tensions between the white soldiers and the Indians. At first, the army allowed the Indians to only play against each other. The Indians formed teams loosely organized by tribes, but often the game would erupt in fights. To counter this, the Army mandated that each team have players from different tribes. When the soldiers played, Indians were prohibited from playing on their teams. Segregation was strictly enforced. But still the army promoted baseball as a common interest of both soldiers and Indians.

As expected the Indians' equipment and playing field, as well as their knowledge of the game, were inferior to those of the soldiers. But this did not stop the soldiers' interest in their games. It was common to see the white soldiers watching the Indian games. That sometimes resulted into gambling, which was against Army regulations; but often tolerated as a form of entertainment. It was just one of many illegal activities that were overlooked.

Jim was thankful to Mansolin for rekindling his interest in the game that his mother loved so much. He rewarded Mansolin by teaching him to better speak and understand English. Jim's language instruction was an important part of

Mandolin's future just as baseball was to Jim. Common interests in things such as baseball and communication had potential to help assimilate Jim, Mansolin and many other Indians into the culture of the Untied States. Unfortunately it took many years with numerous conflicts to change the deep seeded bigotry in the country.

It did not, though, take long for the idea of inter league play to surface. Jim and Mansolin had become friends with a couple white soldiers, Jacob Friendly and Ross Early. Both were captains and graduates of West Point where they played baseball. They had been watching the Indians play and noticed that Jim's team dominated the league. Capt. Jacob wanted to know if an Indian all star team would be interested in playing against a similar team of soldiers. As always, Jim and Mansolin smiled in agreement at anything the soldiers wanted—since they were essentially prisoners on the reservation and in no position to disagree.

Mansolin responded, "Yes, whatever you want."

Both of the officers saw the reply from the two Indians was much like a response to an order. Capt. Jacob spoke again explaining to Jim and Mansolin that this was not an order, but a request for personal pleasure.

Jim, better understanding the intentions of the captains said, "You mean a real game?"

Jacob replied, "Yes. A real game played on the soldiers' field!"

Mansolin took this as good and bad news. The good news was this was the first time in his life that he could recall white men communicating with Indians as equals in a friendly manner. The bad news was the soldiers would beat the living hell out of the inexperienced Indians.

But before Mansolin could respond, Jim asked if this game was okay with the General.

Capt. Jacob replied, "We have talked to the General, and he supports it."

Jim's response was positive; but Mansolin cautioned that they needed to talk with their players first. Jim felt pretty sure there would be interest from the Indians, but Mansolin had some concerns.

Mansolin asked Capt. Jacob, "How can you expect this to be a fair game since your players have all been playing so long? It will be a massacre!" Both Indians and soldiers laughed. And Mansolin said "Bad word."

Capt. Ross responded by saying that they understood and would spot the Indians five runs because of this imbalance. When Jim and Mansolin looked confused, the Captain explained the term.

Jim then spoke up as would a chief, "No runs for us. We will play you even!"

The two captains looked at each other and smiled with Jacob saying, "Whatever you want, but remember we offered."

Mansolin looked at Jim with surprise, not believing that Jim turned down such a fair offer. Without another breath, Jacob smiled and stated that he knew something that would make this game more fun. While Mansolin was already shaking his head "no," Jim asked Jacob what he meant. Jacob said he was talking about money or alcohol. Mansolin was still shaking his head "no" when Jim asked how much?

Jacob and Ross looked at each other, surprised at Jim's interest.

Ross said, "How about one dollar to each Indian player on your team if you win; and if the soldiers win, we want four pints of whisky for each soldier on the team.

Jim chuckled and said, "Not enough. We want two dollars for each Indian player if we win, and we will give two pint bottles of whiskey to each soldier if we lose."

Jacob and Ross replied in unison, "It's a deal!"

Jim qualified his offer by saying that he needed to check with the other Indian players and ask Manso if he would back up the generous bet of whiskey.

As Mansolin backed away from the negotiations, Jim shook hands with the two soldiers and turned to Mansolin. "I know that Manso loves me as a son; but such an amount of whiskey given to the soldiers would really be a test of that love."

Mansolin concern grew more when he heard the two soldiers walking away laughing at what they considered a sure win.

It was obvious that Mansolin was extremely upset with Jim. "Don't you know this is yet another battle that the white man knows he will win—just another battle with different weapons? We will look like the dumb savages they think we are!"

Jim looked at Mansolin, "You worry too much. Be brave and face the challenge. Never lose confidence or else you will lose this war!"

Mansolin said, "Jim, if we lose, your fellow Indians, whose respect you have worked so hard to get, will turn against you for leading them yet into another defeat by the white man."

With all the seriousness he could muster, Jim replied, "Mansolin, you say you love me like a brother. Well, trust in my decision. Even though they may be good, they do not have the power or speed of God's wind at their back as we do. We will win!"

Still upset Mansolin angrily said, "You will end up having us all humiliated by giving into this soldiers' deception just as your father did when he got his tribe murdered."

Such cruel words infuriated Jim, and he struck Mansolin on the chin, knocking him to the ground.

Jim stood over Mansolin defiantly. "Never speak those words to me again! My father did not lead his people into defeat. Because of his overwhelming desire for peace, he was fooled by the army. His spirit now walks with God while the spirits of the soldiers who murdered him are tortured in Hell for eternity. So I go into battle with confidence that we will not be ambushed! We will not lose this game!"

Jim, realizing that anger served no purpose with his friend, helped Mansolin to his feet and apologized for hitting him.

Mansolin responded, "No my brother, I should apologize to you for not having faith in my chief. Now, I see that the son of Lone Eagle is a great Arizee chief!"

They embraced and in their Native tongue repeated their battle cry, "Victory, victory, victory!"

CHAPTER 12

Sensing Jim's confidence, the other Indians players were eager to play this game of baseball. Jim was inspired to see pride and dignity in his fellow Indians, which he feared had been lost with their submission on the white man's reservation.

While the players were an easy sell, Manso was a different story. If the Indians lost, which privately Jim admitted was likely, then he would give up two pints of prime whiskey to each soldier on the team. Jim planned to appeal to Manso's pride in his race. He knew that Manso thought Indians were physically and spiritually superior to the white man, who was weak when compared to the brave strong Indians. So Jim spent the evening in deep thought about how to present this wager to Manso.

The next morning, Jim found Manso sitting outside of his hut, as was his usual custom. He approached the subject gradually, first mentioning how well his Indian brothers played the game of baseball and then telling him of the All Star Game as proposed by the soldiers. Manso, who had become a fan of the game, was glad about the game. He saw it as a step to improved relations. His feelings changed when Jim told him the price of defeat.

Manso jumped to his aging feet and stretched his six foot frame, "How could you promise whiskey before asking me?"

Jim lowered his head, shuffled his feet and mumbled, "I thought you would be proud for Indians to challenge white soldiers in a game that would show them better than white man. But, I said the bet was off if you said no to the whiskey."

Manso raised his head and looked intently at Jim for several minutes. Then he said, "I must meditate and look into my soul for right answer."

Jim knew Manso too well for this to be intimidating, and Manso knew Jim had him in a tight spot. If he said no, then Jim would have to back out of the game causing embarrassment to the Indians. Additionally he knew that if he did not agree, it would show that he had no confidence in his people.

While waiting for a response from Manso, Jim tried another tactic. "If you, Old Wise One, give whiskey in the remote chance that the soldiers win, it will bring you more power and respect."

"Buffalo crap. Indian team is not as good as soldier team. You want to beat the soldiers to give pride back to our people. You showed bravery in accepting the challenge, but wrong to offer my whiskey as a wager without my word. I will not embarrass you or our people. Go and beat the hell out of the soldiers. Increase the wager to three whiskeys for each soldier!" Then he thought a little more and said "Forget that. I am as loco as Eagleson! Wager only two."

Jim was surprised, but pleased by Manso's sudden confidence in the Indian players.

Manso warned Jim, "I have decided that my anger at you will be equal with how much whiskey I have to give soldiers. If I get too angry, I speak to you no more!" He then embraced Jim and whispered in his ear, "Don't lose this game and our friendship."

Jim realized his carelessness in offering something he did not possess could end his friendship with Manso. He was still learning lessons of life that would help him to be a wiser man in the future. Jim thought, *I wonder if my father would be proud of me taking on this challenge.*

CHAPTER 13

After finalizing the wager with Capt. Jacob, it was time to select players for the Indian team. This was not easy since the league's players had varying degrees of talent or lack thereof. Mansolin, realizing that he was on the lower end of the talent scale, quickly accepted an assistant coaching position. Jim, who was the most talented player, served double duty as player and head coach. He wanted the new team to fairly represent the different Indian tribes. So he carefully went about choosing players from all tribes, hoping they could become a cohesive team without getting into serious confrontations.

With guidance from the coaches of the various Indian teams, Jim chose the best players from each of the six teams. Together the players then chose one more player from each team. They made sure that every position was filled by the best player possible. The final Indian All Star Team, as they called themselves, had 12 players. With a monetary reward in addition to their pride, Jim felt sure he could get the best out of the players. His biggest problem, however, turned out to be the Comanche. Mansolin, who conversed in several Indian languages including Comanche, stepped in to help. Jim challenged Mansolin to get the Comanche to participate in the game under the terms negotiated with Capt. Jacob. With a lot of persuasion and some of his grandfather's whiskey, he was successful.

With the players chosen and the Comanche on board, Jim went to Capt. Jacob and officially challenged him to the much anticipated game. The Army Team did not realize that the Indians from the different nations were willing to join with ancestral enemies for an opportunity to win this battle. This was not just a baseball game to the Indians; it was warfare and a way to restore their pride.

Since the Indians had little in the way of adequate equipment, Jim asked for gloves for his players since they only had some old catcher's mitts, which were not suitable for general use. The army distrusted the Indians and felt that quality gloves may be stolen. Additionally the soldiers felt that withholding gloves may serve as an insurance policy to hinder the Indians' performance; therefore only the pitcher, catcher and first baseman were permitted to use good gloves. Jim was not satisfied with the arrangement and negotiated for some older, well used gloves, which were still superior to the ones currently used by the Indians.

The umpire was, of all people, Gen. White. The same General who had helped plan the ambush and the murder of Jim's father and tribe. This was Jim's first chance to face this liar and murderer. Instead of bow and arrow, Jim would use a bat and ball to inflict his vengeance.

Jim talked with Mansolin about his hatred of the General and the government that had carried out the massacre of his tribe.

"Jim your hate is understood and time will heal your pain. It will take many years for masters to trust the enslaved, particularly when they look different and live differently. Masters fear retribution for wrong doing, and that will be for a long time. There was a great war between the North and South fought over the freedom for the black slaves. The white father of the North in Washington who promised freedom won the war. But many years have passed and still the black man is not free and trusted to become equal to the white man. It will be generations before the red man and black man will be free and trusted."

Jim shook his head, not in disagreement, but out of sadness of the situation.

CHAPTER 14

After a week of practice, the day of the big game arrived. The soldiers were comfortable with their knowledge of the Indians' abilities since they watched their games. This was not true for the Indians, who because of security, were rarely allowed to see the soldiers play.

The soldiers were focused on four players, three Arizee and one Cheyenne. Of course, Jim was the leading concern. He was a masterful pitcher and a phenomenal hitter. But it was not only Jim's hitting and pitching that worried the soldiers. Jim also brought an unparalleled level of energy and leadership to the team, which was difficult to measure. He had the ability to inspire and lead the Indians to play as a team, without tribal squabbling. The other players of concern, Jopo, Cochi, and Wyoma, were excellent fielders and hitters. But with enough well placed attention, the soldiers felt they could be neutralized. The other Indian players were good, but did not pose the threat of these four.

When the Indian team arrived at the ball field dressed in their everyday clothes, they were surprised. They had always played on an uneven sand lot. The soldiers' field was neatly groomed and the bases secured to avoid movement. There were seats of several levels for spectators and even benches for players.

To help energize their team, the Indians huddled together and gave out a loud war yell. The armed soldiers, who were there for security purposes, fired their guns in the air as a warning to the Indians.

Jim protested the presence of these soldiers, but Capt. Jacob stated very directly, "The General said he would not umpire the game nor let his soldiers play with a bunch of wild Indians unless they were guarded by these soldiers."

While the Indians were still surveying the field, the soldiers showed up in uniforms. Neither Jim nor his teammates had ever seen such a sight, and without meaning to offend, started laughing. Funny stripped pants too short to cover their legs, long stockings and shoes that had metal pieces on the bottom—a more amusing sight they had never seen. Although comical, it was Jim's perspective the soldiers being in the same uniform projected unity and discipline. This, he knew, would be to their advantage when competing against his multi-tribe team.

Gen. White walked on the field with yet another funny looking uniform with a large pad covering his chest and a mask over his face. Jim guessed both were to protect him from being hit with a ball or bat thrown at him by some "wild Indian."

The General then yelled at Jim, "Take your wild buddies to the bench before I cancel this game."

When their eyes met, Jim felt an immediate hatred for this man. He could never forgive him for the murder of his family. Jim felt that the General was again using force and unfair tactics to insure the soldiers' victory. Jim vowed to win this baseball battle.

The soldiers were boastfully sure of their victory. They openly jeered the Indians as the General named the soldiers as the home team. After all, the General thought the soldiers were playing on their home field. Ironically, Jim believed this home field had been stolen from God, who surely would in time cause the white man to face His wrath.

The General dictated the rules of the game. When he spoke, he directed himself only to Capt. Jacob, the manager of the army team. It was apparent that he assumed Indians did not understand English.

"Capt. Jacob, this game will be played in accordance to the Doubleday Rules of Play. Arrogantly the General continued, "Since I am sure you know those rules, I will not repeat them at this time. Now let's get started—Play Ball!"

Jim spoke up, no doubt surprising the General with his bravery. "We do not understand—Doubleday Rules."

Impatiently the General said, "Well it is too late for me to explain them now. We are ready to play ball!"

Jim shrugged his shoulders and said, "This is not fair, I have never heard of these Doubleday Rules."

Realizing this was yet another benefit to the soldiers; the General ignored Jim and ordered the game to begin.

The General's treatment of Jim irritated Capt. Jacob, who saw no need for his arrogance. But understanding his place as a soldier, one look from Gen. White, and Jacob returned to the bench.

Jim turned and went back to his dugout and told his players of the unknown rules. Once again Jim could tell the white man was using his rules to defeat the Indian. But he told his brothers to ignore this injustice and play their best, speaking kindly to everyone.

When the Indians took the field, they noticed that the stands were full of soldiers, army officers, and civilians, who were most likely rich ranchers, but there were no Indians. Jim assumed that the General felt that the Indians could not even be trusted to cheer for their own. It was obvious that the individuals in the crowd had brought money to bet on the game, as money was being passed from hand to hand. The question in the gamblers' minds was not whether the soldiers would win; it was by how much.

Even though the home team by rule does not bat first, the General decided that they would today. The General loudly suggested that the soldiers would probably bat forever, but it did not take long to discover that he made this prediction too prematurely.

Jim took the mound as starting pitcher to jeers and taunts from the opposing players and spectators. The Indians outwardly ignored the insults and focused on winning the game. But deep inside, their hearts were torn apart by the disrespect.

The first batter for the army was Capt. Jacob who uttered some remarks intended to intimidate the Indians. Jim took this in stride and threw the first pitch, which unfortunately hit the Captain on the arm. Jim knew this was not the best way to start any ballgame especially one that was already tense with racial competition.

Gen. White, after directing Capt. Jacob to first base, peered through his mask, pointed at Jim and said, "Do that again Redskin and the game is over, and your team will forfeit!"

Jim, who had not meant to hit the batter, was pretty sure forfeit meant lose. So he shook his head in the affirmative and prepared to deliver the ball to the next batter. The next batter was unfamiliar to Jim. He later found out that he was part of a contingency of professional players serving at various army forts in the area, brought in to help defeat the Indians. Jim's first pitch was solidly hit for a homerun. The soldiers led 2 to 0.

Jim fast realized that his ragtag team of American Indians was up against a very formidable foe.

Jopo, the catcher came to the mound to help Jim formulate a strategy. "What is troubling you my friend that you throw such bad pitches?"

Jim responded, "The first pitch was a bad one that hit the Captain. The second one was a good one, but the batter was better!"

Jopo said, "We must trick them with different pitches. What was your second pitch?"

Jim said it was a fastball that was not fast enough, otherwise the batter would have swung and missed.

Jopo said, "Slow your pitches down and no more fastballs until I give signal; nothing goes down the center of the plate."

This strategy worked, and Jim struck out the next three batters, at least one of which was a professional players recruited by Gen. White.

As the first Indian stood in the batter's box, Jim noticed that the pitcher was also a stranger. He was a big, ugly guy with a waxed moustache. He threw the ball as fast as the wind and retired the Indians in order, but then Jim returned the favor by doing the same in the top of the second inning.

Jim first batted in the bottom of the second inning. The first two pitches were fast balls, both called strikes.

Gen. White shouted, "Hey, Redskin you going to just stand there looking at the pitches. Remember you have to swing the bat to hit the ball."

Jim just smiled, "Don't worry about me; the next ball is a homerun."

Neither the General nor the catcher took Jim seriously. The pitcher had a big windup and threw his best fastball, ready to hear "Strike Three!" But instead Jim hit the ball high over the heads of the players, out of the field and then rounded the bases for a homerun. His team emptied the bench, screaming, jumping and running out to meet Jim as he crossed home plate. The pitcher and catcher, as well as everyone watching, stared in disbelief. The General, who had a big bet on the game, was furious.

As he walked past the General, Jim simply shrugged his shoulders and said, "Just lucky!" And let out an Arizee yell.

Unfortunately for the Indians, this would be the only run in the second inning. The third inning was without runs for either team. But in the fourth inning, another homerun was hit by the Army player who had hit the homeroom in the first inning. The player, called Big Gus, hit the ball so far it was never found. Now the Captain and General were feeling better with their team up 3 to 1.

No team scored until the final inning. Jim was still pitching and once again faced Big Gus after striking out the first two batters. Jopo and Jim discussed how Jim might pitch to Gus to avoid another homerun.

Jopo said, "Walk him."

Jim could not accept that suggestion. So he decided to mix up his pitches. The first pitch was a changeup to catch Gus off stride. The second pitch, another changeup, was intended to fool him. The third final pitch was a sharp slider thrown like a fastball. The plan worked; Big Gus hit only air in all three of his big swings.

In the bottom of the last inning with the Indians trailing 3 to 1 Jopo was first up and bunted the ball down the first base line for a single, catching the pitcher and first baseman by surprise. The next batter lined out to the third baseman. The third batter drew a walk. A big Cheyenne named Wyoma was the next batter and hit a high fly ball over the head of left fielder. "Foul ball," yelled Gen. White. The Indians felt this was truly a bad call that robbed them of three runs.

Tensions were running high. But Jim, who had cause to hate the General, calmed his players saying. "No tempers. Do not give them reasons for their mistreatment of us."

On the next pitch Wyoma struck out, which brought a deep moan from the Indians. Now it was up to Jim. Because of his successful hitting, the pitcher intended to walk him so he could do nothing to further endanger their lead. The first pitch was outside as the catcher had to reach for the ball. "Ball one!" The next pitch was similar—"Ball two!" The next pitch was another ball; three balls, no strikes. Jim called a time out to consider the situation. He went to his bench and whispered to his teammates to yell out just before the pitcher releases the next pitch.

The pitcher wound up for the next pitch, which would conclude the intentional walk. Just as he was about to release the ball, the Indian bench shouted a "war yell." It was deafening and startled the pitcher just enough to throw him off stride, sending the pitch over the plate. Jim hit the ball over the centerfielder's head. Both base runners scored easily and Jim made it to third base. Pandemonium broke out. The Indians had tied the score and perhaps the next batter would bring Jim home. They were confident of victory, until the General decided that the game would end in a tie due to the inappropriate behavior and unruliness of the Indians. Everyone was stunned. Neither Indian nor soldier wanted this game to be over. Each wanted their chance to claim victory.

CHAPTER 15

Even though the Indians did not win, it was incredible to think a group of raw, untrained Indians who had been playing baseball less than a year, were competitive with a team of experienced and, in a few instances, professional players. Jim proved himself a natural baseball player with leadership qualities worthy of a chief.

Jim congratulated his players on their great accomplishment. Everyone was celebrating when Mansolin asked the obvious, "Who wins the bet?"

In the excitement, Jim had forgotten the wager with the soldiers. Unfortunately the General had stopped the game before victory could be claimed by either team.

Jim yelled over to Capt. Jacob and asked, "Who wins the prize?"

The Captain stopped and shrugged, "I guess no one. The game ended in a tie."

"We did not finish the inning because the General stopped the game, and we both know why—your team was probably going to lose."

The Captain had to agree with Jim that the game did not end naturally, and the Indians could have very well been victorious.

The two of them approached the General and Capt. Jacob asked, "With the game ending in a tie, who wins the bet?"

"No one," he replied.

Jim spoke up in disagreement. Gen. White ignored him as unworthy of reply. But then Capt. Jacob accompanied by a couple of the professional players asked that the game be allowed to continue so as to decide a winner.

Gen. White, not wanting to face possible humiliation of defeat, made a proposal. He suggested the wager be revised so that both teams would benefit from this game. Capt. Jacob and Jim accepted his suggestion.

Jim spoke up saying his players wanted to keep the gloves and be given new equipment. The General objected strongly, "Indians deserve to be given nothing."

Capt. Jacob and some of his teammates, having gained a respect for Jim and his teammates, offered to buy the equipment. In fact while still together after the game, they gathered a considerable sum of money and gave it to the General to purchase new equipment. Gen. White was still furious, but accepted the money agreeing to the demands.

Gus, the big homerun hitter, who was the son of a powerful government official, looked the General straight in the eye and said, "I am coming back to this reservation in a couple of months, and the Indians better have that equipment!"

Gen. White was outraged to be humiliated in front of Jim, but felt he had no choice but to agree to purchase the uniform as soon as possible. After all Gus had connections that could end the General's career.

As Jim walked back to his teammates to deliver the good news, Gus said, "There goes a strong, gentle soul who epitomizes a great baseball player. Baseball teams should have Indian names to demonstrate their might. Hell, one of these days, Indians may even be allowed to play ball!"

Jim and his teammates were bragging about their showing in the game, when Jim heard someone call him. It was Capt. Jacob who wanted to introduce him to Gus and Robert, the big right handed pitcher. Each held out his hand to congratulate Jim on his performance.

Robert said, "If you ever get off this reservation, come east and look me up. I really think you could play professional baseball."

Gus agreed saying, "I have never been fooled by as many pitches as I was today when you struck me out."

Jim was embarrassed and thanked them for the compliments but said it was unlikely that an Indian would be allowed to play professional ball. Both Gus and Robert disagreed saying that public opinion was starting to change. People are becoming more tolerant.

Jim shrugged his shoulders, "Maybe so; but only if God affects the change."

Gus replied, "I think He has already started!"

Capt. Jacob too noticed Jim's talents and talked seriously with him about his abilities and professional baseball. He said the fact that Jim looked part white should be helpful should he decide to pursue this. He suggested that Jim should make every effort to dispense with his Indian lifestyle, perhaps ask to become a scout and move into the barracks. Jim was not very receptive to this because, while he loved baseball, he loved his Indian heritage more.

"Jim, this has to be your decision; but if you ever decide to make changes, let me know. Ross and I will help you in anyway possible."

Jim had obviously made a new friend, which led him to apologize for hitting the Captain with the first pitch of the game.

"No big deal. Heck, maybe you will become a great baseball player, and I can tell my children that I was once hit by a baseball thrown by the great Jim Eagleson."

CHAPTER 16

Jim felt his team made a good showing and demonstrated equality with the white man. He expressed his view to Manso as they shared a drink of whiskey and smoked a pipe. Jim told Manso what Capt. Jacob had said about playing professional baseball.

Jim who respected Manso's wisdom and opinion asked, "Do you think I should try to go out into the white man's world and play baseball?"

Manso was troubled by Jim's question. He qualified his response by saying, "I am an old man now and my experiences with the white man have brought troubles. But, there are good men and bad men in each race. Too many white men think the Indian is not good enough to live in their world. Never forget what happened to your father."

Jim admitted, "I am now very much interested in the white man's game of baseball, but I will always remember the sorrow caused me by the white man. And I understand too the big challenge of trying to be accepted in the white man's world."

Before Jim could speak again, Manso began humming an old Indian chant and speaking in a language that Jim did not understand. This continued for several minutes with Manso's head lowered, eyes closed and his arms outstretched to the heavens. It was as if he was calling spirits for guidance and inspiration. Then suddenly Manso opened his eyes, starred straight ahead and started speaking to Jim in their native language.

"Eagleson, you are a great chief and leader of your people, respected by all people who know of you. You must leave your people and go among the white man. Teach him that you and your people are noble and equal to people of all races. The game of baseball your mother taught you can show you the way. You have played but one game and made friends who will help you succeed in your quest for equality. I must leave you now; but always remember that I love you, my son!" Then Manso collapsed looking very old and weary.

Jim was puzzled, "Was that you Manso? Who was talking to me? Was it my father?"

In a voice barely audible Manso said, "I do not know, but he was strong!" Then he fell into a deep sleep.

Jim was mystified and left to meditate on Manso's prophecy.

Early the next morning, Jim went to Manso and asked again about the incident.

Manso said, "Eagleson, I have visits from the spirit world. I speak but do not remember what I say. Sometimes my words have meaning and sometimes they do not. What did I say to you?"

Jim hesitated a moment then said, "My friend, you told me that I should go among the white man and make my place as one respected by the white man. I believe my father was speaking through you."

Manso said, "That does not make sense. The white man will never respect or look up to an Indian chief. White man has no regard for Indians and does not trust us? Do you think they will accept you as a chief? Great son of Lone Eagle, believe as you wish and do as you must."

Jim was puzzled but told Manso that he believed his words came from his father and foretold his future.

Manso replied, "Eagleson, I do not know who spoke through my mouth. I do not think it was Chief Lone Eagle; but I could be wrong."

Jim was uncertain as to what to think about Manso's prophecy and the more he pondered it, the more confused he became. Had the words spoken by Manso come from his father, giving his wise counsel telling him how to make his way in the world? Jim left determined to find the answer to his question.

Jim pondered this issue all day and into the night. It was still on his mind the following day when he received a letter from his friend, John Thompson. Jim opened it and found some money and the following note:

Jim, my family and I pray you are doing well. Joey talks of you often and says he misses playing baseball with you. From your letters I see that you have grown into a wise and brave chief, but even more importantly, a wise and brave human being. I asked permission from the government to adopt you into my family, but this has been denied. They say it is because of your age and that you are of a different race. I have no choice but to abide by this ruling. This brings sadness to my whole family, and we will fight this injustice of our government. I am sorry, but this is the last money I will be able to send you. My current wage is barely enough to support my family. I am sorry to bring you such bad news. Please remember we love you as a son and brother. Your friend, John Thompson

Jim's life was unsettling; first the prophecy delivered by Manso and now the bad news from John Thompson. Jim hoped that being part of the Thompson family would help him become accepted outside of the reservation. It now looked like that was not going to happen. He knew that if he were to succeed in the white man's world, he would have to do it alone. He wrote a note saying he understood John's circumstances and how much he valued their friendship:

John, I appreciate the love from the Thompson family. I will try to find a way off this reservation. I was told by some professional baseball players that I am good enough to play professional ball. Maybe this is what I should do. Tell Joey that maybe one day we can play ball together. With respect and love, Jim

As Jim wrote about baseball, he felt certain that this was the course he should take. He knew that if Gen. White had his way, he would die on the reservation. He needed help from friends, both on and off the reservation, friends like Capt. Jacob and John Thompson. And certainly Gus and Robert respected him and would be willing to help him.

But for tonight Jim was content to think about the outcome of the baseball game. He felt that the baseball game had given the Indians a renewed sense of pride, something that had been lost by living on the reservation. Maybe even some of the soldiers were starting to see that skin color and cultural differences could be bridged. Jim came away from the baseball game with optimism for the future.

CHAPTER 17

When it came time to settle the bet, everyone seemed happy. The Indians got money and whiskey was distributed to the soldiers. Since it was officially illegal for whiskey to be sold, given or traded between the Indians and soldiers, Manso had devised a plan to take this transaction through the army supply store, which was run by a greedy Sgt. Johnson, who would expect a commission. But since whiskey was given to the soldiers, Manso felt the commission was not in order, although he had concerns that Johnson may not see it that way. On the day the whiskey was distributed, Johnson was on leave. So Manso went ahead with his plan. Johnson's assistant approved the transaction and completed the distribution.

That evening the Indians and soldiers celebrated together. With the whiskey flowing freely, most Indians made themselves scarce to ensure that a difference of opinion between them and some drunken soldier did not ruin the improved relationships. Manso circulated among the partiers to help make sure no fights erupted. When Jim saw Manso telling many of the Indians to leave, he rebuked him as meddling into an historical celebration between the white man and Indian.

Jim, who was with Capt. Jacob and somewhat intoxicated, said "Old father, you are not celebrating with your children?" Jim and the Captain laughed, but Manso did not even smile. He pulled Jim aside to speak to him about his behavior. Jim once again rebuked him, "Old man, why are you so sad and mean on this day of celebration? You embarrass me in front of my white brothers!"

Manso angrily said, "Jim, you act like fool. The white man is no more your brother than I your father. These soldiers' minds are foggy with whiskey. Take it away and you are nothing. They will turn on you." With a raised voice, he ordered Jim, "Leave while you can walk!"

Jim responded rudely, "Look, old man, things are changing with the white man. See they act as my brothers."

Capt. Jacob raised the half empty whiskey bottle in his hand and in a slurred voice said, "Old Man, Jim is right. Look we are all brothers!"

Manso expressed his disappointment in Jim, "You are fool. Listen before it is too late!" He turned and walked away.

Jim went back to the new friends, but his thoughts were on Manso. He realized he may have been unfair so Jim heeded his warning and left the celebration to go home and sleep off his drunkenness.

Dawn was breaking as Jim went to see Manso to apologize. Jim felt badly about his ugly words and realized that the old wise man was speaking from experience. In the morning light he better knew that the whiskey had clouded his mind. When he got close to Manso's home, he heard arguing and cussing. Rushing through the door, he saw Sgt. Johnson hit Manso on the head with an Indian tomahawk. Manso fell to the floor bleeding profusely from a gapping head wound. Jim's eyes flashed with anger as he starred at Johnson, who was angrily starring back.

A drunken Johnson yelled, "Damn thieving Redskins! This worthless old man gave away whiskey without paying me nothing. I taught him a lesson for stealing my money!"

Jim was enraged, "You worthless old drunk. Look what you did to my friend?"

"Worthless old drunk? Who in hell do ya think ya are talking down to, ya thieving Redskin? This old dog deserves to die. He stole from me when he gave away whiskey, and if ya keep staring at me I'll kill ya, too."

Johnson ran toward Jim with the tomahawk ready to strike another lethal blow. Jim defended himself and with his forearm hit Johnson in the side of his head knocking him onto the floor and causing the tomahawk to slide across the floor of the hut. Infuriated, Johnson staggered to his feet pulled out a hunting knife from his boot and charged Jim. This time Jim sidestepped his drunken attacker and pushed him to the ground. When Johnson fell, he groaned deeply and then lay motionless.

Jim went to Manso, only to find the old man lifeless with a massive split in his skull.

Emotionally distraught, he yelled at Johnson, "You killed my friend and God will now see that you die and your soul will be in hell." He walked to Johnson's body and turned him over. Jim was shocked to see that Johnson had fallen on his own knife, which was wedged deeply into his chest. Instinctively Jim pulled out the knife. He looked at Manso and said, "Johnson was mean enough to kill even you; the very person who once saved his life."

A soldier, hearing the commotion rushed in, saw Jim with a bloody knife and Johnson lying dead. The soldier yelled, "Raise your hands above your head and stand away from the white man!"

Another soldier rushed in and checked Johnson's injuries and screamed, "You killed my uncle!" The soldier immediately rose to his feet and hit Jim in the back of the head with the butt of his gun.

Jim collapsed on the floor. The pain in his head was searing. He saw Mansolin rush through the door to his grandfather who was on the floor in a pool of blood.

He cried, "Grandfather, Grandfather," as he embraced Manso's dead body.

As Jim reached for Mansolin in an attempt to comfort him, he felt another sharp pain in the back of his head from a blow by one of the soldiers. This one rendered him unconscious. When later questioned about the incident, both soldiers lied saying Jim turned to attack them with the same knife he used to kill Sgt. Johnson.

CHAPTER 18

As the morning sun streamed through the barred windows of the stockade, Jim slowly woke with a throbbing pain in the back of his head. His vision was blurred, but he could make out a familiar face yelling, "Jim wake up, wake up now."

Blinking to clear the fog, Jim saw Dr. Smith from the Army hospital. He was confused and thought he may be dreaming.

"What happened? Where am I and why are there bars on the windows? My head—my head hurts so bad."

The doctor lowered his voice and said, "Ah, good to have you back, Jim. You had a bad head injury. You will need to lie still for a few days until you can heal."

"Thanks doc, but how did it happen?"

"Jim, you apparently got into a fight with Sgt. Johnson. Can you remember anything about that?"

Jim, looking confused, was gradually able to recall the incident but was unsure of the specifics. He strained to remember.

Dr. Smith said, "Don't worry now. You need to rest. I'm going to give you something for your pain. I'll come back in a while and we can talk more."

As he walked from the cell, he saw Capt. Jacob and Mansolin, who were seeking information about Jim's condition. Dr. Smith told them that Jim was resting, and seemed to remember little of what happened. "I want him to have more rest before he talks with anyone."

Jacob looked concerned, "Doc, Gen. White is really pushing this issue. He has waited two days for Jim to wake up, and he is growing impatient."

Doc replied, "Well Captain, there is nothing I can do to make Jim more alert without possibly killing him. Had he not been hit so hard, Jim would be up by now."

Jacob said, "The soldiers said they were only trying to protect themselves as Jim was trying to kill them, too."

"That has to be an outright lie," the doctor said. "There was no way Jim was attacking the two soldiers. He was hit twice on the back of his head, not the front."

The Captain countered, "I understand the logic, but nonetheless, we have two dead men, one of them white and the other an Indian, along with an Indian standing over the white man holding a bloody knife. While it is difficult to believe that Jim would do this, you can understand how it looks."

Mansolin spoke up, "None of us know what happened, but I know Jim would not kill my grandfather and even though Johnson was disliked by most, I know Jim would not kill him either."

"Mansolin, I respect what you say, but the soldiers who were there tell a different story. Perhaps Jim was provoked and stabbed Johnson out of rage.

My grandfather was killed by a Comanche tomahawk that Johnson was known to carry, and Johnson was killed by a white man's knife that neither my grandfather nor Jim by law could even own. This makes no sense."

The Captain looked into Mansolin eyes. "Perhaps I am not being clear. Gen. White doesn't care what really happened. He will prosecute Jim because he is an Indian who was at the scene of the murder of a white man. I am truly sorry, but he does not care about Jim's life or for that matter Manso's. As the General sees it, Indian killing Indian saves the army the bullets!" This enraged the doctor and Mansolin as Jacob continued. "Doc, you know this isn't my view. I see the Indians on the reservation as human beings who need support to find their place in this country. But my views are not shared by government officials and politicians, and unfortunately these are the men making the decisions on treatment of the Indians."

Mansolin, who was appalled regarding the government's opinion of Indians yelled, "If the government is as bad as you say, when will good people stand up to the evil and destroy it. And if they do not, may God have mercy on their souls when they are judged by Him in death." Mansolin had made his point.

Dr. Smith turned to Jacob and said, "Mansolin is right, God will surely hold us accountable for this. We are cowards who will not speak out against our government in its proclivity to perpetuate the unjust treatment of the American Indian. Our country, established on the premise that we are all created equal, is allowing the unjust treatment of both the Negro and the Indian. God will surely judge us harshly."

Jacob spoke up saying, "One day I will have a hand in changing this; but speaking as an officer in the U.S. Army, today is not the day!"

Dr. Smith nodded his head in dismay," Well then, when?"

The warden, who overheard this conversation, interrupted, "The fate of some wild Indian ain't my problem or yours. In fact, your lack of respect for our government is bordering on treason. If you shut up immediately, I'll try to forget your conversation."

For now the narrowed mindedness of the army would prevail; but Capt. Jacob knew one day honorable men like Jim Eagleson would walk as equals to people of all races.

CHAPTER 19

The following morning Jim was able to recall some of the events surrounding Manso's death. Dr. Smith told Jim to take his time and tell him everything he remembered.

Straining to recount the events, Jim said, "Sgt. Johnson hit Manso in the head with his tomahawk because he was upset that he did not get money from the whiskey given the soldiers."

"It was Johnson who struck Manso?"

"Yes!"

"What else do you remember?"

Jim was trying to recall the details and spoke slowly. "When Johnson realized that I saw him hit Manso, he tried to attack me with the tomahawk."

"Then what, Jim; what happened next?"

Jim said he remembered Johnson rushing at him with a knife. He tried to continue but he was experiencing considerable pain. Doc told Jim to rest awhile and later he would bring Capt. Jacob, who would be very interested to hear what he had to say.

Jim fell into a restless sleep. He heard Manso calling to him from the end of a long tunnel. Manso's head was covered with blood, but he spoke to Jim, "My killer tried to kill you, but failed and fell into hell. You will be blamed. They will never believe the truth. But fear not, your father Lone Eagle is watching over you."

"Jim, wake up, wake up. You are having a bad dream." He opened his eyes to see Mansolin along with Dr. Smith and Capt. Jacob.

"I saw Manso, bloodied, walking in a tunnel telling me that the white man wanted to punish me for killing Johnson. I do not understand. I did not kill Johnson!"

When Mansolin heard Jim recount his dead grandfather's prophecy, he wept and could speak no more. He knew that Jim had not killed Manso or Sgt. Johnson.

The Captain, too, was relieved to hear Jim's account. He whispered to Doc, "How much did you tell Jim?"

Doc said, "I told him very little; but he told me that Johnson hit Manso on the head with the tomahawk, tried to hit him with it and then rushed him with a knife. That was it."

Capt. Jacob sat down on the bed next to Jim and explained, "The U.S. Army is saying that you killed Johnson with a knife that you stole from him after he caught you killing Manso. A soldier overheard you yelling at Johnson that you hated him and wanted to send his soul to hell."

Jim responded, "That is not true. Why would I kill my friend Manso?"

"Remember the argument at the celebration after the baseball game. Word got around that the two of you parted in anger."

"I admit that I had a little too much to drink and was upset with Manso; but he was just trying to help me by telling me to leave before trouble started." Jim paused before continuing, "Capt. Jacob, if you remember, I left soon after that."

"Yes, I remember. I don't believe the allegations the Army is making. But what I have just told you summarizes the Army's case against you. You were mad with Manso and went to his hut to kill him. Johnson saw you, and you killed him, too."

Capt. Jacob, who was a lawyer, told Jim he would represent him before a military court. He explained, "I filed a motion to hear your case in a civilian court thinking it might be a fairer trial, but Gen. White denied it because the crime had been committed on government land against a soldier. I considered going over his head, but realized the politics of such action may cause me to be relieved as defense counsel. I won't leave you with someone who may not be convinced of your innocence or concerned with your welfare." Jacob paused to give Jim a chance to absorb the seriousness of his situation and then continued, "Gen. White will be one of the three judges to hear your case. That by itself will cause us an uphill battle. You know how he feels about the Arizee Indians and you in particular. He should remove himself because of his prejudice, but I know that won't happen."

The General had seen too many soldiers killed in Indian wars to afford him objectivity in any case involving an Indian. Even though Jim had been a leader among the Indians and had never been in trouble, it was clear that Gen. White intended to punish Jim for the crimes of all Indians.

CHAPTER 20

Within a week, Gen. White announced a date for the trial and instructed the lawyers to have their witness lists to the tribunal within five days. Such a time frame made investigation by the defense extremely rushed. The prosecution, having already identified witnesses and assumed Jim's guilt, was comfortable with the date.

Jacob hurriedly prepared his defense. It was decided that Dr. Smith would testify that the location of Jim's head wounds made it impossible for him to have been facing the two soldiers who claimed Jim was attacking them. Mansolin would testify that the relationship between Jim and Manso was that of beloved father and son.

Jacob felt he should play up Jim's heritage. He thought Jim's lighter complexion, brown hair and hazel eyes would help identify him as part white man. He suggested Jim cut his hair and change his manner of dress; but Jim refused, saying he would not forsake his Indian heritage.

The evening before the trial, Jim and Jacob met to review the case.

Jim asked, "Tell me if I have any chance of being found innocent. It seems that Gen. White has made up his mind that I am a killer."

"Jim it doesn't look good, but there are two other judges whose opinions carry equal weight to that of Gen. White. I don't know much about them, but I do know they were not handpicked by White and are accomplished trial lawyers."

"I am an Indian, and we both know that my word does not count for much, especially against testimony of white soldiers."

"This is true, Jim. But I am hoping that testimony by our witnesses and my cross examination of the prosecution witnesses will put doubt in the minds of two judges."

You rest now and I will return tomorrow morning, and we will go to the courtroom together.

The following morning, Jacob found Jim shackled at the wrists and ankles, waiting for the trip to the courtroom. The armed soldiers who accompanied

Jim, Jacob and Mansolin to the courthouse warned if Jim got any ideas of escaping, he would be shot. Jim walked slowly, the shackles clanging with each step. His heart was heavy, but his spirits were lifted when he heard his Indians brothers yelling words of encouragement.

Mansolin said, "Eagleson, listen. Your brothers from all tribes give their support."

Jim yelled, "You are my true brothers. God's blessing to you." Jim thought it was so sad that only part of his heritage was loyal to him.

When Jim entered the courtroom, he saw that all the seats were taken by soldiers anxious to witness the trial and receive vindication for the murder of a fellow soldier. Beyond the seats, there were two long tables. The prosecution lawyer was sitting at the one on the right, and he correctly assumed that he and Capt. Jacob would sit at the other. Soon the three judges, dressed in military uniforms adorned with many medals, took their places at the front of the room. Gen. White called the court to order and introduced himself as chief judge. He then introduced the two other judges, Col. Thomas Slogan and Gen. William Burgess.

Jacob asked that the shackles be removed from the defendant so as not to prejudice the judges. Not surprisingly, Gen. White denied the request citing safety concerns and the severity of the crimes committed by the criminal. Appalled by the presumption of Jim's guilt, Jacob objected to the premature condemnation of the defendant as the perpetrator of the crime.

With a heavy hand Gen. White banged the gavel and said in a loud thunderous voice, "Overruled!"

Jacob feared the ruling would negatively affect his defense. Obviously "innocent until proven guilty" did not apply to an Indian.

Much to everyone's surprise, Gen. Burgess spoke up. "Gen. White, I would ask that your response to the request by the defense be stricken from the record. I do hope that it was a misstatement and not a bias on your part toward the defendant."

Gen. White did not take the reprimand kindly, but agreed to strike the statement. He directed his remarks to the court reporter. "Please strike the comment referring to the crim.... ah, I mean defendant."

Gen. Burgess shook his head in disgust and returned his thoughts to the specifics of the case.

While Jacob was encouraged by Gen. Burgess' rebuke of Gen. White, he knew that he still had a difficult road ahead. As the trial continued, the government produced witnesses who testified to actually seeing Jim kill Sgt. Johnson.

When asked if he actually saw the defendant stab the victim, one witness replied, "Well, I don't guess I actually saw the…"

White interrupted by saying, "Captain, your question is not relevant to the issues because this witness has already testified that the defendant was standing over the victim. It has already been established that this soldier was an eyewitness to the murder."

Jacob objected venomously.

"Overruled," shouted Gen. White.

"But sir, I…"

Before Jacob could say another word, Gen White said, "Counsel, your objection has been overruled. If you continue, you will be held in contempt."

Jacob looked to the other judges for support and with none forthcoming, he walked slowly back to his seat and noticed that Jim was praying.

The prosecution rested and Capt. Jacob called Dr. Smith who testified about the location of the wound on the back of Jim's head. The doctor said that such wound location would be impossible had Jim been facing the soldiers in his supposed attack.

Gen. White interrupted his testimony saying, "The location of the defendant's wound has nothing to do his killing Sgt. Johnson."

Jacob once again protested the defendant's implied guilt and went on to say he was trying to show an inconsistency in the testimony of a prosecution witness.

White restated his position saying," There is no relevance in the location of the defendant's head wound."

Jacob objected again and was once again silenced.

However, this time Gen. Burgess spoke up, "It appears that the defense counsel's questioning of consistency in testimony is relevant to this case and could establish a lack of creditability of the eyewitness accounts."

White was furious with this second rebuke. "This court stands adjourned for 15 minutes while the judges take this issue under consideration."

Jacob turned to Jim, "It does appear that we have a judge who is impartial."

"Yes, but Gen. White has already decided I am guilty and will stop at nothing to convict me."

When the judges returned, it looked like Jim was right. Gen. White announced that it had been agreed by all that the testimony addressing the location of the head wound was not relevant and would not be discussed any further. Jacob looked to Gen. Burgess for support, but Burgess was too embarrassed to make eye contact. In this moment of somber realization, both Jim and Jacob feared Jim's fate was sealed. Jacob still called his other witnesses, but they felt the only decision by the tribunal would be a choice between execution by the hangman's noose or a firing squad.

The final day of the hearing concluded with closing statements by the defense and prosecution. The prosecuting attorney had little to say except that the testimony overwhelmingly indicated that the defendant should be found guilty of this heinous crime.

Jacob's closing statement was an eloquently delivered summation of the lack of conclusive evidence. He pointed out the inconsistencies in the prosecution's case. Jacob felt that his closing remarks had made a positive impact on Burgess and Slogan but knew that White was unaffected.

As the final day ended, the court heard, "All rise," as the three judges stood and walked slowly from the courtroom to deliberate and render a verdict. Jim knew he would be found guilty and was lead from the courtroom to ponder the inevitable.

CHAPTER 21

Jim sat in his small cell meditating and praying for guidance from his father as Jacob sat beside him trying to offer comfort. At times Jim ignored Jacob. It was not out of personal disrespect, but more out of lost hope of ever being treated fairly. Jacob was finally provoked to raise his voice to get Jim's attention. This not only got Jim's attention but also that of the guard, who rushed in ready to save Jacob from the crazy redskin.

"Is everything ok, sir? If that Redskin tries to harm you, just let me know cause I'd love to have a reason to put a slug between his eyes!"

"Yes, yes. I am fine. But, in the future, I expect you to treat this prisoner with respect. Now leave."

The guard left somewhat confused as to why he got a rebuke from the Captain when he was only trying to protect him

Jim looked at Jacob with deep sadness. "That guard was on your baseball team, and after the game he congratulated me saying that I could play ball with him anytime. Now listen to him—he is ready to put a bullet in my brain. Manso once told me that the white man may like you one day and be ready to kill you the next. There is no regard for dignity when it comes to the Indians. So don't ever try to tell me there is fairness in the relationship between the Indian and the white man. It just ain't so."

"Jim, not all soldiers are evil. Not too long ago there was a great war that was fought by this same army to free the Negroes in this country."

This was a bad comparison because Jim knew about that war.

"My mother told me of that war. The Negro was not really freed. She said that when the war was over, the Negroes had no more respect then they had before the war. The white man treated the Negroes just like he did the yellow man in the west when the railroads were being built—cheap labor, nothing more. The white man wanted wealth more than he wanted freedom or equality for people with colored skin."

Jim's knowledge about this ugly part of American history caught Jacob by surprise. As hard as he tried, Jacob could not think of a response to Jim's assessment of racism. With nothing more to add to the conversation, Jacob patted his friend on his shoulder and quietly left.

Jim continued praying.

CHAPTER 22

On Thursday of that week, Jim and Jacob received a message that the judges had reached a decision, and the verdict would be read at 10 a.m. the following day. As Jacob read the note his hands trembled, knowing very well what the verdict would be.

The following morning Jacob walked to the jail to meet with Jim before court. When he arrived he found Mansolin and Jim chanting an Arizee prayer, no doubt asking God's blessing. The eyes of the two blood brothers expressed the sorrow that Jacob felt. All of them knew what Jim would face in the courtroom.

Guards arrived to shackle Jim for the walk to the courthouse.

Jacob spoke, "Jim, it is time to go."

Mansolin was unable to speak, but Jim said, "Capt. Jacob, I want to thank you for all that you have done for me. I think we all know that I will be found guilty today of a crime that I did not commit. With Mandolin's help I have prepared for the time that I will be reunited with my father and mother. While I have failed to meet my destiny, I am ready to die."

Jacob, realizing that he was in the company of a man more wise then his years, said, "Jim, your courage is an example for all of us." He took a deep breath and said, "We need to go. They're waiting for us."

Within minutes Jim and Jacob walked the short distance to the courtroom. Even though they were on time, the judges were already seated. They took in their designated seats, and Gen. White called the court to order. He first addressed Jacob, "Counselor, your tardiness is unacceptable and disrespectable to this court. I have a mind to charge you with contempt."

Jacob expected no less from this soul-wrenching farce. It was no surprise that such a tiny, pathetic matter would be noted in the face of such a serious occasion.

The General turned to the business at hand. He prefaced his verdict by stating the brutality of the crime that resulted in the death of a United States soldier must be vindicated.

Gen. White carefully unfolded the paper he held in his hand and read the verdict. "For the murder of Sgt. Horace Johnson, this tribunal finds the defendant guilty as charged. The defendant will serve 15 years to life in the prison in Oklahoma City." It was obvious that Gen. White was not in agreement with the punishment. "Leniency has been shown because of the position of certain members of this tribunal. Therefore, a killer may be released from prison to one day kill again."

After the court adjourned, a frustrated Gen. Burgess walked over to Jim and said, "I pray you live long enough to be free."

Jim acknowledged the remarks with a nod. Jacob promised Jim that he would file for an appeal, but in his heart Jim knew that he would never be free.

CHAPTER 23

Jim was scheduled to leave for the Oklahoma prison in two days. This left little time for him to say goodbye to his friends. Although they were sad to see him leave and worried about his safety in the notorious prison, they were grateful that Jim was not sentenced to death.

When the day came for Jim to leave the reservation, he was shackled and along with two prison guards boarded a train to begin the long trip to Oklahoma. He looked out the window and was overcome with a profound sense of hopelessness. He felt sure he would never see his friends or Arizona again. Once more Jim's life was changing, and once again it was not for the better. Jim was alone with his thoughts throughout the long ride as the guards spoke not a word to him. He thought about the prison that Jacob said only housed the most violent criminals. Finally he fell into a fitful sleep, with dreams he could not understand. Jim woke suddenly when the train came to a jolting stop. He was taken from the train and shoved into a horse drawn prison wagon. The driver was a small man with a stoic face. He was accompanied by a guard, a burley man with a long beard that still housed remnants of his last meal.

Even though Jim was alone in the wagon, the closeness was stifling. The cage was thick with leftover smells of sweat and urine. The trip was uneventful until three additional prisoners were picked up just before the Oklahoma state line. All three were Indians, two Cheyenne and one who looked like an Apache. The four men, wary of each other, rode in silence until Jim spoke to the Apache.

"My name is Eagleson, son of Lone Eagle."

"I am Bravo, grandson of Geronimo, friend of the Arizee."

At hearing the names of two brave chiefs, the Cheyenne retreated into a corner of the prison wagon while Jim recounted the day he met the great chief, Geronimo.

"When I was a young boy, my father took me to meet Geronimo. It was a life defining moment. After meeting your grandfather I knew that anything less than leading my people as their chief was unacceptable"

Jim went on to relate the incident that led to his imprisonment. Bravo explained that he was recently captured by the Army for refusing to submit to reservation life, adding that many of his people, including women and children were murdered by the soldiers. This only added to Jim's own misery.

The prison wagon came to a stop on the edge of the woods bordering a vast wasteland. According to the guard the prison sat in the middle of this barren land. Such terrain was a definite determent to attempted escapes. An escaped prisoner would not find cover for over a mile beyond the prison walls.

Shortly five soldiers rode up on horseback and began escorting the wagon. Traveling only a few miles, the soldiers ordered the driver to stop the wagon. The prisoners were ordered out of the cage. The driver and the guard seemed confused by this, but nonetheless followed the soldiers' orders. Several soldiers kept their guns trained on the prisoners while they were shackled. The last to leave the cage was Bravo. Jim didn't realize how large Bravo was until he stepped from the cage. He was close to Jim's height and just as powerfully built. Just as Bravo was being shackled, he grabbed the guard around the neck with a choke hold. The guard's eyes bulged and his face turn blood red. Bravo ordered the soldiers to come no closer or he would break the guard's neck. He ordered the soldiers to dismount and lay their rifles slowly on the ground. He demanded a horse, which was relinquished all too willingly. Bravo, with his arm still tight around the guard's neck, got on the horse pulling the guard up with him. Then the horse galloped away with Bravo and his hostage. Rather than hurriedly mounting their horses to follow Bravo, the soldiers seemed unconcerned by this daring escape. A sergeant pulled a very long barrel rifle from his saddle, attached a scope and loaded it with a very large caliber bullet. He climbed on the top of the prison wagon and aimed the gun at Bravo. In what appeared to be no more than target practice, two rapid shots exploded into the desert air. Bravo and his hostage fell from the horse and lay motionless on the ground. Jim stood, frozen in fear. He could not believe what he saw.

Suddenly he screamed, "Why! Why are you so cruel, why do you hate us so?"

The soldiers all laughed and the sergeant said, "Shut your foul mouth, Injun! When I want to hear from ya, I'll let ya know!"

Just then the horse that Bravo took returned to the hand of the man who had surrendered him.

The sergeant continued, "We always have fun like this and get paid pretty good for it. We let a fool Indian think he escaped all the while knowing the boy ain't really doing nothing but giving us some target practice. Today was my turn. We just having some fun. Hell it's only an Injun and a prison guard. Why should we worry about getting into trouble because that Cheyenne over there shot and killed a guard?" The sergeant looked over his shoulder back at the rest of his greasy big bellied gang. He slipped Jim a dark toothless grin and took a labored draw of his cigarette. "Right boys?"

His sidekicks nodded and laughed in agreement staring at the two bodies that were motionless, barely within their sight. Then with a sudden, swift jerk of his elbow, the sergeant pulled his gun from its holster and shot the wagon driver. He fell to the ground with a heavy thud. Jim's instinct took over as he ran to help the man.

"He's not dead!" Jim shouted nervously. "Please we can save him if we just…"

The sergeant then grinned and said, "Hell, boy I can remedy that real fast!"

Pow! Jim felt warm liquid spray his face and arms accompanied by heat and a flash he could see even with his eyes closed tightly. The sergeant watched as Jim looked down at his bloody hands. Thoughts raced through Jim's head. There was simply no way to explain what had just happened; and if he could, would anyone even care. His eyes turned downward to the blooded body. The bullet had ripped a hole through the driver's gut, exposing raw and wicked insides that should have never been allowed out.

The sergeant took the last drag off his hand rolled smoke, its black paper burning orange at the edge of his cracked lips. "Ya think he's dead now?" he chuckled. "Alright, here's the plan boys." He jumped down from his horse and tugged at his pants. "You," he pointed at the one of the Cheyenne. "You're gonna scalp him," motioning to the dead driver. "And you," pointing to the other Cheyenne, "are gonna to scalp that guard out there. And you," he looked at Jim, "your sorry ass is gonna stand right here side me for safekeeping."

With the scalps of the driver and guard securely in the sergeant's possession, He turned to the youngest Cheyenne and told him he was free to run or be shot on the spot. The young man ran only a few yards when the soldier yelled, "Stop!" The Indian turned and was shot immediately.

"I had to get him to turn because I couldn't shoot him in the back. Remember he was attacking us when I shot him!" All the soldiers laughed.

The toothless sergeant then turned suddenly to the other Cheyenne and put a slug right between his eyes.

The sergeant grinned at Jim, "The Apache and Cheyenne bring a big bounty, especially if they kill white men. The bounty on Arizee ain't so high. So you're a lucky devil today. Remember, this is our little secret. Wouldn't want someone to find ya body with fingers, toes or private parts missing. That'd be pretty painful."

The soldiers all laughed. The sergeant hit Jim on the head with the butt of his gun and Jim collapsed.

He did not awaken until the wagon arrived at the prison. The walls were high and topped with wire. The wide heavy wooden doors were securely bolted after the wagon cleared the entrance. The buildings were brick and looked as if they had deteriorated considerably through the years. No doubt the harsh winds of the Oklahoma winters had turned the brick to a dark gray stone. It was by far the largest structure Jim had ever seen and certainly the most frightening.

The soldiers proudly escorted the wagon and ordered the new driver to stop in front of the administration building. Jim tried to sit. As he rolled over and raised his head, he felt someone lying next to him. He looked right into the open eyes of the dead guard who had been scalped. On his other side was the driver's body. Jim retched at the profuse stench of death that permeated every corner of the cage. Then he noticed blood on his shoulder. Looking up he was horrified at the sight of the dead Indians tied on the top of the wagon. Jim collapsed on the guard's putrid body. He heard the toothless sergeant tell one of the prison soldiers his account of the horrible occurrence.

"Me and my men, we tried, but couldn't save their lives. Sir, you can ask that Injun over there in the cage. He saw the whole thing."

Jim was yanked from the cage with a knife discreetly pressed to his back. The sergeant asked Jim to verify the story told by the sergeant. When Jim did not respond immediately, the knife was pressed into this back cutting through his shirt to his flesh. He was forced to cooperate. As soon as Jim confirmed the story, he was thrown to the ground.

The sergeant looking at the guard said, "Two of those Injuns we had to kill were Cheyenne and the other was Apache. Don't that mean we gonna get a bounty for those Redskins?"

The sergeant was directed to the office to file the papers necessary for payment.

Jim, still shackled, lay in the hot sun, his body covered with a combination of blood, sweat and dirt. He lay there for what seemed an eternity. As the sun grew hotter, he called out for water. Then he thought he heard the voice of God reaching out to comfort him. But it was a young officer offering him water.

"Here is some water for you. Take it easy, just a little bit at a time."

Jim felt the coolness of the water as it touched his cracked lips and flowed into his parched mouth.

"Thank you, thank you, sir."

Having just collaborated a lie justifying the killing of five human beings, Jim felt no better than the murderers. He had lost his freedom, but not his honor. Jim told the officer the true account of the killings and how he was forced to lie in defense of his life.

The young officer said. "Yes, we know about their lies. When pressure was applied to one of the soldiers, he confessed and all of them are under arrest."

Even though Jim was still upset over the murder of five defenseless people, he felt better knowing that the killers had been arrested. Jim introduced himself to the officer, and the officer in turn introduced himself as Lt. Peter O'Connor. Capt. Jacob was right. There were good white men in this world.

Lt. Peter helped Jim to his feet and took him through the door to begin serving his sentence. Little did either of them know that today would be the beginning of a close friendship.

CHAPTER 24

Jim was 25 years old on his first day at the Oklahoma prison. His introduction to prison life was distressing. He discovered that all non white prisoners were initially housed in the bowels of the prison. This basement was without windows, dingy, wet and reeked with foul odors. There were three other prisoners, all Indians, who were each kept in cells so small that three steps took them from one side to the other. Each prisoner was given a metal pail as a container for bodily waste. Guards were supposed to come weekly to empty them, but Jim soon found this to be a rarity. Cleaning occurred only once a month and bathing consisted of the occasional pail of water thrown on the prisoners. The disgusting odors saturated the stale air and made eating the daily meal of stale bread nearly impossible. Jim had to sleep on a small pile of straw that had been used by a previous tenant. Filth, hunger and melancholy were vicious reminders of his fate.

Jim spent much of his time in prayer asking God to deliver him from this wretched hole. He thought often of his friend Manso and longed for his spiritual guidance and at times, just one drink of his whiskey to dull his senses enough to bear these appalling conditions. He prayed for the strength to be brave, after all he was the son of Lone Eagle, Chief of the Mighty Arizee.

Mornings dawned without Jim knowing it. Day and night were the same. The only light was from the oil lamps used by prison guards who delivered food or emptied his pail. He tried desperately to keep track of the days, but dates were no longer relevant. Jim's life was stalled in the depressing bogs of the musty stench of his own body and rotting rodents denied a meal by a prisoner who strived to outlive them. Distraught and hopeless, Jim doubted that he would ever be free, must less a chief. These times begged for death.

Such was the dreary situation for the first several months of Jim's incarceration. It was intended to crush his spirit and thoughts of escape. But escape in the conventional way was not in Jim's plans. He felt sure he would gradually die from any number of diseases that fresh air and good food might prevent.

One morning Jim awoke to hear heavy footsteps coming toward his cell. In the dim light from an oil lantern, he could barely see the outline of a giant man. Jim strained to see the soldier's face. As the big man came closer, Jim saw that he had straight black hair and high cheek bones. He was dressed as a soldier, but looked like an Indian.

Jim spoke in Arizee, but the response came in English, "Get up and come with me. The new Sergeant of the prison wants to get to know you better."

After Jim was shackled, he struggled to his feet and accommodated the huge soldier by walking slowly up three levels of rugged stairs. At the top of the stairway, Jim was lead through a door to a brightly lit room. His eyes, which had not seen light for months, were feverishly trying to adjust. Soon Jim realized that he was seeing sunlight and must be on the ground level. He breathed deeply trying to eradicate the stale foul air from his lungs.

"Jim Eagleson, hum! Sound like an American name for a dirty Redskin."

Jim looked at the sergeant and said, "I am Eagleson, Son of Lone Eagle, the Great Arizee Chief. I am also half white," he said hoping that would make a more favorable impression on the sergeant. "My mother was Irish. See I have green eyes and brown hair."

"Well, that's even worse. You are a half breed—bastard son of a white woman raped by a redskin."

With what little energy and dignity Jim had, he lowered his voice to just above a whisper, "My mother was a voluntary wife and mother who was proud to be the wife of Chief Lone Eagle."

The sergeant stood and shouted, "No decent white woman would let herself be taken by a redskin dog! So quit lying less I beat the shit out of you!" The sergeant then struck Jim across the cheek with the back of his hand.

Jim turned his head and then and in a flash put his chained hands around the Sergeant's neck. As quickly as he did that, he released him saying, "Don't talk about things you know nothing about. My father was a great chief and my mother was proud to be his wife."

"How dare you attack a U.S. soldier? Ain't that what got you here?" Speaking to the big soldier, he said. "Take this Redskin out and give him a thrashing with the bullwhip."

But the soldier did not move. He peered in the sergeant's face and said, "I did not see this prisoner attack you; but I did see you attack him and he would naturally defend himself. Now ain't that right Sergeant." The big soldier did not wait for a response. "I will take the prisoner back to his cell now."

As they walked down the first flight of steps, Jim asked the big soldier, "Who are you my brother to be in an army uniform?"

"I, too, am Arizee. My name is Abotoe, and I rode with the Apache before they surrendered to promises of respect and land. When they realized these promises were broken, they fled. But I stayed behind and became a Pony Soldier and was sent to capture Geronimo and his people. We were told that Geronimo would be treated respectfully and fairly, but when we brought him back, he was humiliated even more. The white man had once again lied. Because I captured Geronimo, I live in shame. I am here to guard the Indians and Negroes. I have heard many tales of your bravery and honor and will respect and protect you until your imprisonment is over."

"That will be a very long time. I will spend many years in prison. In fact I may be here for the rest my life."

Abotoe said, "I will be with you. You will make our people proud. One day white men will acknowledge you just as the Arizee do."

Jim felt honored and expressed appreciation for the confidence. "I will do whatever possible to live up to your expectations. I am glad to have you as my new friend."

Abotoe's outward appearance was one of a rough, thick skinned Indian who had seen many a battle, the kind of warrior that one did not provoke. But in actuality he was a spiritual man who was as loyal as the day was long. He was proud, but not arrogant. He was courageous, not afraid to stand up for his beliefs; and he intended to make certain that his chief was treated fairly.

When they arrived at Jim's cell Abotoe handed him two bails of new straw for his bed. After Abotoe locked the door to Jim's cell, he moved a small table just outside the cell within Jim's reach. On the old wooden table, he left an oil lamp, a jar of water and a large chunk of fresh bread for his chief.

After eating most of the bread, Jim rested on the fresh straw. He closed his eyes as he watched the flickering shadows from the oil lamp and focused on his future. Perhaps God had a plan for him. He wanted to believe that his future would continue beyond this prison cell and knew he would do whatever necessary to stay strong until he could leave. Maybe some opportunity waited for him that would again make Indians proud. Jim hoped he could make a difference for his people. To do that he would have to succeed at something that was important to the white man. But what did he even know about the white man? Jim contemplated this for a moment and then thought, *Baseball*! Yes, he knew he was equal in ability to the white players; they had said so themselves.

These thoughts gave Jim hope as maybe he had found a place where he could be equal to the white man.

Jim's thoughts wandered into dreams where he was on a great battlefield with many Indians and hundreds of U.S soldiers poised for major conflict. Jim was in a baseball uniform riding on a small donkey between these two great forces as they readied for battle. Strange, but both sides respected Jim and allowed him to ride in the center of the battlefield. He turned to the Indians and saw his father leading many warriors. Leading the soldiers were Col. Thompson and Capt. Jacob. With Col. Thompson was his young son, Joey who held a ball and bat in his small hands. Jim rode up to little Joey who handed him the ball and bat.

Suddenly the dream ended and Jim woke up, sweating and confused. He wondered. *What did the dream mean? Why were the white and red men lined up against each other as if they were going to wage war? Why wasn't he riding next to his great father ready to fight the white man? Why did Joey hold a ball and bat? None of it made sense.*

He slowly drifted back to sleep only to see that he was not on a battlefield, but a baseball field. The weapons were not guns and arrows, but baseballs and bats. Would he be the link to a peaceful outcome?

CHAPTER 25

"Jim, Jim. Wake up; time for work."

Jim looked out through the bars of his cell to see Abotoe. He was telling Jim that today he would get his first work assignment. After months of staying in his cell all day, a work assignment was certainly a welcome change. Abotoe unlocked the cell door and escorted Jim up three levels of stairs and out a back door into a large clearing surrounded by prison buildings. The sun temporarily blinded him, and he raised his hand to his brow until his eyes adjusted. The air was cool and fresh, a far cry from his stale, stifling cell. He was in the meeting yard where prisoners congregated every morning to be assigned work details. Work details were assigned according to status, which Jim wrongly assumed was based on the severity of the crime. But he soon saw that status meant race. Everything always seemed to come down to race. It was the white man's way of maintaining his superiority.

Abotoe explained the work detail status. "There are four groups of prisoners—whites, Orientals, Indians and Negroes. White men are given skilled jobs, such as carpentry. Orientals work in food preparation and laundry. Indians are relegated to farming and tracking game on prison land while under heavy guard. The Negroes are given the lowest of duties of cleaning latrines, burying bodies and other undesirable tasks. That status represented the very low regard. The government may have passed laws to make the black man free, but he is still not respected, particularly in prison. For all groups, except the white men, duties are interchangeable. When any prisoner, other than white, finishes work, he can be assigned other duties. When white prisoners finish, they can use the library or baseball fields, which are just outside the prison walls."

Baseball fields! When Jim heard the word baseball, he became excited and asked if there were any chance that he might be able to play baseball.

"Don't fool yourself into thinking the warden will ever allow an Indian or anyone with colored skin to play baseball. Being an Indian seriously decreases your rights and excludes you from playing the game even though word has gotten out that you are very good at baseball. So, I am sorry Eagleson; the social order in this prison means no baseball for you. But maybe we can find a place where we can pitch some ball." Then Abotoe grinned as he recollected, "There was a time when the soldiers told me that I would be a good baseball player because I am so good looking. When I finally watched the game, I realized that looks meant nothing to the game." With a smile, the big man said, "Think they were joshing me!"

Jim grinned at Abotoe's story—something he had not done since he left the reservation.

Jim was assigned to the hunting detail. He went into the forest with many heavily armed guards and tracked prey for the guards to kill. When the guards tired or had sufficient game, they brought Jim back to the meeting yard, and Abotoe escorted him back to his subterranean home. Since the game was used for food, Jim felt he had been given a very important assignment.

Whenever Jim was in his cell, he meditated and prayed for the answer to his question—*how can I use the white man's game of baseball to make my people proud and be accepted as an equal?* Although Jim prayed for guidance, none was immediately forthcoming, and his life continued to spiral in an unknown direction.

CHAPTER 26

In the six months that Jim had been at Okie Prison, he had never broken a rule or received any disciplinary action. He was a model prisoner, an example that the warden wished the other prisoner would follow. He even enjoyed his work assignment. Although he was always well guarded, he felt a certain freedom when he tracked the game. He was required to wear a bright red jacket so that he would be easily seen should he try to escape while tracking. With no pony, he used only his feet and wit to pursue the game, whether it was turkey, deer, rabbits and pheasants. Even though Jim was a superior shot, he was allowed to only track the game, leaving the shooting to a white hunter. Except for deer and rabbits, the other prey was new to Jim.

While Jim liked using his intellect to outwit the animals, he enjoyed just being outside even more. Oklahoma was different than his homeland in Arizona. There was more snow and violent booming storms with whirling winds that could destroy everything in their paths. But those were rare and most of the time there were gentle breezes on sunny days. But still, the guards were a constant reminder of his imprisonment as they always watched the Indians closely to thwart any escape.

Another six months passed and Jim turned 26 years old. As a prison trustee, he moved from his dungeon to the ground floor. With this new status, Jim found he was gaining friends among the prisoners, guards and some administrators. He knew from experience that it would be beneficial if he could establish friendships with people in authoritative positions. Even the warden saw Jim as a man of honor and changed his opinion of him. Jim appreciated this, but he realized that such friendships could end at any moment, justified or not.

Abotoe was a loyal treasured friend who once told Jim, "God has told me much about my duty to you my chief. I will be close to you on life's journey."

Jim felt fortunate to have Abotoe as a friend, but memories of lost friendships haunted him.

Jim's new ground floor cell was a definite improvement over the dungeon. Even though the window was too high to see out, he still enjoyed the warmth of the morning sun as it created a brilliant glow in his cell He would close his eyes and imagine the beauty of the glorious sunrises as the first rays of light danced upon the morning dew. He pictured the outside world as he remembered it— the mountainous rocky terrain of his homeland, the widespread desert of the high plains or the lush green life in the low lands of Arizona. Jim used his mind to travel to many places without leaving his prison home.

Since a hunt was scheduled today, Jim dressed in his red uniform and waited for Abotoe. As he sat on a stool, Lt. Peter O'Connor, who was temporarily serving as a prison administrator, walked to his cell door. Accompanying the officer were Abotoe and a beautiful young girl. With her tan skin and high cheekbones, Jim immediately recognized something special about the young lady. She had long brown hair and her eyes that were worthy of stare. She wore her shoulder length hair pulled back and tied with a pretty pink ribbon. Jim thought she smelled like the sweet blooms of the Desert Willow. He knew he had found another of his own. As she and Lt. Peter approached his cell, Jim was embarrassed, as he could not help but stare at this young woman's beauty. He was speechless. The young woman too noticed that Jim was an unusually handsome young man.

Lt. Peter began the introductions. "Gabriela O'Connor, let me introduce you to Jim Eagleson. He is one of our model inmates." Gabriela curtsied with a smile. Lt. Peter continued, "Jim Eagleson, let me introduce you to Gabriela O'Connor, my sister. She lives in Oklahoma City with our parents"

Jim was confused. Gabriela clearly had Indian features, yet Lt. Peter said she was his sister.

Jim bowed and said, "It is my pleasure to meet such a beauty. I mean nice looking female woman."

Both Lt. Peter and Gabriela chuckled at Jim's unusual description.

Jim shook his head in dismay at his awkwardness and apologized, "I am so sorry for that description. I meant to say how very nice and pretty you are to the eye!"

"Thank you Mr. Eagleson for the compliment." Gabriela said with a giggle.

Her friendly manner and warm smile made Jim comfortable as he recovered from the bungled introduction to the most beautiful woman he had ever seen.

"Jim, my sister is of a mixed heritage like you. Her father was my uncle Thomas and her mother was an Arizee woman named Abtha. They left Oklahoma City before either of us were born and went to live in Texas. They had a son, Thomas, Jr. and a few years later a daughter, Gabriela. When Gabriela was eight years old, the Comanche attacked their farm, killing everyone but

Gabriela. Her mother saved her by lowering her into a shallow, dry well. When the army was inspecting the devastation, they heard her cries and rescued her. She was taken to an army hospital and cared for until my parents Patrick and Kathleen adopted her. I told her about you and thought it would be good if you two met."

Lt. Peter told Jim that Gabriela would like to talk with him about their Arizee heritage. The Lieutenant put a chair outside of Jim's cell for Gabriela and asked Abotoe to stay with them until he returned for his sister.

Jim said, "I am scheduled to hunt today so I won't have much time to talk."

Lt. Peter responded. "The hunt has been delayed due to a change in the schedule."

Jim smiled and suspected that the officer had purposely changed the schedule so he could spend time with Gabriela. Jim took a quick review of himself to make sure he was presentable to such an eloquent young woman. He removed his red hunting jacket explaining that he was required to wear it on his work detail.

She laughed and said, "I am glad you told me because I was wondering if you were Santa Claus!"

Not wanting to be rude, Jim smiled, but had not idea who Santa Claus was.

CHAPTER 27

Gabriela and Jim talked for only an hour before she had to leave for lunch with Peter and her parents. But they made the most of their time. Jim expressed his happiness with talking to someone who shared similar heritage, although Gabriela clearly was far more acclimated to the world of the white man. Gabriela emphasized that she was very young when she was adopted and her knowledge of Arizee customs limited. She recalled vague memories of her parents as well as some Arizee traditions she learned from her mother. She wanted Jim to talk about her heritage. Jim felt somewhat inadequate to talk with this lovely young woman who seemed to be very well educated and quite proper. He wondered if she could sense his feelings. However, when she spoke, his fears were dispelled, and he felt at ease.

"Jim, if you don't mind me calling you that, I would like for you to tell me about Arizee people and customs so I can better know myself. I get strange looks from people who seem to be confused as to my birthright, whether I am part Negro or Indian. Neither is good to the white man, even though I must admit, I would rather be facing the future being part Indian than part Negro."

With his experience at the prison, Jim agreed and expressed his concerns about the Negro. "Even after the great war to free them, my mother told me they were still not treated as equals."

Jim knew the plight of the Negro was not what Gabriela had come to talk about so he changed the subject to their Arizee heritage.

"I know you have a desire to learn about the Arizee, but I would like to know more about the complicated white culture. I think if we talk about our past, we can help each other better face the future."

"Jim, believe it or not, my world is really not complex, although sometimes I do admit it seems unjust. Many white people are kind and accepting of differences in skin color. In fact, I think it is more likely for a white person to accept an Indian in our society than the reverse. Racism, knows no specific color. So I will tell you about the bad and the good. I hope it won't be a problem for you to do the same thing."

"No, don't worry about that. I will be honest. I do agree with you there is goodness in some white men. In fact, two of my best friends are white; both were officers in the U.S. Army."

They continued to talk about Arizee culture, with Jim relating stories of customs and traditions. When it was time for Gabriela to leave, she extended her hand through the cell bars to Jim. Not familiar with the custom of shaking hands, he limply held her hand, but felt a firm grip from Gabriela. She said her brother would make a schedule for her future visits.

She smiled at Jim. "I look forward to talking with you again soon."

She asked Abotoe to escort her to her brother's office. On her way out, she turned and waved to Jim.

Jim just experienced one of the most memorable occasions of his life. It had been so long since he had seen an Arizee woman. He was nervous, and felt weak, as if his legs would not hold him up. These feelings were new and strange to him.

Jim had such a pathetically disruptive life since his family's murder; he really did not know how to act with the opposite sex. He was ignorant of what to say or do around a beautiful woman like Gabriela. He could see she was a strong woman, much like his mother. He was confident that she was an influential force in her family, and he felt she could very well be an important person in his life. Perhaps he might even be in love! His thoughts were interrupted by an unfamiliar guard barking orders to get ready to hunt. As he donned his jacket he could not help but think about Gabriela. He started talking to himself.

The white guard could not help but comment. "Who the hell are ya talkin to Redskin?"

"Nobody, just myself," Jim replied.

The guard grumbled, "Damn crazy Indians, all they do is mutter, pray, and chant."

As Jim walked with the guard, the delicate scent of Gabriela's perfume still hung in the air.

CHAPTER 28

Jim lacked concentration during the hunt. Even though he tried to get Gabriela out of his thoughts, he was hopelessly preoccupied with his new friend. He had been so focused on survival that he was totally unprepared for this feeling. But surviving was not nearly as daunting as establishing a relationship with a woman, and for that matter a wonderful woman. As evening fell, he was still not sure how to proceed with a relationship with Gabriela. He spent time deciding what he would say and do, only to fall asleep and dream about how his resolution would fail. He tried praying, only to realize that God had trouble figuring out how to handle a woman, too. Sleep was elusive.

As dawn broke, Jim realized that he had slept for only a few hours. Sometime around midmorning, Lt. Peter and Abotoe arrived at his cell.

"Greetings Eagleson," said Abotoe, "Today you get to be with your new friend—me!"

Jim did not understand. He thought he smelled the sweet fragrance of Gabriela's perfume.

"Abotoe, you are my friend, but you smell like a woman. You are loco."

Abotoe grinned and moved aside. Behind the big Indian was Gabriela laughing so hard she had tears running down her beautiful face.

Jim looked at Abotoe and said, "You should be glad these bars are between us 'cause with your own knife, I would turn you into a wom…" Jim stopped short so as not to embarrass Gabriela. But Gabriela laughed even harder.

Abotoe apologized for his joke, even though he still had a grin on his face. Jim however did not think this joke was funny. He was blushing and embarrassed.

In an attempt to reassure Jim, Gabriela said "Don't pay any attention to Abotoe, he was just kidding you."

To Jim's surprise Abotoe unlocked his cell door and led him to a meeting room where he and Gabriela could talk. Gabriela complained about talking through the cell bars so her brother persuaded the warden to allow a meeting in a well guarded room. Abotoe stood guard in the hall just outside an opened door.

Gabriela began by saying, "Jim, I am anxious to hear more about the life of the Arizee, what things were important to our people. I want to know the good, bad and everything in between. In turn I will tell you what it is like to live in my world."

Jim told Gabriela of the challenges he faced in describing a lifestyle of a simple, sometimes nomadic tribe to someone who has lived a life in one location.

"It is difficult to explain our lifestyle to a person from a society that has so many times diminished the Indians. When our way of life is called savage by the white man, it is hard for him to understand and accept our ways."

His words angered Gabriela, "Jim, don't treat me in this matter with the excuse that I cannot appreciate the special things about the Arizee lifestyle because I have lived with white parents. Look at me; I am as much an Arizee woman as I am a white woman. I am fighting to establish my true identity in this world. I hoped neither of us would let a holier than thou attitude stand between our understanding of each other."

Jim was shocked. He wasn't sure what "holier than thou" meant; but apparently that he was guilty of it and it was not good. Jim knew he was dealing with an opinionated, strong and passionate young woman. His respect for her was growing with every word she spoke.

Jim apologized, "I am sorry if I have upset you!"

He continued in his effort, carefully choosing his words.

"The Indian is but an extension of God. As human beings we were put on this earth to care for His world. All creatures have souls, from greatest Arizee warrior to the smallest creature like the humming bird. God has given them all souls. The relationship between these souls is very delicate. We hunted the buffalo for food and clothing. We took the meat and hides, but we did not kill the soul. It was returned to God as part of His plan. God has directed humans, his greatest creation, to help Him care for the earth and all living things. The Arizee Indian saw the white man as his brother; but soon it became apparent that the white man was here to take God's land as his own. My friend John Thompson told me that Indians were in the way of the Manifest Destiny. So they chose to cleanse the earth of Indians. It will not be many years in the future when the Indian, as a separate people, will disappear. So I must find a way to live in the white man's world."

Gabriela interrupted, "Why do you want to live in the white mans' world when you are treated with disgust?"

"Gabriela, I have no other world in which to live. I am the son of Chief Lone Eagle and am destined to be my father's heir on this earth. I must live up to my father's expectations so that God will be pleased with me. The white man's blood in my body requires me to be accepted. And I must keep trying no matter the disrespect. Should I not do this, my mother and father will be disappointed, and I may not be with them when I die. Now that the Indian way of life is certain to be destroyed, the white man's world is the only one left in which I can achieve my destiny."

Gabriela was perplexed by Jim's lofty goals, particularly in a world that was so foreign and hostile to his existence. She looked sternly at him and said, "Jim Eagleson, you are a fine human being, but your desire to reach your father's status in the white man's world is not realistic."

"I admit it is a big challenge. I might not succeed, but I have to try with all my heart. The only way to make my dream come true is with courage and determination."

Gabriela felt great sympathy for him. Tears welled in her eyes as she saw the utter hopelessness of this great man and other Indians whose destiny would be shaped by the loss of freedom at the hands of the white man.

Jim reached for her hand and asked, "Do my words make you sad? I only want you to know of my ambitions. Please don't cry. It hurts my heart so badly."

Gabriela, touched by Jim's feelings for her, held his hand tightly. "Jim please understand this is the first time someone of my Indian heritage has told me such things. My tears are not only for the struggle you face in pursing your destiny, but also from the joy of knowing an honorable man with such high principles. My Arizee heritage will be a source of pride for the rest of my life. Thank you for helping me see this."

Jim had not known such heartfelt emotion since his family's death. Gabriela awoke feelings of love and affection that were long missing in his life.

He looked into Gabriela's eyes, "I feel much luck to know you. Thank you for bringing me pleasure."

Abotoe knocked on the door saying it was time for Jim to return to his cell. He told Gabriela to wait in the room for her brother, who would be there shortly. She smiled and promised to return the following day. As Jim walked through the door, she called his name.

"Jim, thank you." Then she waved goodbye.

CHAPTER 29

When Gabriela and Jim met the next morning, it was her turn to talk the culture in which she lived. She wanted Jim to know the positives of her life experiences.

"While you have seen the prejudice and cruelty of the white man, I want to tell you of the goodness of the people I live among. I've been very fortunate to be part of a strong, ethical family whose conviction is one of compassion and love, not hate. It may seem strange to you, considering your experiences, but this is not rare. My parents cared for me as their own from the moment they took me into their hearts and home. They taught me to distinguish between truth and deceit. Children are born without hatred and prejudice. They are taught those things. My parents raised me to love and respect my fellow human beings, no matter their differentness."

Jim interrupted, "In the Indian culture, it is foolish to think that a good deed done to the white man will be returned equally. As evidence, look at our own Arizee people. We were scorned by the white man because of our beliefs and the color of our skin. It is difficult to respect when we are treated with contempt. It is difficult to love when we have been met with hate."

Gabriela held her hand up in protest, "I understand your feelings, but you are forgetting your religion. Doesn't it teach love and respect?"

Jim responded, "My tribe saw one God for all people. The white man has determined their white God is the creator of all things on earth, but most of their energies are put toward material possessions, not the spiritual being. It seems very important they have physical proof of God's power to be confident in their beliefs. Spiritualism is more important to us. We believe God created the earth and that God is in all things of nature—the sun and moon, the rain, the buffalo, and most importantly the human being. The Arizee do not need to see God; we feel God. He is all around us. But the white man decided that the Indian is without God, and therefore must be conquered."

While Jim had answered her question, he also disclosed his feelings far more than Gabriela had expected.

"Jim, your beliefs are very inspiring and similar to those of my parents. In fact my mother often says that our society has become so trapped in depicting wealth as a sign of godliness that we can no long see the forest of salvation for the money tree."

Jim looked puzzled and did not understand her response, but continued the discussion.

"Gabriela, what do you think about God's appearance?"

"Even though no one has actually seen God, our Bible says that man was created in God's image. The white man interprets this to means God is white. It makes them feel even closer to Him. But, I think it means we were created in God's spiritual image, which sounds a lot like what the Arizee think."

Jim agreed urging her to go on.

"Even with misguided beliefs, my Christian religion is very loving and caring of all human beings. It is my hope that one day love will broaden the minds of all people to accept and recognize that our God is the same. This could surely help all races live together as brothers. Christian religion teaches us that we should love and care for our fellow man while looking for the good in people, no matter their race. But there are some who do not follow these teachings. I believe that God sent his only son, Jesus to show love and compassion while offering eternal life. Jesus was humiliated and died in disgrace because of what he preached. But only his physical body died. His spirit continues as an inspiration and example through the centuries." She paused a moment and then continued, "Jim, you may be persecuted and discriminated against, but remember it is best to turn your cheek to those who persecute you because your reward will come when you enter Heaven. I think we both believe this."

Jim did not understand her reference to Jesus, but nonetheless he was mesmerized by Gabriela interpretation of religion. He listened to her intently, trying to understand what the white man believed. Gabriela thought it was important for Jim to understand her religion so she talked at length and answered all his questions. He admitted that he too often focused on the evils of the white man while ignoring the evils that were part of his heritage. He needed to understand the differences between the races if he were ever going to be accepted and gain the respect of the white man.

"Yes, I think you are right. Turn the cheek will be my motto. I know this will be a challenge, but one I must accept to fulfill my destiny."

She admired his courage and dedication, even though she still thought his goals were unrealistic. As time for Gabriela to leave grew near, they both knew they had found more similarities than differences in their lives. This strengthened their mutual respect, and both knew they had found a lasting friendship.

Jim was once again escorted to his cell by Abotoe. Jim knew something wonderful was happening in his life—he was falling in love. Gabriela was not only beautiful, but also intelligent and gracious. As Abotoe walked with Jim, he, too, knew there was something different about his friend.

As he locked the cell door, Abotoe said, "Jim, don't worry my friend. Miss Gabriela likes you very much."

"Well, maybe so; but perhaps I got too serious. Maybe she won't want to see me again."

Abotoe smiled, "No worry, Eagleson. You'll see her tomorrow."

Jim sighed, cautiously hoping his big friend was right. He was learning that a relationship with a woman was not easy. Since he was not hunting today, he had all afternoon to drive himself crazy trying to figure out how to cope with his feelings for Gabriela.

Gabriela was concerned about Jim's feelings as well. With deep concern she spoke to Peter about it. "I think Jim is falling in love with me. He looked at me in a most peculiar way, like he was seeing with his heart and not his eyes. He looks to me for direction in his life. I am very concerned."

Peter understood her concerns and tried to reassure her. "Jim's life has been harsh and disappointing. Spiritually he is very mature when it comes to understanding life and death. But emotionally he is still an adolescent, trying to understand his feelings and wanting to mature into a man worthy of his father's legacy. He saw his family and tribe murdered, and his imprisonment is humiliating. Because you are both part Arizee and white, he feels a kinship with you. Your words give him hope. Maybe you are his angel."

Gabriela sighed and became more insistent, "But Peter, he is falling in love with me. I saw it today and felt it when we talked. Jim was different today."

Peter smiled sheepishly, "Sister, do I see that romantic gleam in your eyes. Is Jim seducing you with his charisma?"

Gabriela raised her voice, "Certainly not, I am betrothed to Jacob, whom I dearly love. He will have my heart forever. But if I were not in love with Jacob, I do believe that I could fall in love with Jim—even though he is imprisoned." Then she sighed, "Why does such a man remain in prison? He is so pure of heart. I would give my wealth to free him. He is a very charismatic and spiritually powerful man, and I can easily see why his father wanted him to be an Arizee chief. I can't believe him guilty of any crime."

Peter could easily see in Jim what his sister described and decided to talk with Jim the following morning. Neither said another word, as they retreated in deep thoughts to contemplate Jim's injustice. Peter noticed that tears had stained Gabriela's cheeks. He reached for her hand in an effort to comfort her. He decided to talk to Jim in the morning about his sister's concern. But even more important, he had to find a way to get Jim out of prison, and thought about his future brother-in-law Jacob, who was a lawyer. He would be visiting tomorrow. Peter decided to talk with him about Jim.

CHAPTER 30

The following morning Jim woke early still trying to decide how to cope with his feelings for Gabriela. He felt urgency in resolving this prior to her visit. He truly missed the wise counsel of his parents and Manso. He wondered why God had taken them away. But it was not Jim's place to question God. So he looked within himself for answers regarding his feelings.

Lt. Peter arrived saying that Gabriela was in the meeting room.

"Jim, I need to talk with before you meet with Gabriela."

"Of course, is there anything wrong?"

"Jim I have seen you with my sister, and I am concerned about your growing affection for her and also her feelings of dedication to you. My sister is engaged to another man—a white man. I fear your interest in her is growing into something far different than the friendship I anticipated. So for Gabriela's sake as well as your own, please make your relationship one of friendship of two people who share a common heritage. I hope this doesn't upset you; but I want to protect my sister."

Jim was taken back, but understood his worry.

"What you say makes me sad. I know I would bring problems to her life. So I understand your concern for her happiness. I love her and would not cause harm to her precious soul, so I shall do as you request. Just knowing she is my good friend brings me happiness."

Once again Jim showed that he was a fine human being. But decency was wearing thin the threads that held his fragile emotions in check. This would be very difficult, but he knew he would rise to the challenge.

Like so many others before him, Peter realized that he was in the presence of greatness.

He apologized to Jim saying, "I am sorry to ask that you sacrifice your love."

"No, Lt. Peter, you are correct about Gabriela. She has pledged her love to another and you were proper in what you said. I will honor your request. I look forward to my friendship with my new sister."

Peter shook Jim's hand. "Jim, you are a great man, and God has truly blessed me by knowing you."

Jim said he felt the same about Lt. Peter. He had found another friend to trust.

"There is something else, Jim. Abotoe has told me about your love of baseball. I have talked with the warden, and he has agreed to let you play. However, you will be guarded at all times by Abotoe—both practices and games. I promised the warden that you would not try to escape."

Jim could not contain his excitement. "Escape? Not when I can play baseball!"

Abotoe arrived and flashed Jim a big smile.

"It is said that Eagleson throws the ball like a tornado blows the wind. He is a great pitcher and a great ball player,"

Today God smiled on Jim. He was going to play baseball, and he found a new sister.

Lt. Peter left, and Abotoe took Jim to meet Gabriela. As he entered the room, she greeted him with a big smile.

"Good morning, Jim. How is your day?"

"Wonderful. You've come to see me, and your brother has persuaded the warden to let me play baseball!"

Gabriela was happy to see Jim celebrating the news and was glad that the very frank discussion of the previous day had not damaged their growing friendship. She asked Jim about baseball. He told her about playing ball at the reservation and his friend, an army Captain who said he was good enough to play professional baseball.

Gabriela grew happier as she saw Jim's excitement.

"But you did not come here today to talk about baseball. So tell me more about your family, and I will tell you about mine."

The conversation proceeded easily as they spoke of how the love and dedication of their families positively influenced their lives. Gabriela talked of her happy childhood with the O'Connor family. Jim talked of his early years of being with his tribe. He never experienced discrimination, even with his green eyes and brown hair. It was well known that Lone Eagle would not tolerate it.

Gabriela said, "I can understand why the discrimination by the white man is difficult for you. Please understand that some people have childish minds with adult prejudices. There are cruelties in both words and actions. You must rise above it all as such are born out of ignorance."

"I know what you say is true and realize that I will have to overcome the prejudice toward my race. But I cannot understand the mistreatment of people just because they are different."

"I agree with you, but tell me, Jim when the Arizee took prisoners, how were they treated?"

Jim was surprised and hesitated a moment, "What does that have to do with our conversation?"

Gabriela raised her eyebrows and cocked her head slightly. She was silent for a moment, giving Jim time to answer his own question.

Jim broke the silence. "The Arizee were not compassionate captors. We thought those different from us were mysterious and perhaps evil. They were often tortured or killed." He paused briefly. "I understand. We all discriminate. And we all act out of ignorance."

Gabriela's point had been made and it was a point well taken.

Jim continued, "Your insight and wisdom will help me move forward with my life."

As Gabriela was getting ready to leave, Jim surprised her.

"Gabriela, I love you. I have never felt like this before." Gabriela started to respond, but let Jim finish. "I am a prisoner of your people. I am innocent, an Indian in the wrong place at the wrong time. Because of my circumstances, I can only love you as a good friend and ask for your love and friendship in return until our last days on the earth and beyond."

"Jim, I understand how you feel, as I love you as well. Our common heritage will bond our lives forever. What is so wonderful about love is that is comes in many forms. I will be married soon to a man with whom I share a romantic love. The love we share is different; it is spiritual, inspired by God. I will think of you as my brother and love you always. Our kinship will serve as a unifying force between the races, an example for future generations to be more tolerant."

Gabriela's insight into their relationship left Jim speechless. They held hands and spoke only with their hearts, acknowledging their love was one of affection and devotion, more than just a good friendship. They knew their friendship would be all they would honor. Gabriela was betrothed and was preparing for the arrival of her finance, Jacob Friendly.

CHAPTER 31

The home of Kathleen and Patrick O'Connor was in the heart of Oklahoma City. They moved in the day after their wedding and stayed to raise their family. It was a spacious two story brick home with a beautifully landscaped garden in the back. Their home had hosted many special occasions. Anniversaries, birthdays and christenings had all been celebrated there. Tonight was yet another very special occasion, an engagement dinner. The house was a flurry of activity as Gabriela's fiancé, Jacob was expected shortly.

Jacob, who was a partner at a well respected law firm in St. Louis, fit nicely in the O'Connor family as both Gabriela's father and Peter were career military men. During Jacob's last years in the army, he served as legal counsel and defended many minorities, earning a reputation as a human rights advocate. Due to Jacob's propensity to irritate his senior officers, it was certain that Major would be his highest rank. So Jacob left the army earlier than he originally planned. While his views on civil rights were not often welcomed in the army, they were well received in private practice, where both compassion and compensation were greater. Peter and Gen. O'Connor shared Jacob's strong views on civil rights. Gen. O'Connor had seen too many such violations in the South during the unsettling Reconstruction following the Civil War.

When everyone was seated at the dining room table, Gen. O'Connor offered the blessing and then raised his glass in a toast to Gabriela and Jacob. "May peace and love abide in your lives forever."

After the delicious dinner the men retired to the General's library, which housed his collection of books and maps from his distinguished career. In this austere setting, they shared fine cigars and homemade brandy. After a few minutes Gabriela joined the men. Gabriela had been allowed to join in the after dinner conversations with her father since she had accidentally interrupted a meeting of some esteemed guests and defended the American Indian with regard to the government's doctrine of Manifest Destiny. Gabriela had been so impressive that she earned her place in this typically masculine after dinner ritual.

After finishing the cigars and brandy, Peter said to Jacob. "There is an Indian in the Okie Prison who needs legal representation to gain his freedom. He is a gentleman with a royal heritage, the son of the Arizee Chief, Lone Eagle. His name is Jim Eagleson."

Jacob was startled and responded with a deep gasp, "I know Jim Eagleson! Remember my telling you several years ago that I had unsuccessfully defended an Indian who was inappropriately charged with the murder of a soldier. That was Jim. I tried an appeal, but it was denied. Gen. White, who served as the lead judge, is a cruel man with a vendetta who ruined not only Jim's life, but the lives of many Indians"

Gen. O'Connor pondered the name. "Yes, I remember White. He was politely asked to retire from the army due to some unfortunate indiscretion. To the best of my memory, he bought a baseball team, but I can't remember the name."

Peter asked Jacob to meet with Jim and see what could be done to perhaps win his release from prison.

"Of course; Jim's a fine man and deserves justice."

As they were leaving the library, Jacob asked Peter if Jim were still playing baseball.

"As an Indian, he has not been allowed to play baseball, but just yesterday the warden consented to let him participate in the prison league."

"Great! He is such a good player, and it would be tragic if he could not play." Jacob paused then spoke again, "I sometimes wonder if this discrimination will ever end."

"Probably not in my lifetime," Gen. O'Conner responded.

Peter joined in. "Maybe we can help precipitate the change with Jim. If there is anyone to hold up as exemplary, it is Jim. Now we just have to get him out of prison. Jacob, do you think there may be a chance?"

"The evidence that convicted him was not overwhelming. Jim was a victim of Gen. White's hatred. I know some of the witnesses perjured themselves. Times have changed and opinions have changed, too. I think it's definitely worth a try."

CHAPTER 32

Day after day Jim woke up trying to remember what it was like to be free. It had been so many years since his family was murdered, and he was forced to trade his freedom for the reservation. Now he sat in a prison wondering if he would ever be free. On occasion he still had nightmares of that day of the massacre, but they were becoming less frequent. Mostly he dreamed of freedom.

As he waited for Gabriela, he searched deep in his memory in an effort to remember his life as a free Arizee. Jim's memory was limited by the young age at which he lost his family and tribe. He anxiously tried to recall his family life. He remembered that his father was very respectful of his mother, and for that matter his sisters. He was praying for help in awakening his mind to memories when his thoughts were interrupted by the voices coming from the far end of the hall.

Unexpectedly Abotoe appeared. Gabriela was following with a curious smile. Jim began to think there was going to be something special about this day. Lt. Peter was accompanied by a man with a very familiar presence. Jim shook his head in disbelief. It was Capt. Jacob, his friend who tried so valiantly to get him acquitted.

Jim yelled, "Capt. Jacob! I can't believe it! It's been too long since we have seen each other. How are you?"

"Very well my friend. It is so good to see you again. How are you doing?"

Jim smiled," Pretty good considering I live in a dog pen." He looked at Abotoe, "And watched over by a giant guard dog."

A smiling Abotoe quickly unlocked the cell and the two old friends hugged. It was a joyful reunion. Lt. Peter suggested they go to a conference room where Jim and Jacob caught up on the missing years. Jacob spoke of his law practice and his engagement to Gabriela. Jim felt a twinge of jealousy, but quickly suppressed it so as to enjoy Jacob's update.

Jim's report on his life was much less exciting. "I have done a lot of nothing while in prison, that is until Lt. Peter introduced me to Gabriela. My time with

Gabriela has been wonderful. She is really interested in the Arizee and our customs. We will remain friends for the rest of our lives—just like you and me!"

"Jim, I am so glad you have been able to spend time with her. I hope that she has told you about all the fine white people in the world so that you will have hope for your future."

Jim agreed that she had. He looked at Jacob and asked, "Is there a way I can get out of here before I die?"

Without hesitation Jacob said, "Well, we're going to try. When Peter told me that you were here, we immediately made plans to try and get you out. Then maybe you can play some real baseball. Speaking about playing baseball, Peter told me that you will start playing here at the prison. I don't know if these people know how lucky they are to see you play."

Jim smiled in appreciation, "Captain, I have lost a lot since I last played the game. I am still pretty good at pitching, but I have not hit a baseball since my reservation days."

"Jim, if you play half as good as you did on the reservation, you will be better than any player I have ever seen and that includes major league players."

Jim smiled, "Thanks for the confidence, but time has not been good to me."

Looking at Peter, Jacob asked, "Do you have a starting date for Jim's first game? I want to stay and see him play."

"Next Monday, if I can work it out."

Jim replied, "I love the game, but I will be overjoyed even if you tell me it will be a year from now."

"Well, Jim, hopefully it will be a lot sooner than that.

"I hope so, too, Captain."

"You don't need to call me Captain anymore. Those days on the reservation are over; we are friends. Call me Jacob."

Jim greatly appreciated the courtesy of being able to call Jacob by his first name. "Thank you, Jacob."

"Since it's settled that you will be playing baseball again, we need to talk about an appeal of your conviction. As you remember, I immediately filed for an appeal, but it was denied. Well things have changed in our justice system. I think there is a good chance that I can get an appeal heard in a civil court and not a military one, which I believe would be to your advantage. So if you are willing, it's a good time to consider it."

"Jacob, I am worried that no court will give me a fair hearing. And I do not have money to pay a lawyer. As much as I want to be free and appreciate your interest, I think it will be useless."

"But Jim, we have to try. It will be an uphill battle, but it is worth a try."

Gabriela interrupted, "If for no one else Jim, please try it for me."

Jim smiled, "If you and Jacob think I should do this, I will; but I don't have a lawyer."

Jacob said, "Yes you do. I'll take your case."

Jim thought that an important lawyer like Jacob was much too busy with other cases, particularly when Jim did not have the money to pay him.

"Jacob, I cannot afford your time."

"Yes, you can, Jim. I am taking a leave of absence from my law practice to marry Gabriela, and I intend to work on your case during that time."

"No, I won't deny you of time with Gabriela."

Gabriela spoke up. "Jacob and I have discussed this. You have become a dear friend to me in just a few short days. You are very special, and Jacob and I have decided that we want to spend our time working to get you out of this prison."

Jim was speechless. Other than his parents and Col. Thompson, no one had ever sacrificed so much for him. Tears welled in his eyes.

Gabriela put her hand on his shoulder saying, "My friend, don't cry, it makes me so sad. Be hopeful and smile. You may be out of this prison soon."

Jim, embarrassed, turned away from his friends and said, "I am happy with these tears."

Jacob and Peter left to discuss the appeal while Gabriela remained to talk with Jim, who took a little time to regain his composure before he talked with Gabriela about Arizee women.

When he was able to speak again, he told Gabriela about the women of his tribe. "Arizee women had great influence on the family life and therefore the whole tribe. Many times our women would sit at conferences with chiefs and elders. Their influence in the tribe was immeasurable. It was rarely talked about, but it was obvious to all who knew the Arizee. My mother once told me of a story about an Indian maiden named Pocahontas. She was the daughter of a great chief of the East called Powhatan. She had such influence in her tribe. She is credited with saving the lives of many people, including a white man. So it was with Arizee women. The white man has left these truths about us out of his books, most likely to show the Indian in a savage manner. However, as you reminded me yesterday, we were known to administer cruel treatment to our enemies. So there has been some truth in the white man's portrayal of the Indian. But to be fair, my mother told me of the Europeans who used terrible torture such as impalement, drawing and quartering. So it is not just Indians. We are just easy targets."

Jim's feelings of betrayal by the white man had no limits. Only an understanding friend like Gabriela could comfort this troubled man who had to live with the harsh realities of the world. She did her best to soothe Jim's anger by reminding him that love and kindness must live in his soul, and he must rise above the inhumanities against him and his people.

"Remember our motto. Turn your cheek to the evil!"

Jim was so grateful to have Gabriela in his life. She was a dear friend who gave him insight into the world in which he was forced to live. Gabriela took much from their relationship, too. She learned many things about her Arizee heritage and found a loving friendship in an extraordinary man. In their short time together, they both had become better people because of their friendship.

CHAPTER 33

Jim had a bad case of baseball fever. While waiting to hear from Jacob about his appeal, he kept busy with his work detail and used any additional time to strengthen his pitching and regain his powerful hitting. It had been many years since he played ball on the reservation, but Jim still felt as comfortable with a bat as he did with a rifle or bow and arrow. His father taught him that in order to become skillful with any weapon; it should become an extension of his body. This was also true of the baseball bat. Still Jim was worried about his performance.

Abotoe saw Jim's concern "Eagleson, don't worry too much. You are known to throw harder and hit farther than league players I have seen. So when you get on the ball field, do your best and try your hardest. Show those players that an Arizee chief is better than any other player on the team."

Jim smiled and hugged Abotoe, patting him. "My big friend, I am not trying to show that I am better than the white man. All I want to do is show that I am equal to them both in baseball and in life."

The following Monday, Jim arrived at the baseball field along with his guard, Abotoe. Jim noticed that none of the white prisoners had their own personal guard. He wondered if the warden thought that only Indians tried to escape. Obviously Jim had no intentions of escaping from his chance to play this game.

As Jim walked on the field, he noticed a few familiar faces. In the small wooden stands behind home plate sat Jacob, Lt. Peter and Gabriela. Jim soon found that at least one of these friends would be in regular attendance, which Gabriela said meant that he had a fan club.

Jim was introduced to the manager and coach of his team, Bob Boy Martin.

"Hey, boy I hope ya came ready to play baseball today."

Jim, thinking that he would just be practicing, was surprised to find that he would play a regulation six inning game.

"Well coach, I think I need some practice, but I'll do my best."

Even though Abotoe was a very spiritual man, he smiled cautiously realizing that God would probably only be able to do so much against the experienced baseball players.

Bob Boy Martin played professional baseball when he was younger. Now he was a prison guard, big and gruff with an affinity for chewing tobacco. Before shaking hands with Jim, Bob Boy spit tobacco juice, wiped his mouth and his thick mustache then extended his wet hand to Jim for a hearty shake.

"Boy, I damn well hope you're as good as the Lieutenant says ya are cause Block One ain't doing good at all. We ain't won a game yet which means we found a way to lose ten games straight. We're playing Block Two today so that'll make it eleven games straight"

Having recovered from the wet smelly handshake, Jim said, "Mr. Bob Boy, I will do my best. God is with me."

"Damn, Lieutenant, ya didn't tell me the boy was religious. Heck couldn't hurt. Maybe God will see fit to let us win a game or two!"

Lt. Peter smiled at Jim and Bob Boy, "Who knows, the Lord can do anything He wants, when He sees fit."

Bob Boy was excited about the possibility of divine intervention. Perhaps it was just what his team needed.

He yelled out to his other players, "Okay boys, let's get warmed up."

Jim looked at the players on both teams as they were warming up. He had never seen players running without going anywhere, jumping up and down with arms waving in the air.

Noticing that Jim was bewildered, Abotoe explained. "The players are exercising to get ready for the game. It is a ritual they do so they will be ready to play their best."

"Do you think I should do that stuff so I will be my best in the game?"

Abotoe laughed at Jim and said, "Why not!"

Jim was not very successful at the unusual gyrations of the body. But if nothing else, he gave his teammates a good laugh as he was on the ground more often than not.

Without any pitching or batting practice, the team was suddenly called off the field so the game could begin.

All the players gathered for a speech by the coach when Jim spoke up. "I think I should tell you that I have not played baseball for a long time. I think I need some practice before we start the game."

Laughingly, Bob Boy said, "Ya worry too much, boy. After you see your teammates play, you'll realize that all the practice in the world don't help them.

You'll do just fine and if you don't, hell, nobody will notice. I ain't going to kick you off the team cause of how you play today. By the way which position do you play?"

"Sir, I can play any position. I prefer to pitch, but I will play anywhere you say."

"Good, I like your attitude. You'll start in right field."

With a glove given to him by Jacob, Jim ran out to right field a little nervous, but anxious to play. He didn't have much to do in the first inning as most balls were hit to left field. But that was okay with him, Jim was just happy to be on the ball field playing the game he loved. It was not until Jim's turn to bat that he got a chance to prove himself. The opposing pitcher struck out all but one of the previous eight batters. This meant two things. One, the pitcher was damn good and two, Jim was batting ninth, which meant that the coach had incorrectly assumed he was a poor batter. Jim stepped up to the plate, batting left handed against the right handed pitcher. Bob Boy was shocked. He thought Jim was a right hander. He was positive that Jim threw with his right hand.

He turned to one of his players, "Damn, I bet the boy's a switch hitter. Hell, he may actually be a good baseball player after all!"

As Jim took his practice swings and walked into the batter's box, Gabriela used what little Arizee Jim had taught her to yell, "Hit it hard!"

He looked at her with a smile. Even though the words she yelled meant roughly, "Hug me tight," Jim was appreciative that she was showing her support in their native language. Also, since only Abotoe knew what she was saying, it didn't matter.

The first ball was pitched directly at Jim, and he had to bail out, falling to the ground barely missing a hard ball to the elbow. The short squatty umpire yelled, "Strike One!"

Bob Boy ran to the plate yelling at the umpire with words best not repeated. The umpire stretched his short statue and warned Bob Boy to get back to his bench or be kicked out of the game. Bob Boy, realizing he was pushing his luck, immediately walked back to the bench, mumbling words referencing the umps lack of morals.

Jim appreciated the coach defending him and stepped back in the box after brushing off the dirt and tobacco juice that covered much of the ground around home plate. Through the noise, Jim heard Abotoe yelling in Arizee, "If he throws at you again, step back and hit the ball to the heavens."

For a quick second Jim smiled and glanced back looking for Abotoe. Jim's smile was mistaken for a smirk by Block Two. Suddenly, he was a very unpopular player.

The big pitcher went into his wind up and threw a fastball, inside. Jim stepped back with his left foot and slammed the ball over the left fielder's head. The ball was hit so hard and placed so perfectly that Jim could have run the bases backward and scored before the ball was returned to the infield.

As Jim crossed the plate, the catcher said, "Beginner's luck. Wait until you're up again, sucker!"

Jim's teammates ran to greet the new star. Even though Block One eventually lost the game 10 to 9, Jim's homerun and three hits brought out the best in his new teammates. Bob Boy concluded that it was divine intervention, a true miracle.

Bob Boy shouted in glee, "We almost beat them. Next time we'll do it for sure."

As the teams were leaving the field Jim received praises for his performance. Jim heard someone call his name. It was the big pitcher along with the coach of Block Two. The pitcher, Jumbo Jones, offered his hand to Jim, who reciprocated. Jumbo had pitched in professional baseball and was once considered a prospect for the major league until he was caught taking a bribe to lose a game. He landed in prison, banned for life from professional baseball.

Jumbo said, "Jim, sorry about that first pitch. If I had to do it over, I would hit you in the head!"

Jim was startled.

"Just kidding slugger, you hit that ball damn good today."

Jerald Conroy, coach of Block Two, asked Jim if he had ever played professional baseball.

"No sir, the last 20 years I have either been on a reservation or in prison."

Coach Conroy asked Jim how old he was. When Jim replied 35, the coach said "Damn, that's a shame. With your hitting ability, ya could have made it big in the game."

Jim thanked the two for their praise and surprised both by saying, "I am not too old. I am an Arizee and will be as good a man on my oldest day as I was on my youngest—maybe not as strong, but much wiser."

Coach Conroy looked at Jacob and Peter. "Damn with this boy's ability and attitude, you need to get him out of prison as fast as possible and in professional ball. I think he's ready for the big show."

Jacob responded, "We're working on that right now."

"Well I know a few managers in the big leagues so if you need me to put in a good word, just let me know."

That night as Jim lay on his prison cot, his heart was joyous as he prayed, "Thank you God, and thank you father. Today was a good day in my life. I played baseball." Jim closed his eyes and drifted into a quiet and peaceful slumber.

CHAPTER 34

Baseball was once again a godsend for Jim. In his years living among the white man, it was the only thing that gave him a sense of worth. He contributed to a team effort and was rewarded with praises from white men. Baseball gave him dignity. It also allowed him to escape from the drudgery and disappointment in his life. Each day he played his spirits were lifted and he gained a renewed hope for a better future. Hope that he could live up to his legacy. Combined with his friendship with Gabriela, baseball made Jim think that he could live successfully in a white society. He understood why it was the all American sport.

Had it not been for baseball, the time required to appeal his verdict would have seemed an eternity. Jim knew Jacob was an excellent lawyer and would do everything to get him out of prison. He told Jim that it would take time, maybe even years to get a court to hear his appeal. Jim had been patient since he was 15 years old, while either directly or indirectly imprisoned, so he could wait a few more months or even years to be free, particularly since he had baseball.

Prison teams played games two days during the week, plus once on the weekend. Jim, who had attracted Bob Boy's attention in his first game, had plenty of chances to further impress his coach in practices and games.

During practice for the next game, Bob Boy yelled, "Jim, get your Indian butt over here, I need to talk to you about something important. Your friend Jacob said you had quite a throwing arm. Is that true?"

Jim responded in the affirmative and added, "Coach, I can usually pitch pretty good."

"I ain't talking bout pitching from the mound. I'm talking about throwing the ball to home plate from, let's say out there in deep centerfield. So can ya throw that far?"

"Sure, but I can also throw good from the mound."

Getting a little irritated Bob Boy said, "Listen boy, ya ain't going to be breaking up my pitching rotation. Understand? Breaking the sacred rotation would be too risky just when the team is showing signs of breaking out of a depressing season." Then Bob Boy corrected himself, "What the hell am I talkin' about. Our team has lost 11 games in a row!" He hesitated for a moment and the continued. "But for now, ya just concentrate on centerfield and hitting. Maybe one day I'll give ya a chance to pitch."

Jim nodded in agreement. But in his heart, he knew it was his pitching that would win games for his team, as well as get him into professional ball. In the meantime, Jim went to the deepest part of centerfield and practiced throwing to the infield. Bob Boy was most impressed.

One of his assistants said, "Coach, I ain't never seen anything like that. Damn, that boy can throw strikes over the plate from centerfield as accurately as most pitchers can from the mound! Are you gonna let him pitch?"

Bob Boy looked at his assistant, "What the hell do ya think? Of course I am. And I'm gonna figure out how to use him as much as possible. Damn, I never thought it'd be so hard to manage talent!"

Bob Boy watched Jim and wondered how good he was when he was younger. Even if he could get to the pros, which was doubtful with him being an Indian, he was too old to play much longer.

Turning to his assistant he said, "Ya know, we gotta do something about not letting Indians play in professional leagues, Negroes, too. Look at Jim. He is the best baseball player I've ever coached, and the only reason he's playing now is because of a couple of decent white folk pulled some strings for him. It's just ain't right."

The assistant took offense, "The reason them wild Indians ain't playing is because they all still want to kill us white folk for taking their land. Ya just can't trust 'em."

Bob Boy retorted, "Whatcha talking about? There ain't a better mannered, more decent person on that field than Jim Eagleson."

His assistant was not about to be convinced to the contrary. So Bob Boy turned away, shaking his head in disgust, "It's a damn fool world we live in."

Jim played centerfield in the next two games. Runners, who were trying to stretch singles into an extra base, were surprised to find that Jim's throwing made it impossible. He also continued to display his ability at the plate, getting three hits in four times at bat in both games, two of them homeruns. Jim's effort helped his team win both games. Block One team was happy to have Jim as part of their team, and Jim was thrilled to be part of the team of white players who admired him so much.

Several more games into the season, Jim finally got his chance to pitch. Unfortunately it came as the result of a shoulder injury to the team's best pitcher, Louis Degold. Because his team had only a few pitchers, Coach called on Jim to relieve Louis in the game. His nervousness showed. The first two pitches sailed over the head of the umpire and evoked taunts from the opposing team. When he finally got the ball over the plate the batter hit a homerun. Time out was called and both the coach and the catcher went to the mound and talked with Jim.

"Just calm down boy; I know ya got it in you."

"I do, but I'm just a little nervous."

"Well get over it boy; you got some batters to get out."

Jim took a deep breath remembering the words of his father. *Make the weapon an extension of your body.* Jim went on to strike out the remaining batters. But even though no more runs were scored, Block Two won the game five to three. After seeing Jim pitch, Bob Boy decided to make him the new starter and, if needed, a relief pitcher.

When he told Jim this, he asked, "Does this upset ya? I know ya just want to be only a starter, but I think you'd be equally valuable as a reliever to close our games with saves."

"Coach, you don't need to explain anything to me. You're my coach and friend, and I trust your decisions to be for the good of the team."

Bob Boy was so impressed, "I think I see why people think so much of you. Ya aim to please and are truly a team player."

The following day Jim once again started in centerfield and batted fourth in the clean-up position. He had a great hitting day, starting with a double and an RBI, scored in the early innings. But in the bottom of the last inning, his team was losing 6 to 5. Block One's first batter got on base, only to be thrown out on a double play when the second batter tried unsuccessfully to bunt. The third batter, Creek Martin walked. So now the pressure was on Jim to produce a hit that resulted in at least one run to tie the game.

Bob Boy called Jim over for a little encouragement. "Ya know what ya need to do. Show everyone how ya handle the pressure. I know ya can do it."

Jim batted left handed against a big, husky right hander. He hit the first pitch, a fastball, down the right field line. The runner on first easily scored, tying the game. By the time the ball was relayed to the infielder, Jim rounded third base and headed for home. The infielder fired the ball toward home plate; Jim avoided the tag by using a hook slide which propelled him around the catcher's tag.

"Safe!" yelled the umpire.

There was wild celebration. The bench emptied and Jim was the hero, vaulted on the shoulders of his teammates. Here he was, an Indian on the shoulders of his white teammates, riding the tide of victory. Life was looking up for Jim.

CHAPTER 35

The season ended successfully for Jim and his team. He not only used his talents but also sportsmanship to make his teammates better players. He strived to be an example for others to follow. Baseball was his vehicle for self expression and acceptance in the white society. This is how he wanted to live the rest of his life, whether free or imprisoned. But Jim was still holding out for eventual freedom. He felt that if he could do as well in professional ball, it would be his means to succeed in white society and achieve his destiny.

Peter, Jacob and Gabriela came to most of Jim's games and also visited him frequently at the prison. Jacob credited himself with discovering perhaps the best baseball player of all times and always had tips for Jim about his game. With Jim's immense respect for Jacob, he studiously listened to all of his advice, after which Jim would inquire about the appeal.

But a day came, when both Jacob and Gabriela visited, that Jim did not want to talk baseball; he wanted to discuss the progress of his appeal.

One of his concerns was that Gen. White would be a judge in the appeal.

When he asked about this Jacob replied, "No, Jim he is no longer a judge. The General is retired and working in professional sports."

"Does that mean that he can stop me from playing professional baseball?"

"Unlikely, since there are many teams and Gen. White does not have the power he had in the army."

"Jacob, I hope you are right."

Jacob moved on to his explanation of the appeal process.

"We'll file your appeal with the courts and hopefully you can get a retrial. A retrial will be similar to your original trial, except you may choose to be tried by a jury instead of a judge. That means that a judge alone will not decide your guilt or innocence, but 12 citizens, who in your case may be more prejudiced against an Indian than a judge. If you are not granted a retrial, we will take your case to a higher court. Of course, the best thing to happen would be that the appeal court overturns the verdict, in which case you will be freed immediately. I strongly suspect that one way or another you will be a free man when this is over."

Jim asked a few questions, and said he understood what Jacob said. He was more optimistic than he had been in years and found considerable comfort in knowing that he could be close to freedom.

Now that Jim's questions had been answered, Jacob changed the subject.

"Jim, I need to talk with you about your dream of playing professional baseball. Don't get too optimistic. I worry that you expect baseball to change discrimination in this country. That won't happen anytime soon. Racism is so much deeper than you realize. It is a negative force that persists in men's souls. So don't think your accomplishments in baseball will end bigotry. Be prepared for obstacles."

Gabriela interrupted, "Understand what Jacob is saying. The abuse you have received because of your race is unfair and cruel. You have experienced this many times in your life, and baseball will not necessarily put an end to it. We want you to be prepared for prejudice that you will surely face. So remember your motto."

Although Jim did not like what he heard, he promised his friends that whatever happened, he would be prepared.

"Yes, I remember. I will turn my cheek."

Gabriela touched his hand. She was glad he remembered and hoped that he would practice it. She had no doubt this remarkable man would try.

CHAPTER 36

A month passed since Jacob and Jim talked about his appeal process. Jacob had filed the appeal and tried to explain the bureaucracy in government which often impeded the wheels of progress.

"Jim, this is the way our government works. We can't rush anything. And if you are granted a retrial, it appears now likely to take as much as two to three years for the court to hear your case."

Jim did not understand most of what Jacob was saying concerning the bureaucracy, but he did understand his appeal could take a very long time. He also realized that it may be many years before he could play baseball as a free man. His face was a mask of sorrow, and Jacob was almost certain he saw tears in Jim's eyes.

After a painfully long pause, Jim spoke. "Jacob, I will be patient and wait for my freedom. But I don't have much time left to play professional ball. My bones and muscles hurt so much after a game now that I have to drink pain medicine from Abotoe. What will it be like when I am even older?"

"What do you mean pain medicine?"

"Just some stuff that Abotoe's friends make from cactus juices and corn."

Concerned for Jim's health, Jacob scolded him. "Jim, don't drink that stuff. It will kill you if you are not careful."

"Jacob, I am an Arizee. I have been drinking spirits since my reservation days. The water was bad so we drank Manso's whiskey instead."

Jacob continued his warning, "You better stop now. You can easily become addicted. You don't need that stuff to make you feel better. If you have pain, I can get the doctor to see you."

Jim peered into Jacob's eyes and in a rare show of anger said, "That's easy for a free man to say!"

Jacob thought about all the bitterness in Jim and wondered if he would ever be able to succeed in a complicated world that was so foreign to him; only time would tell, and time was not on his side.

CHAPTER 37

It was almost six months after filing for Jim's appeal that Jacob brought the good news that his appeal had not been rejected.

"So Jacob you think by next year this time I might be free. One year—that's not too long"

"I certainly hope so. But let's not get too confident. We still have a long difficult road ahead."

Jim had waited for many years and he could hang on for just one more. So while waiting for the court's decision, Jim concentrated on playing baseball. He used this time to improve his pitching and hitting because in his heart he knew baseball would help him earn the respect of the white man. There were rumors of professional baseball scouts slipping into the prison to check out the players. Jim was of particular interest to them.

Jacob and Gabriela continued to work very hard on preparation of Jim's case. They finally made the decision to officially postpone their wedding. This change in their plans made Jim very sad and angry, but they would have it no other way. Jim's freedom was now the most important thing in their lives.

Almost twelve months to the day, a letter addressed to Jacob Friendly, Esq. arrived from the court. Jim had asked that any news on the appeal be read when all three friends were together. So Jacob and Gabriela went immediately to the prison.

When they arrived Jim had just hit a homerun to end a tough game with a victory for Block One. His team now had a good shot at the championship title. When Jim saw Jacob waving an envelope in the air, he slipped away for the celebration. Jim, sensing what Jacob had in his hand, dropped to his knees with great emotion and prayed, *God please let this be good news so I can be free to make my father proud.*

With great deliberation Jim slowly opened the envelope, unfolded the letter and read silently. Jim was unsure of what the letter said, so he handed it to Jacob for an explanation.

As Jacob read the letter, first he smiled and then he yelled, "We got the appeal hearing in six months! The court saw merit in our argument. Jim, we have hope!"

Jim looked toward the heavens and yelled something in Arizee, giving thanks to God. The players saw the excitement and rejoiced with him. Even the manager of Block Three was celebrating. He told Bob Boy that the news was worthy of celebration because he was hoping Jim would get out of prison before the championship games began! With Jim gone, Block Three had a good chance at the title.

Jacob turned to Gabriela and said "I hope these people aren't celebrating too soon. We have a lot of work a head of us and victory is not assured."

Later Jacob expressed these thoughts to Jim, but Jim refused to remain anything but optimistic and eagerly began working with Jacob to prepare for the hearing.

CHAPTER 38

While preparing for Jim's appeal, Jacob fought an uphill battle to gain access to the army's files from Jim's military trial. The Army was in no rush to provide an aggressive lawyer any information that could reverse a military court decision.

Jacob knew he was facing a case that was very challenging since it involved an Indian who was found guilty of killing a white soldier. The sensitivity to the subject of a racially debated case could dissuade the most liberal judges from reversing a military court's decision. However, Jacob remained confident that at the very least he could win a retrial. He was committed to this appeal, since it could be Jim's last chance for freedom.

Jacob was feverishly working on Jim's case when he got word that Gen. O'Conner had suffered a heart attack. He rushed to the hospital where he met Mrs. O'Conner, Peter and Gabriela. Throughout the night Jacob waited with Gabriela and the family for news of her father's condition. Fortunately, good news was forthcoming. Gen. O'Conner had survived the heart attack and was resting comfortably. But Gabriela still worried about her father's health. So she and Jacob decided not to wait to get married. Fortunately, Jacob had made good progress in his work on Jim's appeal, and Gabriela and her mother had already completed most of the plans for the wedding. While her father recuperated in the hospital, the rest of the family busily worked on the wedding details.

The wedding date was three months prior to Jim's hearing. With the guest list numbering over 500, this was a wedding Oklahoma City society would not soon forget. Gabriela had chosen her sister, Elizabeth as her maid of honor and her best friends, Sandra and Anna as her attendants.

Jacob's decision about his groomsmen was more difficult. Even though his parents had come from large families, they married outside of their faiths. Jacob's father was Irish Catholic and his mother of Jewish decent. So this breech in family relations had materially reduced Jacob's contact with his relatives. He asked his father to be his best man, his future brother-in-law Peter and his law partner to be his groomsmen. He also dearly wanted Jim to serve as the other groomsman, but he knew getting permission for Jim's release to attend a wedding would indeed be difficult, if not impossible to obtain from the prison warden.

Gen. O'Connor's considerable influence with prison officials was invaluable. So with the General's persuasive powers and clout, Jim, who was already on trustee status, was allowed to leave the prison to participate in the wedding. The warden specified that Jim would be accompanied at all times by Abotoe. Since that was settled, Jacob now turned his attention to the proper attire for his groomsmen. Jim, not knowing exactly what he was getting into, eagerly anticipated the wedding.

To prepare for the wedding Jim was introduced to the bathtub. It was the first time he had bathed in a tub and found it quite relaxing. Next he was scheduled for a haircut. For his friends' wedding, Jim was willing to look like a white man. In fact, once Jim cut his hair he never let it grow to the long length he had maintained since his youth. He saw this as an important step to gain acceptance in the white society. Next came the tuxedo. Jacob and Gabriela took Jim and Abotoe to the tailors for the fitting. Up to the fitting of the trousers, Jim did not find the process particularly distressing. But when the tailor put his hand near Jim's crotch to measure the inseam, Jim grabbed the poor man by the neck, calling him "loco."

Jacob immediately removed Jim's hand and yelled, "Jim, the man was only measuring the length of your legs to make sure your pants fit properly!"

"Then why can't he measure from the outside and not the inside?"

Jacob shrugged and looked at the tailor for an answer.

The tailor who was just now regaining the color in his face muttered, "Ah, because this is a more accurate measurement."

Gabriela and Abotoe were snickering. Jim smiled at Gabriela, but stared fiercely at the tailor, who was not comfortable with the safety of his life until he finished this dangerous assignment. The tailor cautiously finished measuring and promised that the tuxedo would be ready by 3 p.m. that afternoon. With this unholy indoctrination into civilized life over, Jim left the shop with his friends, Jim had recovered from the inappropriate situation and wondered why Gabriela still found it amusing.

He looked at Jacob and asked, "What is so funny to her?"

Jacob, who could hardly refrain from laughing said, "She's loco, too."

Jim grinned, "Yes, that's right, women can be loco. My father once told me that. Now I understand."

Later that afternoon, Jim and Abotoe stopped at the tailor's to pick up his tuxedo. The wary tailor was concerned that Jim was only accompanied by the large Indian. He preferred that Jacob was there, too. He was somewhat relieved, though, when Jim apologized for his actions earlier in the day. The tailor retrieved Jim's outfit and timidly asked Jim to try it on to assure the fit.

The tailor, who was relieved, sighed deeply, "Ah, it looks very good on you."

Jim disagreed. "The pants do not fit well in the crotch. You must measure again!"

Not again, the tailor thought. Sweat began to appear on his forehead as he bent to one knee to measure again.

As he began, Jim yelled, "Boo! Just kidding, the pants are just fine."

Jim and Abotoe laughed at Jim's joke, but the tailor saw no humor. After recovering, he packaged the tuxedo and gave it to Jim. He smiled somewhat timidly; happy that he would live to measure clothes another day.

CHAPTER 39

On the day of the wedding, Abotoe and Jim arrived at the church early. Peter, Jacob and his law partner, Tim Wilkins, were already there. Jacob asked Jim if he needed help with the tuxedo.

"No, I have already been fitted by the tailor, who by the way, I had to scalp because he put his hand on my crotch again."

Jacob was momentarily shocked by Jim's story, but before he could say a word, Jim laughed, "Just kidding, I wanted to make a funny."

Jacob smiled and realized that Jim was starting to manage just fine in the sophisticated civilized world.

With help and encouragement from Abotoe, a frustrated Jim finished dressing. He commented to Abotoe, "Why does the white man make something as simple as marriage so difficult. From what I can recall from my youth, there was a simple ceremony, then off to the hut for man and woman to make babies."

But then he stepped in front of a full length mirror and saw a completely new man. He thought, *maybe a big ceremony with fancy clothes does make a wedding more special.* Although Jim initially liked what he saw, he was frustrated by the identity crisis going on in his mind. He turned to leave the church not feeling he belonged there but stopped when he reached the door. Abotoe sensed Jim's crisis of seeing himself as a white man.

"Go back to the mirror and have another look at yourself!"

For a moment, both men stared at Jim's reflection.

Abotoe finally spoke with wise counsel, "Whether you are dressed as an Arizee or a white man, you are Jim Eagleson. It is not what is on the outside, but who you are inside." Abotoe continued with a chuckle, "My brother, if I was not on this earth, you would be the best looking man in the world."

Taking Abotoe's words to heart, Jim rushed to the wedding hall feeling very confident, but conscious of the irony of an Arizee chief in a tuxedo.

When Jim joined the other groomsmen in the vestibule, Jacob was amazed at Jim's transformation. "I am darn glad Gabriela met me before seeing you."

Jim laughed, but deep down he too wished he had met Gabriela sooner. Of course it did not matter since Jim loved both Gabriela and Jacob and would do nothing to threaten their relationship. After the groomsmen were given instruction as to their responsibilities, they entered the sanctuary for the ceremony.

Because of Jim's good looks, he received many admiring stares from the female wedding guests. He was sure that most did not realize that they were seeing an Arizee Indian, who under different circumstances would make them cringe in fear and repulsion.

As the wedding began, the bridesmaids walked slowly down the aisle of the old church. Elizabeth entered the sanctuary just prior to Gabriela, who on her father's arm, made a grand entrance to the sounds of the Wedding March. Her long two-tier veil cascaded from the pearl and diamond tiara that was worn by Mrs. O'Connor on her wedding day. Gabriela wore a long sleeve lace jacket with pearl buttons over a satin dress with embroidered beadwork. She carried a bouquet of white roses and ivy. Gabriela was truly a beautiful bride who commanded the attention of everyone in the church.

She could not help but notice Jim's bright smile. For one quick moment she pictured Jim standing where Jacob was. But she quickly blocked the thought and continued down the aisle to the other man she loved. She stood beside Jacob, tears in her eyes. As her father kissed her cheek, he gave her hand to Jacob.

It was a lovely wedding with an elaborate reception. Guests were entertained with music, hors d'oeuvre, champagne and a three tier wedding cake. No one noticed that Jim was having difficulty enjoying the happy occasion because of his feelings for Gabriela. To help him get through the day, he often sipped champagne as well as whiskey from the small bottle tucked in his pocket. As the happy couple left for their wedding trip to Pennsylvania, they were met with good wishes along with a shower of rice.

Jim was lonely with his two friends gone. His thoughts turned to Gabriela and how he wished she had married him. But he did not allow himself to dwell on the negative. He gladly discarded his tuxedo and donned more comfortable clothes even though they were prison issue. As he reflected on the day, he was glad he went to the wedding, not only because he wanted to be with his friends on the happiest of day of their lives, but because for the first time he was treated as an equal in a situation other than baseball. He hoped this was but a glimpse of the happiness he could expect as a free man.

CHAPTER 40

Gabriela and Jacob had a wonderful honeymoon. She had never been east of the Mississippi and was thrilled to see new and exciting places. Jacob took her to Philadelphia to see Independence Hall and the Liberty Bell where she ran her finger down the crack she had heard so much about.

When they returned, they renewed their work on Jim's appeal. Jacob wasted no time in visiting the prison to discuss the case. Instead of talking about his appeal, Jim wanted to know about the wedding trip.

"When the Arizee marry, they go to their hut and start making babies. Why do people in your society need to go away from home to do this?"

Jacob did his best to explain the wedding trip was not only for that purpose, but Jim did not buy it. "You are a good man, and you are smart. You and Gabriela will have many babies."

Jacob laughed. "Jim, you are a clever man and have shown me many ways in which the Arizee and white man are alike."

Jacob then turned the discussion to Jim's case. He told Jim that he had sworn depositions from all witnesses and experts who testified at the original trial.

"I have some very good news. I found Pvt. Johnson, nephew of the deceased sergeant, who said he witnessed the murder of his uncle. He is currently serving a prison term for attempted murder of an army buddy. While in prison, it seems that Pvt. Johnson became a Christian, and has changed his original testimony. In his deposition, he stated that when he entered Manso's hunt, he saw his uncle lunge at you with his own knife. Missing you, his uncle fell on the knife, which plunged into his chest, killing him. He also admitted that he never saw you make any attempt to physically attack anyone. He said that his uncle was drunk when he went to see Manso. Sgt. Johnson told his nephew that he was going to confront Manso for distributing spirits to the soldiers without sharing the profits and said he was going to kill the old Indian if he did not get his money. The Private said he lied at the trial because the vices of the devil were channeled through his sinful mind."

Jim was excited to hear this. "Well this is good news, but also very sad." This news, while breathing new hope into Jim's appeal, also revealed the sad fact that such a wise man as Manso had been killed over whiskey profits.

But, even with this new information, Jacob warned Jim not to become over confident. Jacob admitted he had seen cases like Jim's where witnesses who changed their testimony were thought to be chronic liars and unreliable.

"I don't see how the law can be so damn confused as to the simple truth."

Jacob shrugged his shoulders because he actually had no explanation.

"Jim, I honestly don't know. Our country's courts continue to search for the truth you are talking about. Hopefully one day, they will find it in your case. So we will submit this new evidence and see what happens."

Jim was confused and somewhat discouraged over this whole question of truth.

When Jim was alone in his cell that night he looked to the heavens and prayed, "Oh great father of mine please speak with God and ask him to see me through this most trying time. Give me the courage to face my future for I most certainly know the road will be difficult and paved with hardships."

CHAPTER 41

Jim played baseball until the weather became prohibitive. His outstanding performance continually pleased Bob Boy and his teammates, but irritated and amazed his opponents. Bob Boy and the other managers had nothing but praise for Jim's athletic ability as well as his sportsmanship and moral values he demonstrated on and off the field.

At 37 years old, Jim's aches were more frequent and intense. He never acknowledged the talk of baseball players' careers ending by the mid thirties. He did not wanted to show his pain, so he never sought care from the prison doctor or even Jacob's personal physician. To help he relied on Abotoe's pain medicine, which was smuggled into prison. Realizing that this pain medicine wasn't much more than pure alcohol mixed with water, both Gabriela and Jacob warned Jim of the possibility of dependency and serious health problems

Jim was always defensive. "I am an Arizee chief. I am strong and do not worry about that nonsense. I am only using the medicine to help with my pain. Abotoe has been drinking the brew for many years, and he's just fine."

Jacob tried to warn his friend. "Jim, aside from the dangers of alcohol, a professional team would not tolerate any player drinking as much as you."

Jim still showed little concern. In fact, Jim was already an alcoholic in denial. And because of that, his drinking would haunt him for the rest of his life.

The three months since the wedding passed slowly. When Jacob received news from the court, he once again visited Jim to relay this information.

Jacob explained, "This is good news. Pvt. Johnson maintains his revised account of the night his uncle died. But the court still has questions that are unanswered and needs additional time."

With Jacobs's explanation and more delays, Jim grew less confident that he would be freed from prison. Even though Jacob tried to give encouragement, Jim was becoming despondent. Visits from Gabriela helped somewhat, but Jim knew that the only thing that would give him complete satisfaction was being released from prison and playing professional baseball.

It was January before Jacob finally received notice of his hearing date. Jim remained hopeful but prepared for disappointment.

Jim's case was heard before the appeals court on a cold windy day in February. Along with Jacob and Gabriela, he was escorted by Abotoe. He also had other friends to support him, the warden, John Stephens and Bob Boy. As Jim stepped into the courtroom, he could not help but recall his military trial and the decision that put him in prison. Jim and Jacob took their seats at a long table near the judge's bench. Promptly at 9 a.m. the bailiff rose and asked everyone to stand for the Honorable Harvey Hadwell, Judge of the Appeals Court. With the judge seated, the bailiff was asked to read the specifics of the case. As the bailiff read, Jacob noticed the

U. S. attorney, who would normally be readying himself to object to Jacob's request for the military court's decision to be set aside, was sitting at his table without any files.

Jacob whispered to his friend, "I have a mighty positive feeling, Jim."

After the bailiff finished, Judge Hadwell, asked the U.S. attorney if he had any objections to the request that the original verdict be set aside. The attorney rose, "No, I do not."

The courtroom became a buzz of excitement. The judge let the gavel fall, threatening to clear the courtroom if the disorderly conduct did not immediately end. When silence ensued, the judge asked Jim, along with Jacob to, approach the bench.

"Jim Eagleson, upon the review of your military court proceedings it is the decision of this court that you should be released from the Oklahoma Prison as soon as possible."

For a second time Jim's supporters began to rejoice, but the judge again squelched the celebration with a threat.

He continued, "Mr. Eagleson, I do not know you, but I must say that based on the errors and inconsistencies of your original trial, I deeply apologize for your unjust incarceration." As the judge dropped the gavel for adjournment, the courtroom erupted with joy. Finally Jim Eagleson, Son of Lone Eagle was a free man and had been exonerated. There was going to be a life for him beyond the prison walls.

As Jim embrace Gabriela, he whispered, "It has turned out just like you said, I am free because of you and Jacob, because of your prayers and hard work. Turning to Jacob, he said, "I love you and Gabriela. Thank you my eternal friends"

CHAPTER 42

Jim was returned to the prison to await the completion of the paperwork necessary for his release. He had no problem waiting a few days for his freedom. The fact that he knew the day would come was enough for him. His only concern now was if he could find a baseball team that would let him play.

Abotoe, while happy for his good friend, felt he needed to have a serious talk with Jim before his release. One evening, Abotoe sat with Jim to express his concerns.

"Jim, you have gained freedom to live among the white man. I worry how you will handle your life. It has been many years since you were free. I think you should go back to the reservation to live for a while before going out on your own. This will give you time to make plans about your life. You have no experience living in the white man's world, and I worry that you will be treated unfairly even though you have a few good white friends who want to see you succeed. You are a man of honor who treats all men with respect, even though it may not be deserved. I pray that when people see this in you they will overlook your skin color. I wish you much luck as you make your way in this new world and fulfill your destiny. Remember whenever you need me, I will be there."

"Abotoe, my friend, you have taken care of me for many years here in prison, and I know what you tell me is true. We will always be friends and you will be with me wherever I go."

"Yes Jim, friends forever."

"Jacob and Gabriela have invited me for dinner to discuss the same concerns you have talked about. The warden has given me permission to go, and I would like for you to go with me, as my guard, and as my friend."

Abotoe stood, "I am deeply honored that Jim Eagleson, son of Lone Eagle shares such an important event with me. I'm a very lucky man!"

When Jim and Abotoe arrived at the Friendly residence for dinner, they were both handsomely dressed.

When Gabriela opened the door, she said, "Gentlemen, may I help you? If you are selling something, I do not have time to talk with you now because I expect two friends for dinner."

Both men looked surprised and wondered why Gabriela had not recognized them.

Not being able to maintain a serious face, she giggled, "Don't worry boys, I recognized you. I was just kidding. Although I must say that the two of you are so handsome that my eyes were temporarily blinded."

Jim thanked her for the compliment. But, secretly Jim hoped that what she said about being handsome was true—at least about him and not his big lug of a friend, Abotoe.

Jacob was laughing when he greeted them and welcomed them into his home. Gabriela and Jacob shared the love of laughter, and their marriage reflected both their devotion and deep friendship. Jim prayed that when he met the right woman they would be best friends, just like Jacob and Gabriela.

After a scrumptious dinner prepared by Gabriela, the three men adjourned to the parlor; and Jacob handed out cigars. Jim had never smoked a Cuban cigar. Once, he had smoked some type of weed in a pipe, but it was not nearly as pleasurable as the cigar. Abotoe was a snuff man, but graciously accepted Jacob's hospitality.

After Gabriela finished her work in the kitchen, she surprised Abotoe and Jim by joining them and smoking what she called her girly cigar. It was a much smaller, milder one made with tobacco raised in Virginia. It was grown in a small farming village in Virginia called Varina. It is similar to another mild tobacco grown in Spain.

Jim found himself quite confused with this explanation and asked, "Where are Cuba, Spain and Varina?"

Jacob said, "It doesn't matter; what's important is the pleasure the cigar brings you. And speaking of pleasure we want to give you a box of these cigars to celebrate your new life."

Just then Gabriela brought several more boxes from behind the desk and said, "Jim, Happy Birthday! Since you are not sure of your birth date, Jacob and I have decided that it will be today!"

"So what are the boxes for?"

"They are birthday gifts, and they are for you," She then explained the custom of giving gifts to celebrate one's birth.

Jim smiled, realizing that he may have found another benefit of living in the white man's world. He ripped the wrapping paper with a fury to see what his friends had given him. There were shirts, pants, food and even money. Jim greatly appreciated their show of affection, but jokingly said, "What do I do with all these gifts? I still live in a prison!"

"Why Jim you can keep them here. Jacob and I have room."

Abotoe, who was aware of the surprise, also had a gift for Jim. He handed Jim a long wooden box that he had given Gabriela earlier for safekeeping. Jim carefully opened the box and found a calumet with Arizee ornamental carvings. He was overwhelmed with its beauty and recognized that the carvings indicated it had been the property of a chief.

Abotoe explain the origin of the pipe. "Jim, our friend Mansolin found this calumet inside the old wooden box that belonged to Manso. There are many religious carvings, but there is one that makes this pipe very special. See, it indicates that this was your father's pipe, a gift from the Geronimo. Mansolin said that his grandfather most likely got the pipe through a trade with soldiers."

Jim wiped several tears that had escaped from his eyes. "This pipe will be an inspiration to me through the rest of my life. I will always cherish it along with you and Mansolin. This is the greatest day of my life. All of you have made me very happy!"

Jim carefully placed the pipe back in the box and the birthday party continued with cake and ice cream. Gabriela told Jim it was tradition that he make a wish and blow out the candles on the cake. Sucking in a big breath, Jim exhaled and extinguished the candles with one blow. Everyone knew Jim wished he would make his father proud, but Gabriela told him to keep it to himself so it would come true.

CHAPTER 43

Jim was anxious for the administrative paperwork to be completed so he could finally be free. While contemplating his future, Abotoe arrived with a message from the warden.

"Jim, there are some important people coming to see you today. The warden says they are a politician and an Indian agent. I also heard that Jacob is coming. I am worried. I hope there is no trouble with your release."

Jim, too, was concerned and wondered if he had once again become a victim of injustice.

"My big friend, I've had many good things happen over the last month, I will not worry until I know for sure that I have something to worry about. Jacob would have told me if there was bad news."

Jim elected to skip breakfast and dressed quickly. Abotoe accompanied him to a meeting room where he saw Jacob and Mr. Stephens, the warden, Bob Boy, prison managers, along with other men who were unfamiliar. Mr. Stephens began by introducing the Honorable Thomas Saunders, Governor of Oklahoma and Pete Napier, Indian agent for the state. Jim knew about Indian agents, but wasn't too sure about a governor.

Abotoe, sensing this, whispered in his ear, "The governor is a big chief to the people of Oklahoma."

Both men shook Jim's hand after which the Governor noticeably wiped his with a handkerchief. They stood on either side of Jim as a small bald headed man stood behind a black box that was on top of three legs.

The small man said, "Please freeze."

Jim immediately dropped to the floor and covered his head with his arms.

The Governor laughed. "For God's sake man, get to your feet; you have nothing to fear from this box. It is not a gun. It is a camera for taking pictures so many people can remember this special day."

The Governor leaned to the warden whispering, "In addition to being a savage, he's also stupid."

The warden chose not to address such ignorance on this joyous day.

Jim jumped up and stood with the men for the picture. He flinched when the box went boom accompanied by a flash and smoke. Jim was still not sure this box was harmless.

The warden asked Jacob if he would introduce the other guests.

"Jim, honored guests, I'm pleased to introduce Robert Owens. He is a scout for the St. Louis Spartans. Mr. Owens, would you please explain why you are here?"

"Jim Eagleson, I'm here representing the owners of the finest baseball organization in the country, the St. Louis Spartans. I have been authorized to offer you a contract to become a member of our organization and play for our team in Phoenix."

Jim whispered to Jacob asking him to explain a contract.

"It is an agreement so that you can play baseball with his team—the professional baseball team."

That got Jim's immediate attention. Mr. Owens continued, "The contract specifies that your salary will be negotiated by your agent, Mr. Jacob Friendly."

At that time the bald man with the black box appeared and began taking more pictures. Flash, boom, more smoke circled from the black box and lingered above the guests.

Jim tried hard to control his excitement so as not to appear to be the wild savage some people thought, but soon found that to be impossible. He and Abotoe excitingly shouted an Arizee yell. Appalled by their performance, the Governor asked for quiet so he could say a few words on this momentous occasion.

"Jim Eagleson, you should be very proud of what you have accomplished against odds that would destroy most men. You and your lawyer have challenged a miscarriage of justice and won. A considerable part of that bravery is characteristic of your native Navaho people."

Jacob cleared his throat and quietly told the Governor that Jim was an Arizee.

The Governor, his hand shielding his words from the audience, turned to the warden and said, "Whatever, they are all the same." Turning back to his audience he continued, "Excuse me, Arizee. Jim, we are very proud of all that you have accomplished. You are a hero for all young Navaho boys, and we feel certain you will become an inspiration to all young people."

The Governor speech left little doubt in anyone's mind that his appearance was primarily ceremonial and for the advancement of his political career. He did not in any way seem sincere in acknowledging Jim's achievements.

After the Governor's political performance, the Indian agent had a few words to say.

"Jim Eagleson, you are proof that with diligence an American Indian can achieve success particularly with the aide of the current Indian agency system."

The Indian agent was no better than the Governor. He was praising an Indian agency system that was miserably failing too many American Indians.

The warden spoke next. "Jim, when we first met, I saw you as a murdering savage, only to find that I was completely wrong. You are an exceptional man and a fine human being. You have earned the respect of guards, prisoners, as well as me. You have demonstrated determination and bravery to withstand the hardships of prison life. I now proudly tell you that as of today you are officially a free man. I personally want to apologize for the many years of injustice. You are free to leave this prison."

Jacob in closing added, "Yes, my good friend, you are now free to show this country the courage and greatness of an Arizee chief. I consider you a credit to the human race."

Guest and prison officials clapped loudly showing their respect.

Jim was visibly moved by the words spoken. He thanked everyone and once again received well deserved applause.

Then out of the corner of his eye he saw Gabriela standing in the crowd. She was beaming with pride for her Arizee brother.

After the dignitaries left, Gabriela congratulated Jim with a big hug and a friendly kiss. Jacob could not help but notice the special relationship that existed between the two friends. Some husbands would have been intimated by this, but Jacob knew that the friendship was one between fellow Arizee's, too important and sincere to criticize. He was truly happy for the friendship they shared.

Bob Boy was also on hand to congratulate Jim on his release from prison and his baseball contract.

As Bob Boy shook Jim's hand he said, "Even though it's hard as hell to accept I'm losing my best player; I can honestly say that I've never known a baseball player, red, yellow, black or white, as good as you. You got that balance of discipline, skill and love of the game that makes a complete player. I wonder how good you'd be if you were younger. I guess I will never know, but I do know one thing. In due time, your name will be a household word in America, especially with those who love the game of baseball."

Bob Boy turned to Jerold Cason, "You know we're gonna miss Jim"

"Not me! Hell, maybe now we can beat your butts like we used to."

"That may be true, but we've all had the opportunity of watching a truly great player. Now if we wanna see him play, we're going to pay for that pleasure."

Both Bob Boy and Jerold were the reason that the Spartans took notice of Jim. They even had to sneak the scout into prison to watch him play. Mr. Owens commented that this was the first time he ever heard of any one trying to break into prison. But it was worth it, for the Spartans had recruited a talented player who they knew would give his all to the game.

Jim left the celebration to gather his belongings. He took off his prison clothes for the last time and laid them on his cot. They were part of his past, a sad remembrance of injustice. He put on a pair of pants and a shirt that Gabriela and Jacob have given him. He wished he had a mirror to see his new image.

He reported to the warden who accompanied him from the administration building to the prison gate. As he walked from the building, Jim saw Lt. Peter, who saluted him and his Block One baseball team who lined the steps and waiting to say goodbye. As they approached the prison gate, Jim saw more prisoners and guards standing waving goodbye to him. Some were white men, some Indian, Chinese and Negroes. Not everyone knew Jim personally, but they all knew him by reputation. To them Jim was a hero. He was an honorable man who fought almost impossible odds and finally won. As Jim passed through the gate to freedom, he turned and looked once more at his home for many long years. He could see his big friend Abotoe, standing above the crowd, waving and yelling his best wishes. After many years of confinement, Jim was finally free.

CHAPTER 44

Jacob and Gabriela met Jim outside the prison and took him to their home. He had accepted an invitation to live with them until he reported to the Spartans team in Phoenix. Gabriela showed Jim to the guest room and gave him time alone to unpack and rest. The first thing he did was look in the mirror to see how he looked in his new clothes. He liked what he saw and was confident in his future success.

The following week, a large envelope and box addressed to Jim arrived at the house. Gabriela pointed out that it was from the Spartans. Jim, who relied on Jacob for advice on his baseball career, decided that he would not open them until Jacob returned from work.

A few hours passed during which both Jim and Gabriela stared at the box. They couldn't wait much longer.

When they saw Jacob walking up the sidewalk, they opened the door and ran to meet him. Gabriela told him of the delivery.

"Jacob this box and envelop arrived today for Jim. He wanted all of us together when he opened them."

"Well, let's not wait any longer," Jacob said.

Jim anxiously opened the envelope and read the letter. He gave it to Jacob to interpret. Jacob explained that the Spartans had sent a contract. The salary was not as much as he had asked for, but Jacob felt it was fair considering Jim had been assigned to the minor league team in Phoenix, Arizona, which was not far from the reservation where Jim had once lived.

"Jim, there is also a train ticket to Phoenix along with an advance on your salary."

The money was almost secondary to Jim because just playing in professional baseball seemed reward enough. Jacob handed the box to Jim for him to open.

In the box there was a Spartan's uniform, complete with shirt, pants, socks, shoes and a hat. Jim was elated. It was his first real uniform since the tuxedo.

Jacob explained that the ticket was for the 10 o'clock train on Tuesday. Jim signed his contract and changed into this Spartan uniform. He then asked Jacob to take him to the prison so he could show Abotoe.

Abotoe was duly impressed. "When you get to Phoenix, get me one of those shirts! I want as many people as possible to know that I am a friend of the great baseball player, Jim Eagleson."

Jim gave his friend a hug saying, "Don't worry; I'll do my best to see that you have your own shirt."

When they returned home, Jacob spent time with Jim explaining professional baseball. "It gives the individual teams a means to develop talent for the major league while providing baseball teams to smaller cities who do not have the population to support a major league team. So there are major and minor league baseball teams. Jim, in your case, the Spartans will start you on one of their minor league teams since you are an unproven talent in professional baseball."

Jim said he understood and would be willing to start at any level just to play professional ball.

Jacob applauded Jim's good spirits saying, "The best thing you can do is go to Phoenix and knock their socks off."

Jim interrupted, "Knock their socks off?"

"That just means really show them how good you are."

Jim nodded.

"Anyway, knock their socks off so they have no choice but to put you on their major league team. It'll be a difficult road for you. There are only a few American Indian playing in baseball. It will take a lot of patience. Your friends have confidence in you and will always be here when you need us."

"I know it will be very difficult for me and I'm prepared to do whatever it takes to succeed in my dream."

While Jim said he was ready to accept the challenge, he had no idea the depth of the challenge or the discrimination he would face. Trial and tribulation would continue to mark his life.

CHAPTER 45

Jim headed to Phoenix leaving most of his worldly possessions at his friends' home. Parting with his friends was not easy. He suddenly realized that while he was free from prison, he would miss time with his close friends. But leave, he must. He had his find destiny and time was getting shorter with each passing day.

He kissed Gabriela goodbye, and Jacob took him to the train station. He enjoyed the ride as the train twisted and turned through the canyons and the plains. Compared to the train ride to prison, this trip as a free man was far superior. Jim was not accustomed to sleeping in a bunk bed, so he laid a blanket on the floor of his Pullman compartment and let the motion of the train lull him into a peaceful sleep. He awoke just in time the following morning to witness Nature painting an exquisite sunrise upon the Arizona sky. The colorful intense brushstrokes dripping with emotion and memories poured into Jim's soul as if he were a living, breathing canvas, and he was now part of what was once only a memory. It was alive now, it was real, and while Jim was immersed within its mesmerizing beauty, a sweet song from within resonated through his body, and it sang to him, he was home.

When Jim arrived at the Phoenix railroad station, he looked for the Spartans' scout who was supposed to meet him. He expected Mr. Owens, but instead saw a man with a big sign, "Jim Eagleson" in letters so large even the blind could read it. The man introduced himself as John Cherokee, who Jim quickly discovered was an errand boy for the team. Jim noticed the man's skin and features were similar to his. So with a few questions, Jim found out that John was part Comanche and Mexican. He assumed the Spartans thought that he would be more comfortable with an Indian driver. Unfortunately, if someone really wanted to send a friendly face, it would not have belonged to a Comanche. The Arizee had never been friendly with the Comanche. But that was another time and place, and Jim did not hold grudges in his new life.

John gathered Jim's few pieces of luggage and helped him into the motor car. A few minutes into the drive, Jim said, "Isn't Cherokee a name of an Indian tribe in the east."

John replied in the affirmative.

"Well if you are Comanche and Mexican, why are you called John Cherokee?"

John grinned, "The Spartans gave me the name because they could not pronounce my given name. The coach was from the east and Cherokee was the only Indian name he knew. Then, I guess wanting to give me a first name, they called me John because I had to use the john so much when I first got here. I had a bad case of diarrhea and it took weeks to get over it. So they started calling me John Cherokee."

Jim could not help but laugh and hoped he would not have a similar problem.

As John drove through the city to the clubhouse, Jim noticed the large number of non white people. This was encouraging. For the first time since leaving prison, he did not feel like the few; but one of the many. Such good feelings, though, were short lived once Jim met his new baseball family.

Arriving at the Phoenix Spartans' facility, John pointed out the location of Mr. Owens's office. Before John hurriedly left, he showed Jim to a room and told him that Coach Larson McCoy or one of his assistants would be there soon to familiarize him with the place. Jim had waited for a very long time when John Cherokee popped his head in the room.

"So Jim what did you think of the place. Pretty impressive, huh?"

Jim told him that he was still waiting for one of the coaches to show him around.

"Heck, Jim I can do that. Come on let's take a quick tour."

The first stop on the tour was Jim's living quarters. Jim was given this room because it was difficult to find housing for an Indian that was close to the stadium. Other than a strong smelly odor, the small room was adequate. There was a bed and a kitchen area with a hot plate for cooking, but no privy.

John explained. "You can use the bathroom in the locker room. It ain't bad. There's a nice shower there, too. Heck, up until yesterday, your room was a cleaning supply room, but don't feel bad; it is bigger and better than mine." Jim assumed the cleaning supplies were responsible for the strong odor

Next stop was the locker room where Jim would keep his uniform and baseball equipment. John pointed to Jim's locker, which was the last one at the far end of the room. Unfortunately it did not have a lock, but John promised to get that fixed for him.

Jim looked worried, "All I have is my uniform. I don't have a glove or a bat."

"Don't worry; the team will supply everything you need, including a jock strap."

"Jock strap? What's that?"

"Protects your private area."

Jim wrinkled his brow, "When you say private area, are you talking about my big pants warrior?"

John laughed, "Yeah, I think we are talking about the same thing."

The tour continued, but Jim saw nothing remarkable until they walked into the ballpark. He was staggered by its size.

John described it. "The stadium holds up to 5,000 fans and is only five years old. But fan support is growing quickly so before long we'll need a bigger one."

Jim was amazed. He had never been in a professional ballpark. "With all those fans, how do the players hear each other?"

"Well," John explained, "We use hand signals."

Jim said he knew of those. They were used a little in prison ball.

"Come on Jim, let's go to the top seats here on first base side. This place seems really big doesn't it? But the field is regulation which is probably the same size of any field you have played on. So don't ever let the size of ballpark scare you. Say, have you ever played in a park with walls in the outfield?"

"No, why have walls? All you have to do is hit the ball over the outfielder's head."

"Well things are a little different in professional parks. It's a homerun when the ball goes over the wall. You don't have to race around the bases like you did in a field without walls."

"Okay. So all I have to do is to hit the ball over those walls and I can walk around the bases if I want!"

John shook his head in agreement.

Thirty minutes went by before Jim and John returned to the locker room, where a good number of players had arrived for an afternoon game. John walked into the room through a barrage of dirty laundry thrown by some of the players. He said, "Don't worry they don't make you players do the laundry. That's my job."

Coach McCoy saw them talking and yelled to his newest player, "Boy, where the hell were you. Your ass was supposed to be waiting for me to take you on the tour and introduce you to everyone."

John spoke up, "Coach, he left because I told him to. He had been waiting such a long time so I took him on the tour."

"Well, then you're a dumb tail hole. I'm supposed to do that. No wonder you are the grunt boy around here. Even at that ya don't take orders well."

Jim was surprised at the language directed at John, but wisely remained silent.

"Yes sir coach, you're right. I won't interfere again, just thought I was helping."

"Well, don't think and get ya ass out of here before I beat it white."

Coach McCoy quickly realized that he was inappropriate with John in front of the new player. "John, don't mean to be so gruff, but I gotta get my point across when you screw up."

"Yes, sir, I understand."

Jim continued to hold his tongue thinking about the "turn the cheek" advice from his friend Gabriela. But he thought that when he was a great ballplayer, he would make sure that no coach degraded any of his Indian brothers.

McCoy turned to Jim as he lit a cigar. "Come on boy, let's go to my office."

Coach said he had five team commandments and pointed to the wall behind his desk where they hung in a large frame.

1. You will be expected to do everything Coach McCoy asks of you, on and off the field.

2. As a member of the Spartan organization, you will act respectfully at all times.

3. You must learn all hand signals.

4. Show respect for the flag of the United States of America and show reverence to all Christian prayers.

5. There will be no smoking or drinking alcohol and you are not to engage in sexual relations during baseball season.

Jim quickly realized that these rules applied only to players as Coach McCoy was currently smoking a cigar and drinking what appeared to be a beer.

"You understand, boy? If you violate any of my commandments you will be punished and may find yourself kicked out of the Spartan organization."

Jim intensely disliked being called "boy," but he politely replied, "Yes sir, Coach McCoy, whatever you say."

"Ok, now let's get down to business. I see you did not bring any equipment; which means you will be expected to buy it. The cost will be deducted from your paycheck."

Jim politely informed Coach McCoy that he understood that the equipment would be given to him.

"Well yes and no. If you prove that you are good enough to play for us, we'll refund your money. But you gotta make the team first."

With a look of surprise, Jim replied, "But Coach McCoy, I thought I had already made the team?"

"Look here boy. Your contract says that you'll be paid for services rendered to the team. If you ain't good enough to provide those services, then you don't get paid."

Jim could not hide his disappointment that he may not be playing baseball.

Coach picked up on his worry, "Hell, if you are half as good as I've been told, you can make the team easy! Now we have more business to attend to."

Jim listened intently as the Coach explained how he would receive his pay and told him about the away games.

"What do you mean away games?"

"Damn boy, you're dumb as a bell. I mean we don't play all of our games here at this ballpark. We have to travel to other cities."

When Jim thought about it that did made sense. Not all the teams in the league were located in Phoenix. Then Coach added a bit more of unwelcome news.

"Some towns don't necessarily like non whites using their facilities. So you may find that you will not be allowed in the same hotels or restaurants as our white players. You may have to sleep on the bus. I guess I could say I am sorry, but there ain't a damn thing that I can do about it. It's the law in some cities."

"Coach McCoy this is disappointing, but I'm here to play baseball and will do what I have to in order to play the game. But tell me sir, is it because people think that I'm inferior?"

"I respect you for asking that. I would like to tell you the answer is no, but I would be lying to you. Maybe you can help change that."

Jim was disappointed in the response, but knew he could prove himself equal, if given the chance. And it seemed that coach thought that way, too.

"One more thing, boy; because you didn't wait for me as you were told, you'll be the equipment boy in tomorrow's game. John will help you. Now let's go meet the players"

Equipment boy! Jim could not believe what he had heard—he was relegated to equipment boy and not a player. This is not what he dreamed about all those lonely nights he spent in prison.

CHAPTER 46

The Spartans had a long home stretch in Phoenix. Jim was glad because it gave him time to adjust to his new life and hometown. Before every game the team, including equipment boys, ate together; something about camaraderie, according to Coach. The food was much better than anything he had on the reservation or in prison. In fact, he had gained almost eight pounds, which were really needed since he had experienced a significant weight loss in prison. There was also the matter of his new teammates. Jim handled this just as he had in prison. He was very humble, expressing the honor of knowing such fine men. The players saw Jim as friendly and cooperative and a few accepted him, but only as the equipment boy, not as a fellow player. But he soon discovered this was not the same as respecting. Jim could not help but hear the racial comments about him being a half breed Indian and the snide remarks about his appearance and how he ate. Jim once again thought about what Gabriela said. He must turn his cheek and rise above the insults; but he didn't know how long he could continue to overlook the cruel remarks.

Also frustrating to Jim was the delay in actually playing baseball. The only time he handled a bat or ball was when he was performing his duties as equipment boy. Days passed and he had yet to pitch or hit. While the team was taking hitting practice early on a game day, Jim decided to ask Coach McCoy of his status on the team.

Coach was reviewing the starting line up when Jim asked, "Coach McCoy, when do you think I can play with the team?"

The coach, with his mind obviously on the game, spoke to Jim as he never heard a word he said. "Damn, Jim! How ya doing? How are things going for ya?"

Jim, who took this to mean that the coach had no immediate plans for him to play baseball, replied, "Just fine Coach McCoy."

Two days later, Jim asked the coach the same question.

"Well Jim you gotta be patient, buddy."

Jim had to admit that "buddy" was better than boy, but coach's response didn't seem to get him any closer to playing baseball.

So Jim became more insistent. "Coach McCoy, What are your plans for me? I gotta play on the team!"

This sounded like an ultimatum to McCoy. With his small dark eyes glaring, he rose from his chair in disgust, "Listen boy, you'll play baseball when I say ya play and not one damn minute sooner!"

That pretty much told Jim where he stood, and now he figured that Coach McCoy hated him for even asking. That week ended just like the one before, without Jim playing baseball. He assumed that he would remain an equipment boy right along with poor John Cherokee. Jim felt his dream disappearing; but he tried to keep faith, thinking God must have another plan for his life.

CHAPTER 47

The first away game was in two days, and it was traveling day for the Spartans. They broke even for the two-week home stretch, which wasn't bad since prior to that they had a losing record. Now they were heading to Amarillo to play the best team in the league. Coach McCoy was upset that the top prospects he had hoped would propel them to a championship season were nothing but disappointing. He was particularly disillusioned in the relief pitchers and clutch hitters. Jim watched game after game from his seat in the dugout. He knew if Coach would give him a chance that he could help win games for his team. He didn't understand why moving equipment was more important than winning.

While Jim and John were stacking the equipment bags in front of the clubhouse to be loaded for the road trip, a large bus with the Spartan's name pulled up in front of the clubhouse. It had racks on top for equipment and a door on the side which held the players' luggage. Other than the train, Jim had never seen anything that big with wheels.

As they were loading the equipment on the team bus, Jim marveled at the inventions of the white man—trains, cars and buses, magnificent buildings and even superior guns and cannons that they used to defeat the Indians.

John spoke up "That bus is really something, huh?" John replied, "Times are changing, Jim. You know we gotta keep up with the progress. If we don't, it will only serve to make us Indians look even more inferior."

"John Cherokee, you are a wise man. Our people have to figure a way to become part of this progress so we can move forward with the white man."

"But Jim I'm just not sure how we do that."

"Well I think my way is baseball."

John replied, "Trust me, Jim; baseball ain't no way to do it. Look at us. You and I can play ball, and they have us loading equipment."

Jim replied, "I intend to do something about that. My loading days are numbered, just wait and see!"

"They may be numbered, but not anytime soon." John paused then added, "By the way, I was told to stay in Phoenix because you would be in charge of equipment on the road. Does that make you feel more equal?"

Jim was truly disheartened by that news. He shook his head, "Naw; I guess I really did make coach mad."

John left Jim to load the last of the equipment. A few of the players arrived and tossed their luggage to Jim as if he were their servant. When Jim finished the packing, he stood next to the bus not knowing what he should do. Should he get on? Was he even going to be allowed to ride on the bus?

Just then Coach McCoy yelled, "Get you ass on the bus, boy. Ya plan on walkin' to Amarillo?"

On the bus Jim saw a long aisle with benches on either side, just like the train. However, there was not a seat left for him.

Tom Thurman, who was one of the more promising rookies, occupied a seat toward the front of the bus. He yelled, "Injun boy, what's ya problem?"

"Just looking for a seat."

Thurman shouted, "Well look closer. There it is in the very back where you get to sit by your lonesome Injun self. That's because Injuns stink and the real players don't want them up front."

The other players laughed. Jim looked to Coach McCoy for support, but the coach sat with his head down apparently working on some strategy for the next game. Jacob was right; being an Indian in the white man's world wasn't going to be easy.

Once again Jim wisely remained silent and took his seat in the back of the bus. Throughout the trip he sought solace from his miseries in whiskey; this time with the help of John Cherokee and his connections to a few bootleggers in the area.

Jim's drinking problem was shared by many of the Indian men. Discrimination, along with the lack of education and available jobs, almost assured a second class existence. Whiskey seems to make things more tolerable for the Indians. Jim thought baseball would boost his status, but so far that hadn't happened. So Jim found himself in the same circumstances that most Indians eventually faced.

The bus finally came to a stop in the heart of Amarillo. Jim unloaded the luggage. The players picked up their bags and went into the hotel to register. Coach McCoy was right. Jim was not allowed to sleep in the hotel with his teammates. He both slept and ate his meals on the team bus. McCoy ordered food for Jim and brought it to him whenever he got around to it. Once when

Jim tried to order a hamburger, someone from behind the counter shouted an obscenity and threw garbage at him.

Jim did as he promised Gabriela, but as he walked out of the restaurant, he heard someone say, "Good riddance! We don't need no thieving Redskin smelling up this place."

Everyone in the restaurant laughed. Jim walked away without saying a word.

Depression lead Jim to consume enough alcohol in the morning to get him through the day and even more at night to chase away the nightmares of failure. He was following in John Cherokee's footsteps, whose addiction to the spirits had caused an estrangement from the team. Between Jim's excessive drinking and melancholy, his prospect of being a baseball player seemed all but dead.

CHAPTER 48

Several months passed since Jim reported to the Spartans. The team showed even more improvement. They were in second place in the Southwest League, although still nine games out of first place. This was a tremendous margin to overcome, particularly with so few games left in the season. Hitting was improving steadily, but relief pitching remained a big dilemma with no resolution in sight. The Spartans often managed to go into the late innings with a lead, only to lose because of their pitching staff, whose stamina was insufficient to hold the opponent scoreless.

Jim was often too drunk to be concerned about the team's performance. Half the time he did not know if they were winning or losing. He took his morning drink before dressing and delivering the equipment to the field, and then retired to the dugout where he would alternate between dozing and going to the bathroom to sneak a drink.

One evening after a loss at home to the Amarillo Tigers, Coach McCoy sent a message for Jim to come to his office. Jim, who was so detached from the team because of drinking, had no idea what coach had on his mind. And truthfully at this point he didn't care.

Jim knocked on the door, and without waiting for a reply he entered. He took a seat in a chair, slouching as if he were ready to nap. "What ya need Coach?"

McCoy's face was stern and angry. "If ya think you're fooling us, you're dead wrong. Everybody round here knows about your drinking. Ya not only look drunk; ya smell drunk; and you are drunk!"

Jim tried his best to focus on what Coach was saying and was frankly surprised that anyone noticed anything about him.

Coach continued, "Remember my commandments. No alcohol or you'll be fired? Well Jim," with his thumb almost touching his index finger, "you are about this far from being fired."

Jim drunkenly responded, "Well Coach, ya gotta do what ya gotta do!"

This enraged McCoy. "Ya know if I told the owners of the Spartans what sorry shape you're in they'd fire your red ass and take back all the money they've paid you. You're very close to being kicked out of baseball for the rest of your life?"

"Hey, right now I'm not playing baseball so if you fire me; it won't be a big change for me."

McCoy softened his tone and said, "Jim perhaps I went too far not letting you play ball. But honestly, I wanted to see how you could handle things; you know, kinda see what you were made of. There are only a few professional teams that have any Indians or Negroes playing in their organizations. I wanted to see how ya could withstand the ridicule before I put ya in a game and face the fans and players. You gotta be tough to take the ugliness from narrow minded people and strong to stand up under the pressure. Ya can't succumb to your inner doubts and resort to drinking to cover your disappointment, which no doubt was made easier by your association with John Cherokee. I know he must've told you of his failure, perhaps making you think that you, too, will fail. But here's the truth about John. He joined us when he was a lot younger. But we soon found he was a drunk with very limited talent. So we made him equipment manager, and he's lucky as hell he has a job. You, Jim are different. I know ya got the talent to make it in this game. So I'm going to give ya a chance. You'll pitch batting practice tomorrow. Show them your good stuff. But if ya don't lay off the alcohol, it'll be the last time ya play with this team."

Jim tried to thank Coach McCoy but was too soaked in alcohol to manage his emotions. Even in his drunken haze, he understood that he was finally getting a chance to show off his pitching; and if he didn't stop drinking, it would be his last.

"This is your chance, Jim. We need a closer and if you can throw some decent pitches during practice and maybe in the next few games, you might just be our man. The scout who saw you play in prison said you have a mean change-up and a blazing fast ball. So tomorrow show me what you can do."

The following morning Jim came from the dugout in uniform and more sober than he had been in months. He was going to be pitching in preparation for an afternoon game with the Amarillo Tigers. He felt proud, but very shaky because of his withdrawal from the spirits. He hoped his pitching with John Cherokee on and off over the last month had helped to keep him sharp.

Bill Foster was first up and made fun of Jim, as was his usual custom. His taunting got so bad that the coach yelled at him to shut up or consider himself benched for the game. Many of the players were pleased that the coach had finally admonished Bill. His cheap slurs had grown old.

Bill, who was embarrassed by coach's remarks, decided to get his revenge on Jim by hitting every one of his pitches, which was much easier said than done.

Jim was nervous as he threw his first professional pitch, even if was only practice. The pitch was a disaster, bouncing once in front of the plate. This brought a barrage of heckling from the few fans that had arrived early to watch the practice or get autographs. The second pitch was no better as it traveled over the head of the batter and the catcher.

Bill yelled, "Damn boy, can't you see the plate. Want some spectacles?" He pointed to the plate with his bat. "Here it is. Is it too small for squinty Indian eyes?"

Jim was feeling the pressure and anger from Bill's taunts. The catcher, Joe Dominic came to the mound. He told Jim to concentrate on getting the ball across the plate and ignore the batter and the fans. "He's a good hitter, but he doesn't even know the difference between the men's and women's john."

Jim laughed, but secretly wondered about the difference. When Joe got back to the plate he looked directly at Bill and said, "Don't you start up with him again. I won't be as well-mannered as Jim; I'll come after your ass!"

Jim stepped back on the mound, took a deep breath and ignored the heckling to deliver his third pitch. Bill swung at the fast ball and missed it by a good foot. Bill Foster, as well as the next two players, was eventually able to get solid hits off of Jim; but he was not the pushover they expected. Next up was clean up batter, Tom Thurman. This big mouth from the bus walked to the plate taunting Jim. Coach McCoy thought it best that he talk with Jim before he pitched to Tom, so he took a trip to the pitching mound.

"Jim, relax and don't listen to Tom. He's a big mouth blow hard. But he is our best batter. Throw some easy stuff before ya give him your best pitches. Let's see what he is made of." Coach grinned and patted Jim on the butt saying, "Go get him chief!"

Well, chief was a hell of a lot better then boy and buddy so Jim did as Coach asked. Thurman almost knocked the cover off the balls hitting all of Jim's slower pitches for line drives and homeruns. Now it was time for phase two of Jim's plan for Thurman.

In a rare display of name calling Jim yelled, "Hey big mouth. See if you can hit this!"

"Red boy, watch who you call big mouth. You done pissed me off so I'm gonna to slam one down ya throat1"

Jim starred at Thurman and released a fast ball. Thurman swung and missed so badly that it sounded like the ball hit the catcher's mitt before he even swung.

"Lucky pitch; try that again and see what happens!"

While Thurman was watching for a fastball Jim threw him a changeup, and Thurman swung before the ball crossed the plate. He was speechless and walked back to the dugout, embarrassed and angry.

Jim pitched the remainder of practice and mixed his pitches up so coach could get a sense of his abilities.

Coach McCoy was waiting to shake Jim's hand when he returned to the dugout. "See boy, just like I said, ya got what it takes to be a big time ball player. It's just a matter of time before you're in the big league."

"Thanks Coach for having faith in me. I'll do a lot to help the team win the rest of the games."

"Ya damn right ya will. And I will help ya get to the majors; but time is passing and ya ain't getting any younger. Be ready to close tonight's game."

Jim sat in the corner of the dugout and bowed his head. The other players walked by him without the usual taunting. Strange, Jim was still an Indian; he had not changed. But his teammates had changed. They saw him pitch and that made him worthy of their respect. Life in this world was sure confusing. His teammates sat in silence, wondering if Jim were praying. They chose not to interrupt him, especially if it might help them win.

Jim was praying for the strength to be his best against the opponents. He knew the answer to his success was in God's hands. Suddenly, like the lightening strikes, Jim felt a sharp pain in his stomach. It only lasted a moment, but it was excruciating and made it difficult to stand. His hands were shaking. He figured it was the alcohol talking to him. Jim knew he had to be strong and fight his craving so that he could play ball tonight—his first real game. He had finally made it to professional baseball.

CHAPTER 49

The game that night against the Amarillo Tigers was a tough one. The Spartans were losing by three runs going into the bottom of the eighth. Since the bottom of the Tiger's batting order was up, coach let the starter, Tom Cotton, begin the inning, but signaled his pitching coach to have Jim warm up. His plan was to call on Jim, if Tom started having problems. The first two hitters flied out, deep in center field. The next two batters walked and Cotton was struggling. Time was called, and Coach McCoy went to the mound.

"Coach, I'm starting to aim for the plate. You know what that means, one blink and the ball's hit into the next county. Think that Indian boy could take over for me?"

Coach took the ball from Tom and said, "Damn if I know, but I guess we'll have to give him a chance." He waved for the right hander. Jim Eagleson was in his first game.

Jim sprinted to the mound eager to get started. After he finished his warm up pitches, Coach put his arm around Jim shoulders and said, "Jim, this ain't no different from batting practice. You threw to the same home plate less than two hours ago, and you were damn good. Now stick it to the Tigers." Coach patted Jim on his butt and said, "Go get 'em chief."

Jim looked up into the sky in hopes that his father was watching.

He stepped off the mound and gave the ball a good rub.

Then the catcher, Joe Dominic, stepped in front of home plate and yelled, "It is two out. All we need is this one!"

Jim stepped back on the mound and delivered his first pitch. It was a fastball that whizzed over the batter's head. The base runners took advantage of the wild pitch and advance bases. Runners were now on second and third bases. The Tigers' bench erupted in laughter. Jim tried to ignore their amusement and concentrate on the game. With the ball in his hand, he remembered his father saying that he should make the weapon an extension of his body.

Jim's second pitch was a fastball down the center of the plate, swung on and missed by a very bewildered batter. The next pitch was another fast ball, hit foul. "Strike two."

Tension grew as the batter and Jim eyeballed each other. The batter was going to be ready for a fastball that he could turn into a homerun. Joe flashed the sign for a changeup and Jim nodded his approval. Jim wound up and threw a changeup that caught the batter off guard. He swung hard, but well before the ball crossed the plate. "Strike three!"

The inning was over. At first there was disbelief, but then the Spartans' bench erupted in celebration. Jim was a hero after facing only one batter.

It was the top of the ninth and the Spartans needed four runs to win the game. Jim's performance seemed to inspire his teammates, even though they were facing one of the best closers in the league. The first batter hit a line drive down the left field line for a double. The second batter promptly singled the runner home. The Tigers' coach and catcher went to the mound to talk with the pitcher. Whatever transpired out there on the mound, worked because the next two batters struck out on just three pitches each.

The whole Spartan team was feeling the pressure because they knew that Roscoe Emmaus was coming to bat. Roscoe was in a bad slump that he just could not seem to shake. Coach felt it necessary to give Roscoe a little pep talk.

"Now son take ya time. Make sure the pitch is a strike before ya swing. Ya got a damn good eye—so wait the pitcher out. I got confidence ya can get a hit." After returning to the dugout, McCoy told his assistant, "Damn, we're gonna lose this game!"

The pitch to Roscoe was a slider across the outside of the plate. He swung and fouled the ball down the first base line. Then on a fast ball, he slapped a lazy liner into right field just out of reach of the first baseman. The runner on first ran to third, and Roscoe rested confidently on first base. The Spartans' bench went wild. The tying runs were on base. Victory was within their reach.

McCoy called a timeout. Jim was up next. He had not taken batting practice and coach was not sure he could depend on Jim in a tight situation. The umpire was getting anxious to finish the game and made his feeling known rather loudly.

Coach called Jim. "Jim, the scout said you're one of the best clutch hitters he's ever seen. That right?" Before Jim could say anything, Coach continued, "Well boy, hope he's right because I need ya bat right now! I used all my decent pinch hitters, which means you're the only player I got left."

There was no time for Jim to respond as the umpire yelled, "Play ball!"

Jim randomly picked up a bat and walked to the on deck circle to take a few swings when he felt a tap on his shoulder. It was Tom Thurman, the big mouth who had made all those disparaging remarks about Jim.

"Jim, I'd be proud if ya used my bat. Hopefully ya can do more with it than I did tonight."

Jim was taken back and graciously took the bat from Tom.

He repeated his father's words, "Make the weapon an extension of your body, and you can control it like you do your hands."

Feeling support from the bench, Jim had the confidence he needed. Because he was facing a right handed pitcher, he decided to bat left handed. Coach called a quick timeout to make sure Jim was not confused.

"Don't worry, coach. I can bat left handed. I've done it lots of times."

Apparently no one told McCoy that Jim was a switch hitter.

Once again the umpire yelled, "Play ball!"

As he walked back to the dugout, Coach shook his head, "Should've let him take batting practice. I hope he knows what he's doing. Damn, I hope he can hit like he pitches."

Jim set himself in the batter box waiting for the first pitch. It was a fastball over the plate for called strike one. He stepped out of the box and took a deep breath. The crowd roared, but Jim wisely did not let it distract him from his mission. The next pitch was a slider—strike two! Once again Jim stepped out of the box and looked at his bench. Coach held his head in his hands, no doubt very anxious. Jim asked for a timeout and walked toward the dugout.

Coach McCoy ran to meet him. "What's wrong boy? Why did ya call timeout?"

"Don't worry. I have this pitcher figured out. You look desperate, and I wanted to make sure you were looking because I'm about to hit my first professional homerun."

Coach was astonished. He couldn't believe what he was hearing. "Well if nothing else you're the most confident boy I ever coached. So go ahead, knock the cover off and bring the runners home."

Jim nodded and returned to the plate. When he stepped into the batter's box his stance was different. He thought maybe it would throw the pitcher off a little. And that's exactly what it did. Next pitch was outside for ball one.

Coach nervously held his head in his hand. "Oh God, why am I letting this boy bat?"

The following pitch was a fastball that Jim's bat met solidly. The ball easily went out of the ballpark, but was called foul. When Jim saw the coach applaud

GEORGE DAVIS

his effort, he pointed at the coach and then toward center field. Of course McCoy was not the only one who saw that. The Tigers' manager signaled his pitcher to throw the pitch inside. He was not about to let this arrogant player call the shots. The pitcher threw the ball high and inside, narrowly missing Jim's head. The count was now two and two. Not to be outdone, Jim stood firmly in the box with his eyes blazing a hole right through the pitcher who threw a changeup. Jim's keen eyes picked up the slight delayed motion by the pitcher and knew what was coming. He hit it perfectly. The ball sailed over the centerfield wall. The team was yelling as Jim rounded the bases. They met him at home plate with their congratulations. His homerun gave his team the lead, which was enough to win the game as Jim retired the batters in order.

! Jim, the oldest rookie in baseball, played in his first professional baseball game. If he had aches and pains because of his aging body, he sure didn't feel them.

CHAPTER 50

Jim stayed sober and saw more action in the remaining games that season. He was the closer the team needed. Coach also played Jim in the outfield, because his batting was extremely valuable to the team. Even though Jim's abilities helped spark the team's efforts, it was too late for the Spartans to end up in first place. However, they finished second winning 13 of the remaining 15 games since his first game against Amarillo. He saved 10 of those wins and his earned run average was .91, just below one run per game. His batting average was .396 with six home runs. Those statistics were good, but not good enough to get Jim called up to either the Triple A or major league team. Two of the players, Tom Cotton, a pitcher, and Tom Thurman were invited to the majors. Jim was disappointed, but not entirely surprised by his exclusion. He knew his success thus far had been too brief for recognition. But even that aside, he realized as an Indian, he faced an uphill battle to get to the majors.

With the season over, Coach called Jim into his office.

"Jim you're truly a great player—just as I hoped. Ya clearly outclassed many of the other players in our league. Because of that, I've got you're a new contract; and there is a substantial pay increase."

Jim thought that sounded good, but said he needed to talk with his lawyer Jacob before he could accept it. Coach McCoy, of course, understood that process.

McCoy continued, "Jim, at this time, I wanna be honest with ya about a few things. There are two things currently keeping ya from the major league. You're an old man to be playing this game. Teams don't want to invest a lot of time and money in a player of your age. Secondly and probably most important, you're an Indian. I honestly don't know, even with your talent, if ya can overcome that. Your race may exclude ya from ever playing in the majors; but I still aim to do everything possible to help ya get their. But even with my help, it's gonna be difficult. Truthfully the owners aren't anxious to have an Indian in the majors. They don't mind having one in the minors, but don't want to risk fan support in the majors. But if ya ask me, it's not the fans; but the owners who don't want

Indians. The fans are going to come whenever the team wins, and I know ya could see to that."

Jim was once again disillusioned with the reality of life. Even though he had been warned of this by many people, Coach's bombshell about racism still was extremely disappointing.

"Thanks for your honesty, coach. This just means that I'll have to try harder, work longer and practice more. I'm the son of a great chief, and I have a destiny with greatness."

"Damn, boy, I gotta believe if there is anyone who can do it, it's you. And I want ya to know that I really mean it when I say I'll help all I can." McCoy continued, "I want ya to know, too, that as long as I am with this organization, you'll always have a place on my team—whether it is as a player or my assistant."

Coach then hesitated for a moment before he commented on one more thing that was bothering him. "Jim, before you leave I need to apologize for not letting ya play sooner than I did. I know I was wrong. Had I let ya play sooner, hell, we may have won the title."

Jim responded, "Look Coach, all that's over; but we'll bring home the title next year."

He shook Jim's hand and gave him a pat on the back.

Knowing that Jim had come to baseball from prison, Coach inquired of Jim's plans for the off season.

"I'm going to see my friends, who live in Oklahoma City, and then I'll go to the reservation. I got some good friends there that I want to visit."

"If any of this does not work out, lemme know." With a grin, Coach said, "I think I can get ya a spot on the team bus!"

Jim smiled, "I'll remember that. And thanks for giving me a chance. I'll never forget what you've done for me."

CHAPTER 51

Jim took the money he saved during the season and went with McCoy to buy gifts for his friends. Since coach was an old military man and Jim an American Indian, the gifts were somewhat unusual. For Gabriela and Jacob he bought a picture of Custer and the great Sioux warrior, Crazy Horse at the battle of the Little Big Horn. Jim thought with Jacob's interest in history and Gabriela's Indian heritage that they would like the picture. Mansolin and Abotoe each got a Spartan jersey and a white man's pipe. Jim also bought Coach McCoy two fine cigars for helping him shop. When all gifts had been purchased, coach asked Jim if he wanted to visit his homeland since it was so close.

Jim thought not. "I won't return to my homeland until I have proved myself worthy of being a chief."

"I don't want to discourage you, but how do you plan to be a chief without an Indian tribe?"

"When I'm admired as being a wise and deserving man, I will be worthy."

"And exactly how will ya know when that happens?"

"When the multitudes know of me and acknowledge my worth even if it's on my deathbed. I will know when God and my father declare that I have fulfilled my destiny."

"You've already become respected by your teammates and coaches as well as your friends. I'm not quite sure what greatness ya talking about; but you sure seem confident you'll know it when ya see it. So, I wish ya the best."

Jim telegraphed Jacob and Gabriela his travel plans. He packed a few things in a new black suitcase and boarded the train for Oklahoma City.

As the train pulled to a stop in Oklahoma City, Jim looked for his friends. Gathering his luggage and packages, he stepped from the train and heard a familiar voice. He knew immediately that it was Gabriela. She ran and jumped into his strong arms. Jim twirled her in circles until he almost lost his balance.

"Jim, I'm so happy you came to visit us. I've missed you terribly, as has Jacob. We are so proud of how well you did this season."

Finally he put Gabriela down and looked around for Jacob. "Where's Jacob?"

Gabriela did not immediately answer. She looked away. Jim took his hand and gently turned her face to his.

"What is it, Gabriela?"

She took a deep breath. "Jacob has been very sick. He wasn't strong enough to travel to the station."

"How sick?"

Tears spilled from her eyes and stained her delicate cheeks. "Jacob has cancer."

"Cancer; is cancer bad?"

Gabriela lowered her head and in a broken voice said, "Yes, very bad. He may not be with us very much longer."

Jim was stunned and deeply saddened by this news. To steady himself, he sat on a bench. "How can this happen to my friend. He is the reason I am alive and playing baseball."

Gabriela sat beside Jim and hugged him, explaining Jacob's illness and offering comfort. They both were grieving for a future without Jacob.

"Jim, we mustn't allow ourselves to show sadness around Jacob. He's trying to be strong, and we must support him as he comes to terms with his illness. He doesn't want our pity."

"I can understand that. I'll enjoy our friendship and not dwell on his illness."

After a short ride to her home, they put on the happiest faces they could muster. When Jim walked through the door, he saw Jacob. His body that was once muscular and strong was now thin and frail. His eyes were weakened by disease and pain. Jacob could no longer walk by himself so he sat in a chair with wheels.

"Jim, my good friend, so good to see you, welcome to our home. We hope when you leave you will be happier than when you arrived."

Jim walked to Jacob and wrapped his arms around his friend and said, "Jacob, it is so good to see you again. I've missed you."

Jacob was even thinner than he looked. There seemed to be so very little between Jim's hug and Jacob's bones.

Jim noticed tears in Jacob's eyes, but Gabriela not wanting Jacob to be embarrassed said, "Look Jim, Jacob has tears of joy at seeing you again."

Jacob replied, "How true Gabriela. It's so good to be in the company of a great baseball player who's also my good friend."

Trying to bolster the mood, Jim said, "Oh, I almost forgot. I've got gifts for you."

So Jim hurried to the front porch and returned with a large, flat box, tied with a big red bow. He handed it to Gabriela who sat it on the table next to Jacob. She energetically ripped off the paper and her beautiful eyes grew big as she showed the painting to Jacob.

"I thought you both would be pleased. It shows both a brave soldier and Indian warrior in battle, knowing that one must die, but showing respect for each other."

After Jim said those words, he thought the gift may not be appropriate. Of course, he had no idea that Jacob was dying when he bought it.

He was about to apologize when Gabriela said, "The painting demonstrated much bravery, something we all need."

Jacob agreed saying that he could not imagine a better gift.

Jacob looked at Jim. "Please come sit near me. We have so much to talk about. Gabriela, you come, too." Jacob needed to explain his illness. "I am sure Gabriela has told you that I'm dying of cancer. The doctor gives me little chance of living to next spring, but I refuse to be depressed. I'm focusing on the goodness in our lives, past, present and even future. So let's make the most of our time together by concentrating on the positive. Okay?"

Jim replied, "That sounds good to me because you know you've been part of some of the best times in my life—particularly when I hit you with the baseball!"

All three laughed at Jim's comical reminder.

Jacob wanted to hear all about Jim's season with the Spartans. Jacob told him that a friend in Phoenix had sent newspaper clippings of the games and how disturbed he was that it took the Spartans so long to use Jim's talents.

"Yeah, Coach McCoy admitted that he made a mistake by not playing me sooner. I think he was waiting for the players to accept me. He said the owners were not pushing for me to actually play, and they probably won't promote me because they worry about the major league fan support."

Gabriela interrupted. "That's not fair. You talents are wasted once again."

Jacob agreed with Gabriela's assessment. "Your point is painfully true, dear. But Jim's heritage is a big determent to his future in baseball."

"That's what coach told me, and he also told me that my chances of making it to the majors were also slim because of my age. So it seems I've got two strikes already."

Jacob shook his head. "Unfortunately, your coach could be right. But if I know you, you will never stop trying. Someday there will be Indians and Negroes in major league baseball. There is no one better than you to be the first."

"I will never stop trying. Somehow I'll get into the majors, whether by luck or the help of God. And with my friends to help me, how can I lose?"

Jacob smiled, "Now that sound likes an Arizee chief."

Gabriela left the room briefly and then returned announcing that dinner was ready. They all moved into the dining room where Gabriela was serving roast beef, a favorite of both Jim and Jacob. Gabriela had also made creamed potatoes with gravy, lima beans, roasted butternut squash and stewed tomatoes. Jim sampled everything and took seconds on the roast beef and potatoes. He ate until he could not take another bite; but noticed that Jacob had eaten very little, he assumed because of the cancer and his strong medicine.

As Gabriela was serving the apple pie, a smiling Jacob looked at her and said, "Do you want to tell Jim or should I?"

Gabriela quickly accepted the responsibility. "Jacob and I are expecting a baby!"

Jim jumped up and let out a yell. He was so happy; it was as if he were going to be a father. What great news for two wonderful people.

Jacob leaned toward Jim and whispered, "There is something that I need to talk with you about."

Gabriela, who knew what Jacob wanted to say, left the room because the subject was too emotional for her.

"The baby is due in about five months." Jacob paused, then continued in a broken voice, "I'll probably not live to see my child. Jim, you have to promise me that you will be a father for my child. I know this is unfair to ask of you, but please give me your word that you will do it."

Jim rose from his chair and took Jacob's frail hand. "Of course I will. I'll always be here for you and Gabriela, as well as your child. I'll do whatever you ask."

"Thanks Jim. I trust you to guide the child through life. Teach our child right from wrong and pride in its heritage. There is no one better than you. You are the person I want as a role model for our child."

"You can depend on me. I am honored, and it will be my pleasure."

"I know. That is why I asked you, Jim."

CHAPTER 52

Jim stayed with his friends for a couple of weeks doing all he could to bolster their spirits. Jacob reviewed the new contract and told Jim that only the salary had changed. So Jim signed it and mailed it back to the Spartans.

The end of his stay was nearing when Jim told Gabriela that he would be leaving for the reservation to spend time with Mansolin. On his last day in Oklahoma City, all three friends realized that it would probably be the last time they all would be together. When Jim and Gabriela were alone, he talked with her about what Jacob had asked him.

"Jacob fears he will die before you give birth. He has asked me to help you raise your child. You must promise me that you will let me know whenever you need me. I will return after the season and spend time with you. You're my best friend, and I consider it a privilege to take care of you and your child."

Gabriela took a deep breath, hugged Jim and said, "Both of us will need you, but we won't come between you and baseball. You have a monumental struggle to make it to the majors and that won't leave you much time to care for a widow and a child."

"I do love baseball, but I love you and Jacob more. You gave me freedom. Without you and Jacob I would be but dust in the desert. You're my family and it will be my privilege to help you."

"Jim you are wonderful. Jacob and I are blessed to know and love you. Thank you and I promise to do as you ask."

Hand in hand they walked into the living room where Jacob was resting. Being a brave soul, Jacob smiled when he saw them. Jim saw that Jacob was wearing a Phoenix Spartan baseball cap.

"That looks great on you. How did you get a team cap?"

"Oh, I have a friend here that makes baseball uniforms for some of the teams. I had him make hats for me, Abotoe, Mansolin and Gabriela, and a tiny one for our baby."

"Thanks. I'll give these to my friends with your regards."

When it was time for him to leave, Jim tried to reassure his friends.

"Jacob, God will be there for you when you pass. He will give both you and Gabriela comfort. It may seem very bad, but Jacob, you'll find that it's the beginning of a new life." Then looking at Gabriela, he added, "Though you feel alone, have faith in God. He will reunite you again. Please believe that what I tell you is true. It will comfort your souls through the trying times. I love you both dearly."

Jacob replied, "Jim, you be strong, too. I have confidence that you will make a place for yourself in this world."

"Thank you, Jacob. That means a lot to me. And thanks for my freedom. I'll make you proud, and will love your child as my own."

Jim hesitated a moment studying Jacob. He knew he would never see his friend on this earth again. Jim asked Gabriela if she would accompany him to the prison to give Abotoe his baseball cap. When they arrived, Jim saw many of his friends; but was surprised that Abotoe no longer worked there. He was told by an unfamiliar guard that Abotoe left his job somewhat unexpectedly, and he did not know his whereabouts. Jim found that news troubling, and he tucked the cap into his suitcase. He decided he would make inquiries about Abotoe when he reached the reservation. Perhaps he had been reassigned or maybe left the army.

He and Gabriela headed to the train station, arriving just as the train was pulling in. Before boarding, Jim hugged her, and she managed a small heartfelt smile.

"Get word to me when Jacob passes. I will come immediately. I will be on the reservation until time to return to Phoenix for next season."

Gabriela promised she would and kissed him on his cheek. Jim boarded the train quickly to avoid the strain of a long goodbye. As he waved to her from the train, he could see the tears that spilled from her eyes. Jim thought about how fragile life was. He and Gabriela both faced a future of uncertainty, and they would need to rely on their friendship, as well as God, to get them through the difficult days ahead.

Jim rode the train to just over the Arizona border, where he purchased a horse and a pack mule, and changed into his Arizee clothing, including his leather trail boots, and headed for the reservation. He found little had changed. Initially he was stopped and cleared by an army officer. As he rode through the gates, in the distance he saw a large soldier walking toward him. He feared he would again be questioned to see if he may be a renegade who was running from authorities. But as he drew closer he saw that it was none other than Abotoe. After hearing the news at the prison, he feared he would never again see his big friend.

"I went to the prison and was told you had left unexpectedly".

Abotoe smiled, "Jim, I quit that job so I could come here to live on the reservation. I knew you would come back here. I work for the army and the reservation is my assignment."

"Come, let's find Mansolin."

"Where's his home now?"

"Not far, we can catch up while we walk."

Just then they saw Mansolin walking toward them. Jim knew that he was not in good health and could see by the way he walked that he was ailing. He looked frail and tired. Although they wrote occasionally, it had been a while since these two old friends had seen each other. As was the custom, visitors needed to register. The three friends went to inform the commander of Jim's plan to spend several months on the reservation. It was generally accepted that the reservation would be available for any Indian who had nowhere else to live. That, of course, assumed reservation life was considered living. But to Jim, being with his Indian brothers, even under adverse conditions, was certainly more appealing then the team bus! Jim thought of it as a refuge where he could live among his people. But to the Indians who had no place to go, it was by no stretch of the imagination a refuge.

Abotoe walked with his friends for only a short distance saying he had important business to attend to. As Mansolin and Jim continued on, they walked by Jim's old home, which was now in ruins, used as a trash dump. They hesitated and Mansolin explained that when Jim was sent to prison the army tore down his hut and began using it as a dumping ground.

"I guess it was a message to the rest of us that we should not defy the white man's laws. Well, that only made us more defiant."

Jim responded, "There are some men who will always feel they have to teach the Indian the hard lessons of life. But I have found white men who are different, ones with whom I share spirituality."

Well, as for me, Jim, I have only seen that in Capt. Jacob."

"Trust me, my friend, there are others, maybe more than you can imagine."

As they continued their walk to Mansolin's, they approached a newly built hut. Jim commented that it was perhaps one of the finest on the reservation

"You really like it?"

"It's great. Best looking place I've seen. You must be planning to take a wife and bring her here to live."

"I do have a woman friend, but we won't live here, because it is yours! Jim, this is your new home. When you wrote me that you were coming back to the reservation, I wanted you to have a nice place to live. You have suffered many hardships and deserve this. In fact, I was hoping that you would find a nice Indian girl to share it with."

"I already have a family or at least I will in the near future. Unfortunately it will come as the result of Jacob's sickness. He has cancer and very little time to live. He's asked me to help Gabriela raised their child. I'm honored and will do my best. So I am not ready to choose another woman. My life is dedicated to Gabriela and her child."

Mansolin was saddened by the news that such a fine man would never live to raise his child. But he knew Jacob has chosen a fine man in his place.

"They are wise to choose you. Once again your father would be proud."

Jacob's illness was still very difficult for Jim so he changed the subject and went inside his new home. It had to be better than most housing on the reservation, and Mansolin has seen that it was furnished quite well. Before moving on to Mansolin's hut, they sat a while and reminisced about the days when Manso was alive.

"You know Mansolin; your grandfather was a very special man. I believe he was a prophet. Remember my telling you about the time my father spoke through him. To this day, I believe he was telling me of my father's wishes. Those words gave me the courage to look deeply into my feelings and gain a clear understanding of how I should live my life."

"Yes, he was a very wise man. But I sometimes wonder if those were actually your father's words."

"I don't know, and it doesn't really matter. But whatever the case, Manso was a guiding force in my life, and I miss him."

Mansolin shook his head slowly, "I do, too."

Silence ensued, both men thinking about the loss of their dear friend and grandfather.

Jim was the first to speak. "Where are you living these days?"

"I moved into my grandfather's home so I can keep the family business going. I am now the reservation wise man and the whiskey maker!"

"Well I hope I will get a chance to sample some of your spirits."

"I'm planning on it; how about now?"

When they arrived at his friend's hut, Jim thought it looked much larger than when he last saw it.

"This is larger than I remember. I've tried to forget as much as possible, though. This is where my freedom ended when I found your grandfather dead, and I was attacked by Johnson."

Mansolin replied, "Such memories haunt us all, but that's in the past and I say enough about the past! Let's get some whiskey and talk about your future."

As they walked toward the back of the hut, which had previously been forbidden territory, Jim saw the still for the first time. He had no idea where the old man had gotten all the metal tubes and barrels, but it was impressive and produced some good whiskey.

Jim caught a slight movement out of the corner of his eye. It was Abotoe sneaking a drink of a recently brewed batch. By the way he swayed in his chair; it appeared he had been tasting since he left his two friends. Jim crept closer and gave a big shout, which caused Abotoe to fall out of the chair

Jim scolded, "I thought you had important business."

"Well what could be more important than this? And if I weren't so drunk, I would scalp both of your red asses. But right now I see too many of you and am not sure which one to scalp first!"

Jim and Mansolin could not help but laugh.

They joined Abotoe and sat down with a jar of sprits to continue their talk. Jim spoke of the treasured pipe that had once belonged to his father.

"It's something that I always keep near me. I feel I have something important of my father's that can give me the determination to continue my quest to become a chief. But I hold nothing more important in my life than the love of my close friends."

Abotoe told Jim about his new love life. Seems he had met a Cheyenne woman and was going to marry her.

"She's a hell of a cook and has a broad bottom so she can have many babies for me."

Jim laughed at Abotoe's prophecies on his future domestic life.

Mansolin told Jim of all the time it took him to adjust to the loss of Manso. He admitted to having a special woman friend, but not much time for her since he was busy with the family business.

The three friends reminisced far into the darkness and then finally fell asleep.

Jim began the next morning like he would so many mornings that fall. He occupied his time recounting tales of his baseball experiences to old friends, often repeating the same stories. But since more often than not, most of the men on the reservation where full of spirits, repetition was easily tolerated. In reality there was nothing much else for the men to do. There was little land for farming and game was scarce. Alcoholism and crime were rampant among the Indians who lived on reservations. Only the bare necessities of life were provided by the government, and Indians had no education to find employment off the reservation. All of this gave the government control of the Indians, both their present and their future.

CHAPTER 53

Jim's addiction mirrored that of his Indian brothers on the reservation. Before his own addiction gripped him, he often warned his friends of the dangers of alcohol; but he was now addicted as much or more than his friends. He used racism and social injustice, as well as the pain from baseball injuries, as excuses for his drunkenness. With plenty of drinking buddies on the reservation, Jim was drinking daily, going from highs to hangovers, often ending in depression.

To make matters worse, Jim received a letter from the Spartans that informed him he had been assigned to a Spartans' team in Louisville, Kentucky. He felt betrayed by Coach McCoy, whom he considered a friend and saw the new assignment for what it was—a demotion. Feeling deeply depressed, Jim went to Mansolin's for whiskey and stayed drunk for days on end.

When Mansolin and Abotoe confronted him about his dependence on whiskey, he said, "My life is over. I have nothing to live for. Baseball was going to be my way out, and I have failed in that! Look, I have been demoted."

Even though Jim was distraught over the trade, Mansolin knew he had to give his friend more bad news. He handed Jim a telegram from Gabriela.

My dearest Jim, Jacob died Tuesday. Please come as quickly as you can. Baby due soon! Your loving friend, Gabriela

Abotoe took the jar of whiskey from Jim and he and Mansolin tried desperately to comfort their distraught friend. Words seemed useless.

Jim could not be comforted. "How can I handle Jacob's death and the demotion by the Spartans? I'm not strong enough."

"Jim, you don't have to face all this alone. Abotoe and I are here for you. Remember you are, Jim Eagleson, son of Lone Eagle, the great Arizee chief. If your father saw you now, he would not know you. Do not disgrace your father. Get yourself cleaned up and sober."

Reference to his father gave Jim strength to tackle many difficulties in the past, but he was not so sure it would help him on this day.

Mansolin urged Jim to go to Gabriela.

"That's where you are needed. Leave your worries about baseball for another day. I will write Coach McCoy about your trade."

Jim realized his friends were right and accepted their advice and help. Mansolin, who made coffee as well as he did whiskey, brewed a strong pot and insisted that Jim have some. Abotoe helped him pack and accompanied him to the train station, where he purchased a ticket and boarded a train for Oklahoma City. Jim's hangover from days of excessive drinking was still with him. He had a headache and a burning in his stomach that he assumed was from the drinking binge. The long ride helped sober him up and gave him time to think about positive things in his future. When the train pulled into the station, he was feeling stronger. As he stepped from the train, the cold winter wind was blowing snow across the platform. Jim pulled his woolen scarf tight around his neck and put on his hat and gloves. It was definitely winter in Oklahoma. The snowfall became heavier, as Jim walked the short distance to Gabriela's. When he arrived, he knocked, but there was no answer.

"Gabriela, Gabriela, is anyone home?"

Without an answer he tried the doorknob and found it unlocked. He was beginning to worry. He walked throughout the house calling her name, but there was no answer. He was about to leave when he saw a note lying on the hall table.

"Jim, Jacob was laid to rest yesterday, and I am with my parents. Please come. They live at 1 East Main Street. It is just two blocks east. With love, Gabriela"

With a deep sigh of relief, Jim hurried from the house and made his way to her parents'. His knock at the door was answered by Mrs. O'Connor, who did not immediately recognize him as he had changed considerably since she saw him at the wedding.

She hesitated and then asked, "Jim, is that you, Jim Eagleson?"

"Yes madam, I'm Jim. I want to give you my deepest sympathy in the death of your son-in-law. He was my good friend and I owe my life to him." Jim had practiced those words but was still somewhat nervous as to whether he spoke them correctly.

Thanking him for his thoughts, Mrs. O'Connor politely directed Jim to the parlor and asked him to wait there while she woke Gabriela from a nap.

"Please don't wake her up. I am sure she needs a lot of rest."

"Well then please come into the parlor and have a seat. I will let Patrick know you are here."

Gen. O'Connor joined them and welcomed Jim to their home. Jim once again expressed his sympathy.

Before Jim could say another word, Gen. O'Connor spoke, "Both Gabriela and Jacob told us about their wish for your involvement in their child's life. I want you to know that Mrs. O'Connor and I fully agree with their wishes."

Jim, who was relieved to know their feelings, accepted the General's offer of a cigar. The two men talked about baseball and Jim's career. He was too sad to tell the General about his setback of being traded to another team."

Gabriela, who had not slept well since Jacob's death, awakened to the sound of male voices. She found Jim with her father in the parlor.

She rushed to Jim and sobbed uncontrollably. Gen. O'Connor excused himself to give the two some privacy. For a short time neither spoke.

"Jim, thank you for coming so quickly; this has been so difficult for me. I loved Jacob so deeply. I feel as though part of me died with him. I am so empty. I don't know what to do."

"We both loved Jacob and will miss him beyond what our words can describe. He was a great friend."

"Jim, you know he had so much respect for you. He saw you as a man of honor and commitment. He wanted you as a role model for our child."

"I appreciate Jacob's confidence in me. I had great respect for Jacob, too. He faced his illness and death with courage and dignity."

"Yes, he was a great man, and God has rewarded him with a place in Heaven. The pain and embarrassment he suffered the last months of his life were almost unbearable. We prayed together for God to take his soul. Jacob and I both were reconciled to the need of his passing."

As strong as Gabriela sounded, her loss was still devastating. Jim offered his handkerchief to dry her tears.

"I often wake in the middle of the night dreaming of Jacob and longing for his touch. I feel he is watching over me and is pleased you are here. Jacobs's last words were of his child and your importance in its life."

Gabriela and Jim spent most of the evening consoling each other with tears, intermingled with laughter at fond remembrances of Jacob.

For the next several weeks, Jim was her constant companion as she trudged through the last few days of pregnancy. He packed up Jacob's clothes and even helped ready the baby's room. Gabriela grew wearier with each passing day. Her due date came and went. But then on a sunny day in February, when the previous night's snowfall covered the ground, Gabriela, gave birth to Jacob (Jake) James Friendly. He was 7 pounds, 2 ounces, and 21 inches long. He made his way into this world like most babies, kicking and crying loudly. To all that were listening, Jim proudly said that the screaming was an Arizee yell. He said it was Jake's way of demonstrating his heritage. Jake was a handsome baby with high cheek bones, an olive complexion, and a good crop of straight dark hair.

When Jim first took Jake in his arms, he said, "I'll tell you everything about your father so you will know what a great man he was. You'll be a son he would be proud of."

Gabriela seemed to weather the birth well and was very happy being with her new son. Even in the joyous times after Jake's birth, she would often think of Jacob and how she missed him. Each time she held her precious son and looked into his eyes, she saw Jacob. Sometimes in the middle of the night when she was feeding Jake, she felt Jacob's presence watching over them.

Several weeks after Jake's birth Gabriela and Jim spent an evening together while little Jake slept in his mother's arms.

Gabriela spoke, "As you know, Jacob wanted you to become Jake's father."

Jim gently corrected her, "I will always love and care for Jake, but Jacob will always be his father."

"Jacob meant more than that. He knew of our deep love and devotion to each other. He did not want either of us to travel through life alone."

"What do you mean?"

"Jim, I have loved you since I first met you years ago. Jacob knew of our feelings for each other. He wanted us to be happy, and he gave his blessing should we later decide to marry." Overcome with emotion, she paused and then continued, "I want to respect Jacob's wishes, but I am so consumed with grief over the loss of my beloved husband. I want you to know how Jacob felt, but it is too soon for me; I am too distraught over my loss."

Jim concurred but felt a bit uneasy with the discussion. He loved Gabriela and certainly wanted to be her husband. But he, too, felt it was too soon to move in this direction. They spent the rest of the evening in the parlor talking about Jake and remembering Jacob.

Since Jake was Jim's first experience in dealing with a baby, he was surprised at all the work involved in taking care of such a small person; but he took his promise to Jacob very seriously. He was busy both day and night, which left little time to worry about being traded by the Spartan's. But when a letter arrived from Mansolin, Jim was very nervous. He anticipated that Mansolin may have found something about his demotion. Jim anxiously opened the envelope. He learned that McCoy was furious about the situation. In fact, he didn't know about it until after the fact. When he found out, he went straight to management and raised such a fuss, including threats of resigning. Well apparently it was enough to convince management. Jim was back in Phoenix, and he had two weeks to report for training. The good news was just what Jim needed to get excited about the new season.

When the day arrived for Jim to leave Gabriela, she and Jake accompanied him to the train station. Gabriela would have preferred that Jim stay a little longer, but she knew that baseball was very important to both his pride as well as his wallet. Jim hugged and kissed Gabriela and Jake. It was one friend saying goodbye to another. Right now it was too soon for anything more.

During the train ride, Jim pondered this new phase of his life. He would definitely stop drinking. He hoped when he returned after the season, that Gabriela could talk about a deeper commitment. He looked forward to a relationship that would grow into more than just friendship. Their talk that night in the parlor gave Jim hope for a future with her. He knew that he could wait as long as Gabriela needed. He loved her since the day they first met. Whatever happened in the previous years of their friendship, he knew the rules were changing. His life would never be the same. With Jacob's blessing he would not only be a father to Jake, but maybe a husband to Gabriela.

CHAPTER 54

When Jim began his second year in professional baseball, he was 38, more than twice the age of some rookies. Jim was easily the oldest player in the league. But that didn't discourage him in the least. Jim's pitching earned him a place on the starting rotation. On days he was not a starter, he was available for relief as a closer. He was one of the most successful pitchers in the league. He won 20 games and had 25 saves. His ability to hit the ball placed him third in the starting lineup. His batting average was .380 with 18 homers, which led the league. Even with such a successful individual season, Jim was most proud of his team winning the league championship. Jim had fulfilled his promise to Coach McCoy. But even with his individual record and a championship, Jim did not get the call he had hoped for.

Coach McCoy explained. "You were very important to our winning the championship, but your chances of moving up still ain't good. Of course like before, it's your age and race."

Coach paused, then continued, "However the team in Kansas City, whose season ain't over yet, needs a reliever and good pinch hitter. When I got the call from the coach there, it took me about two seconds to recommend you. The coach is Lars Benson, a rough-edged old veteran. I must tell ya though that he asked about ya being an Indian and all. I told him your race won't important. You could pitch and hit and that was all that mattered." Coach hesitated then said, "He seemed satisfied with that."

Jim felt this was the chance he had been waiting for. Before he could open his mouth to thank McCoy, the coach added, "This is a great opportunity for you. You'll be playing in a league championship game. So go to Kansas City and show them whatcha got, chief."

The following morning Jim boarded a train for Kansas City. Maybe this was his chance to prove that he was ready to move up in the Spartans' organization. After a long, uneventful train ride, Jim was met by Coach Benson, who admitted he was pleasantly surprised.

Laughingly, he said, "Damn boy, ya look just like all of us. Guess I was expecting you to have feathers and moccasins. They told me you was an Indian."

Jim smiled, "You have heard too many stories about Indians that just aren't true. The source is often people who are ignorant of the Indian ways with too much prejudice born out of hatred."

Benson wasn't sure whether or not he personally fit into that area of ignorance Jim talked about, so he simply did not respond to the whole damn subject. Instead he told Jim that he wanted to give him a quick tour of the facility and introduce him to the players. The ballpark was quite impressive, and most players responded to him much like Benson did—surprised and reserved.

He saw his old friend, Joe Dominic, who was now a catcher for Kansas City. Joe extended his hand and welcomed Jim. "Glad to see you again, Jim. I'm looking forward to working with you again."

Benson interrupted, "Look here, Jim. Tonight's game is the championship game, and I'm low on pitchers. There's only a 50/50 chance that you'll pitch, but you gotta be ready to work just in case. I mean two or three innings, hitting and pitching. I might have to call on you to close the game."

Jim nodded and said he was ready for anything the team needed.

"There's another thing I gotta warn you about. Since this will be the first time our fans have seen an Indian play, you may hear some name calling. Ignore it and stay focused on the game."

"Don't worry. I pay no attention to name calling. Those people don't know me. I'm here to help the team win, and I will do it with pride and honor."

Benson looked at Jim. "Damn boy, I can see why old man McCoy likes you so much. You're quite the gentlemen. But I'm paying ya to get out there and kick ass."

"I hear you coach."

Both smiled and shook hands as Jim left to get ready for the game.

Jim did not have to wait long for the ignorance he spoke of. In fact it came from his one of his teammates. Jim was busy getting dressed when a player shouted, "Look, the nigger is here from Phoenix."

Jim, trying to diffuse the situation, said, "Yes, the nigger is here and ready to kick some ass. So let's go out there and win this game."

His teammates were speechless. No one said another word. They finished dressing in silence and walked onto the field. Even though Jim tried to make light of the comment, inwardly he was deeply hurt and disappointed.

CHAPTER 55

When Jim entered the dugout, he saw his teammates taking up all the space on the bench. He politely walked the length of the bench and asked if someone could slide down to make room for him. Several players sitting near ignored him and when he asked again, three players chose to stand so as not to sit next to him. Just as in Phoenix, he was shunned and would have to prove himself worthy of respect.

The Kansas City team was playing the Columbus Kings, a perennial power in minor league baseball. They were part of the New York Titans' organization and considered by many to be the most successful in baseball. In the first eight innings the Kings lived up to their reputation. They scored three runs in the first inning and another three in the second. By the end of the third inning, they had chased two Spartan pitchers from the mound. For each of the next five innings, Coach Benson put a new pitcher on the mound, and it worked as they held the Kings scoreless. The Spartans sparked a couple of rallies to score five runs. So going into the ninth inning the score was 6 to 5, in favor of the Kings. Unfortunately Coach Benson had no more regular pitchers to call on. His pitchers were either injured or worn out. Benson had reservations about using Jim. So Paul Fisher, who had pitched the eighth inning, continued into the ninth. If he faltered, Jim would get the call. So he sent Jim into the bullpen to warm up. The inning began with a single from the Kings' first batter. The second batter struck out. The next batter hit a double down the third base side, resulting in a man on second and third with only one out. That was enough for Coach Benson. He called Jim's number.

Jim jogged to the mound as he had so many times before and threw some warm-up pitches. It didn't take long for the cheap racial comments from the hometown fans who showed very little confidence in Benson's choice of pitchers.

Some young boy just behind the Kansas City dugout yelled to Benson, "Damn Ben, whatcha you doing bringing an Injun in to let the Kings win?"

ARIZONA SON RISE

Coach Benson felt he had to talk to Jim and walked out to the mound. He repeated Jim's words that comments are made out of ignorance and should be ignored.

"Ignorance, just plain ignorance; show them you're as good as any other player on the field. No, show them you're better."

On his way back to the dugout, the coach had the foul mouth twelve year old and his drunken father escorted from the ballpark.

Out of habit, Jim stepped off the mound and rubbed a new ball. Apparently he lingered too long, and the home plate umpire yelled, "Hey you gonna to pitch that ball or rub it down to a marble."

The batter laughed and prepared to show Jim a thing or two. Jim stepped on the mound and got the sign from the catcher, Joe Dominic—a fastball high and inside to get the batter's attention. Jim buzzed a fastball within two inches of the batter's chin, which did not set well with the batter or his teammates. "Ball One!" The batter pointed his fat index finger at Jim threatening him if another pitch came that close to him. Jim's next pitch was another fastball, but this time on the outside corner of the plate. "Strike One!" The next pitch was hit foul down the right side of the field. Then Joe called for another fastball, but Jim shook it off. Then he signaled for a slider, down low. Jim thought *Good call*. He delivered the slider; the batter swung and missed for the second out of the inning. Suddenly the fans had more confidence in their Injun pitcher.

Next up was a powerhouse hitter, Boss Driver.

Joe met with Jim on the mound. "This guy is trouble. I have seen him easily hit the ball over the center field fence. Don't make any foolish mistakes. He can hit a fastball, but he's sucker for a changeup"

Jim nervously positioned himself on the mound, and Joe took his place behind home plate. Jim's first pitch was a slider on the outside corner. Boss hit the ball foul. The crowd was on their feet. The next two pitches were both balls. Jim knew a pitch on a two/one count was a hitter's pitch. Not a good position for a pitcher. He was so nervous about Boss hitting a homerun that his next pitch was another ball.

Now Benson joined Joe for a trip to the mound.

Benson had a plan. "Ok, Jim. Boss wants a homerun, and he'll go for it. Give him a slider on the outside corner. Hopefully he'll hit it foul. I think the runner on second is stealing our signals so on the next pitch when Joe signals a changeup, shake it off. Then Joe is gonna signal a fastball. Let Boss think he's getting a fastball; but you throw your best changeup."

This seemed like a good plan. Jim pitched a slider on the outside corner just as Benson had directed. "Strike Two!" Boss' dark eyes stared angrily at Jim, as if he was willing Jim to throw the homerun ball. Jim got the signal for a fastball He went into his windup just as if he were going to throw a fastball. Boss Driver was ready. He could almost smell victory and was planning on hitting the homerun to stretch the Kings' lead. By the time the pitch got to the plate, Boss had already swung and missed. Strike three and the side was retired! The fans screamed so loudly that they could be heard two counties away. Boss Driver inspected his bat looking for a hole that allowed him to swing and miss. In a rage, he threw the bat hitting Joe in his right thigh, who fell down immediately as the coach, team doctor and Jim ran to his aid. The umpire ejected Boss Driver from the game, and Joe hobbled back to the dugout in pain. Hopefully it would only be a bad bruise.

Going into the bottom of the ninth the Spartans had two major problems. They needed two runs and the catcher, who was barely able to walk, was due to bat second. Benson conferred with his assistants and decided that Tom Thurman, Jim's early nemesis from Phoenix, would pinch hit for Joe. This would now force Coach Benson to use Jim as his third hitter.

The inning started with a line drive that fell in for a single. Tom Thurman was up next. He was visibly nervous and wanted a homerun to end the game, but instead he walked on a three/two count. Now it was Jim's turn.

Before he took the field, Coach Benson said, "Boy just hit the ball like ya did for McCoy down in Phoenix."

Jim could not have been more nervous; but he covered it well. He knew it was an important game for him as well as the team. The winning runs were on base, and he had a chance to bring them home and win this game.

After taking a couple of swings, Jim headed to the plate and positioned himself to bat right handed. The Kings' coach displayed his coaching strategy and called in his right handed reliever to pitch against a right hander hitter. The reliever finished his warm up. Then to everyone's surprise, Jim changed position in the batter's box. The reliever thought, *Damn he's a switch hitter!*

The Kings' coach fumed, and Benson smiled.

As Jim stood waiting for the first pitch, there were insults from the Kings' dugout. Beads of sweat hung on his face, and he suddenly had a painful spasm in his stomach. When the pain subsided, the umpire had already called a strike.

He stepped out of the batter's box to compose himself and wipe his brow when he heard the catcher say, "What's wrong Redskin? You scared of the pitch? Watch out for a high fastball, it might scalp you!"

Jim thought he even heard the umpire laughing. After a few seconds, the spasm subsided. Before he went back to the batter's box, Benson called a time out.

Coach, thinking that Jim was just nervous, decided to talk to him. "Don't pay no attention to those turkeys gobbling. Concentrate on getting a hit. Remember they're ignorant!"

Jim smiled and nodded in the affirmative.

Coach ended his talk by saying, "Now kick ass, boy."

And kick ass he did.

The next pitch was a blazing fastball which Jim hit down the right field line going ample distance to score both base runners. The Kansas City Spartans won their first league championship 7 to 6 over the seemingly unbeatable Columbus Kings.

The fans ran onto the field in disbelief. As Jim ran off the field he was met by his teammates. He proved he could compete in this league. When Coach congratulated him, Jim felt sure this would be his ticket to the majors.

CHAPTER 56

Jim returned to Phoenix with renewed hope of being called up to the majors for the next baseball season. But unfortunately after Coach McCoy congratulated him on his game, he gave Jim the same speech he heard last year.

"Jim, you are one hell of a ball player. I told Benson you were his ticket to the championship, and you didn't disappoint him. I don't think there is any doubt ya can play with the big boys. But nothing has changed since last year. You got the same problems. Even though ya had a great showing here and in Kansas City, things still ain't looking good getting to the majors. You ain't getting any younger and you ain't getting any whiter. But that said, play your best and don't give up your dream, for one day we may see a miracle because Coach Benson and I ain't done trying."

Jim appreciated Coach McCoy's honesty and not doubt what he said was true. He continued to play the best he could—just like Jacob had said.

Showing a renewed spirit, Jim exclaimed, "Coach, you know I'm dedicated to the Spartans and determined to make our team better."

Jim left the meeting not knowing that this would be the last time he would see his coach.

Jim was glad the season was over. He was tired. He had played in every game that season, plus the game in Kansas City. He was having more trouble with stomach pain and nausea, and the numerous bouts left Jim weakened. So he drank more whiskey hoping to dull the physical and emotional pain

He planned to spend most of the off season with Gabriela and Jake and then have a brief visit with Mansolin and Abotoe on the reservation. He wired Gabriela when to expect him and asked her to meet his train. He was anxious to see Gabriela and Jake and looked forward to his new responsibilities. It made him feel more civilized to know he would spend the off season helping Gabriela raise her son, instead of a senseless drunk.

When the train pulled into the station, Gabriela was waiting on the platform. She looked as beautiful as ever. He wondered, *Will she ever want me for her husband?* Jim knew the love between Jacob and Gabriela reflected deep passion and mutual respect. He knew he could never entirely replace Jacob in her heart, nor did he want to. But he was hoping to have a chance to be a loving husband. He wanted to be with her at night, watching her sleep; and he wanted to be the one to hold her in his arms when she was afraid. Jim tried in earnest to put those thoughts aside as he had come as a friend, not a suitor, to help her. Gabriela had made it clear that she was grieving for Jacob and not ready for any romantic involvement. But still she was in his thoughts seemingly every day.

When the train rolled to a stop, Jim jumped from his seat, rushing by the other passengers eager to meet Gabriela. The two friends embraced and Gabriela seemed truly happy to see Jim again.

As they stood face to face, Jim stuttered something that did not make sense and then said, "I missed you."

"We've missed you too, Jim. You look very handsome and irresistible to this young Indian girl."

Jim blushed. "You look so beautiful. I'm so glad to finally be here. Where is little Jake?"

"Oh, he's at home with his nanny. He's quite a handful these days, so I felt it better that he stay at home." Jim hugged Gabriela again and whispered, "I love you, my Indian girl."

"And I love you, my brave chief."

This reunion was everything Jim had hoped for. He had a family that he loved. His personal life was good, but his career was still a big concern for him. He would not be satisfied until he made it to the major league.

The nanny met them at the front door holding Jake. Jim was certainly partial when it came to Jake. He thought Jake was as handsome a baby as he had ever seen. He had the Arizee high cheekbones and the dark hair of his ancestors. His blue eyes, though, came straight from his father. Gabriela took Jake from the nanny and handed him to Jim. Jim held him tenderly and whispered in his ear. Jake starred at Jim for a moment, then smiled and touched Jim's face. Jim patted him gently and sang an Arizee lullaby.

"What's that song you are singing to him? He seems so content and happy."

"It's a little lullaby that my mother sang to me each night as I feel asleep. In English it means, "Sleep softly my sunshine."

Gabriela was deeply touched by Jim's tenderness.

She whispered, "Jim, thank you for being here for us. I know you will be the father that Jacob wanted for his son."

Watching the two together, Gabriela could tell that Jim was obviously smitten with Jake, who in turn seemed very happy to be with Jim.

The next few months went by quickly. Jim and Jake became inseparable, and Gabriela was pleased to see the two "men" in her life so happy. As days passed, the deep loss of Jacob's passing seemed to become more manageable for her. She still missed Jacob at night when he would hold her in his arms and make her feel safe. She also missed the romance they shared. Gabriela sensed that her relationship with Jim was changing. She was beginning to have the warm romantic feelings that a woman and man share. It only made sense that this new phase of their relationship should be nurtured. During the off season, Jim worked for Gabriela's father at his construction company. The job, which required physical strength, helped Jim stay in shape for the next baseball season. His stomach problems persisted, and he drank more thinking it would ease the pain. It concerned Gabriela so much that she confronted Jim.

"Jim, I have noticed that you drink more than I remember. Are there reasons that you feel it necessary?"

Jim laughed it off, "It is just something most of my teammates do to pass the time. There's no harm and besides it helps me cope with my aches and pains."

"You know how I feel about you, and it concerns me that you drink so much whiskey. You will become addicted to it, if you don't stop."

"Gabriela, I think you're over reacting to this. My teammates call this medicinal drinking, and I see no harm in it. The work with your father is hard and a little whisky helps my aching muscles. I can't go into next season with aches and pains."

"But Jim, this will do nothing to help your baseball career. And even with that aside, I hope that we'll marry some day, and I don't want an alcoholic as a husband or as Jake's father. I want the wonderful man I met all those many years ago."

"I'm still that same man. I love you and Jake, and would never do anything to hurt you. You and Jake return my love; but with baseball, the love is not returned."

"What do you mean, the love is not returned?"

"Baseball doesn't love me. It's because I am not white. I will probably never play in major league ball. My coaches have told me that the powers in baseball will probably do all they can to keep the Indian out of the major league. They fear the fans will stay away from the game. So I fear I'll never achieve what my father wanted. Never become a chief of any people. I am doomed to be a failure."

"Jim, that's not true. This country is the land of opportunity where anyone can pursue a dream. You have come so far, and I know you will be the person you so desire! You mustn't give up. You will succeed."

Jim hugged her. "My love, I wish what you say were true. Failure is in my future, and there is nothing either of us can do about it." Not wanting to press the issue further, Gabriela changed the subject.

Over the next few weeks, though, they had many conversations about his drinking and success, or as Jim saw it, his failure in baseball. The talks, intended to inspire Jim, did little to soothe his troubled soul. She tried to convince him not to judge himself based on a goal that may be unattainable. He had already proven himself many times over, and he was loved and respected by everyone who knew him. She reminded him that his coaches told him he was good enough to make it to the majors. But Jim knew the decision not to promote him came from the pious, bigoted owners and that doomed his chances.

One evening Gabriela, who was frustrated with her lack of progress concerning Jim's drinking problem, said with much conviction, "You are already a leader, a chief. You are a great man, no matter what baseball does or does not give you. And more importantly, Jake and I think you're a great man. Your father would be proud of his son, but if you don't stop drinking, the alcohol will destroy yourself and our love!"

As much as Gabriela tried, she knew that she could only offer so much inspiration to Jim about his drinking or his baseball career. But, in her soul, she knew he still had the Arizee determination to achieve his goals and there was no replacing his desire to be a chief among men, even if those men were white.

Late in the evening before he left for the reservation, while Jake slept soundly in his bed, Jim and Gabriela had another very serious conversation. Jim was open about his love for her. He told her that he wanted her as his wife and mother of his children. It was the first time Jim had been so forthright about his desires. Gabriela said she wanted the same things, but being a widow with a young child thought it proper to wait until they were married to consummate their love. Even though this was frustrating, Jim concurred; he could wait. It seems he had been waiting for things most of his life. He was a very patient man.

When time came for Jim to leave, Gabriela and Jake accompanied him to the train station. Jim gave Gabriela some of his savings to help out with the household expenses. Even though it was not needed by his new family, Gabriela took it with appreciation and saved it for Jake's education.

Jim boarded the train, waved and blew a kiss to both of them. Leaving was becoming increasingly difficult.

CHAPTER 57

Jim's visits to the reservation were an important cultural trip for him. However as he gradually transitioned into the white man's society, the trips were becoming less crucial. But he still looked forward to seeing his friends. This year when he arrived, he was met only by Abotoe, who looked very solemn.

"Where is Mansolin?"

With tears swelling in the big man's eyes, he replied, "A sickness came to the reservation several months ago. The white man calls it consumption. It has killed many of our people, including women and children."

"Is the disease still here?"

"There has not been any new sickness, although there are some, like Mansolin, who are still fighting the disease. He is very sick."

As they walked through the camp to Mansolin's hut, Jim could tell there were fewer people. When he entered Mansolin's home, he was shocked by his friend's appearance. He was pale and very thin and his eyes were barely open. It was hard to imagine how the person he saw before him was alive. Jim sat beside Mansolin, who slowly opened his eyes and greeted Jim.

"My brother, you have come to see me. We must drink to your good health and safety."

Jim replied, "You rest now. We'll have plenty time to drink and be merry."

Mansolin, whose body was sapped of energy, smiled, "Eagleson, my chief, you are very kind, but not truthful when you say we have much time."

"I don't want to hear that. God doesn't need another Indian warrior just yet. He will keep you here with me for a while."

Mansolin, too weak to respond, closed his eyes and fell asleep. His breathing was labored as he struggled for every breath. Jim and Abotoe left the hut of their friend with many bottles of whiskey to drown their worries. Jim remembered Gabriela's words and made an effort to reduce his consumption, but this latest sorrow made the effort difficult.

Over the next few days, Jim spent many hours reminiscing with Mansolin. He knew his friend had but a short time to live, and Jim wanted to stay by his side until his last breath. So day after day he and Abotoe sat in old rocking chairs beside Mansolin's bed. Jim drank as much as possible to dull the pain of facing the inevitable loss of his friend. He was sure Gabriela would understand.

Abotoe knowing the end was near spoke to Mansolin, "I fear the end is near my brother. Soon it will be time for you to be with your grandfather."

Mansolin, whose breathing was more labored, spoke in a voice that was barely above a whisper. "Jim, I have been to see my grandfather. He tells me of the love and peace my new life will bring. He is in a wonderful place. There is no pain, no sorrow. I also saw your mother and father. They are very proud of you." Mansolin had to stop for a moment as he started coughing and blood spilled on his lips. Jim held his head and wiped blood from his mouth with a damp cloth. He spoke his last words, "Eagleson, I love you."

His lifeless body released his soul to rest in peace with his grandfather. Both Jim and Abotoe cried, but not for Mansolin. He was with God. They cried for their loss and once again succumbed to alcohol. Jim stayed drunk for the remaining days on the reservation, even on the day of his friend's burial.

When the day came for Jim to leave, he left a small sum of money for Abotoe, who had appointed himself the new whiskey maker, reservation wise man and spiritual advisor. Abotoe and his son, whom he named AJ, which was short for Abotoe Junior, were alone now. His Cheyenne wife had also died from the consumption.

Jim patted AJ on his head, "Looks like you will be great warrior like your father."

The boy smiled and hugged Jim. As he rode off, Jim looked back and yelled, "Keep yourself and the boy healthy. I have lost too many friends. See you next year."

Abotoe looked at AJ and said, "There goes a great chief and an even greater man."

CHAPTER 58

Jim was greeted with more sadness when he arrived in Phoenix. Coach McCoy passed away a week earlier. He had a heart attack that took him quickly. This was a tragic blow to the Spartans and Jim in particular. He was glad that coach did not suffer with cancer or consumption that had so slowly taken the lives of Jacob and Mansolin. Jim knew that coach supported him in his desire to play in the majors and was probably his only hope of moving up. Now with the death of his mentor and good friend, Jim sobered up enough to visit an Arizee Holy Ground in the nearby mountains, where he fasted for three days, asking God to accept the souls of his friends and to give him strength to face his deep sadness.

Jim wished Gabriela were with him so she could hold and comfort him through these difficult times. He wrote her of the loss of Mansolin and Coach McCoy. She sent him letters expressing her sympathy and love, trying to raise his spirits by writing about Jake and her dreams of their life once they were married. Her letters gave Jim renewed hope in the most dire of times. But with Gabriela so far away, Jim was ultimately left to face life alone, comforted only by his whiskey.

When the new Phoenix coach was named, Jim felt somewhat better. He learned that the new coach would be Coach Benson, whom Jim had played for in Kansas City. At least the new coach knew Jim and had seen him play.

At the start of the new season, Benson called a meeting of the players.

"I want you boys to know that Coach McCoy was not only my good friend, but also my mentor. So I will be coaching you just like he did. I won't be able to replace such a great man, but with your help, I'll damn well try!" Coach Benson looked around the room. "I have scouted, coached or evaluated most of you in this room. And I will tell you that I had the absolute pleasure of coaching your own Jim Eagleson for one game last year. If there was one reason we won that game and the championship, it was Jim."

Jim got applause, pats on the back and congratulatory words from just about everyone in the locker room.

Coach paused a moment and then continued. "I guess some of you are wondering why I left Kansas City to take this job. Well, it's none of your damn business, so quit speculating and concentrate on winning games."

When the meeting was over, Benson called Jim aside. "Jim, as I recall you are almost 40 years old. We both know that your age and race are detriments to your being promoted to the majors. But I want you to know that I will continue McCoy's effort and try my best to make it happen. You are a damn good player and deserve a chance to make it to the big league. I understand that one of the owners is thinking of retiring and the other one wants to sell. The new owners may feel differently about you. I will make sure they take a close look at you."

"Thanks Coach. I miss McCoy, but I want you to know that I couldn't be happier with his replacement."

Coach continued, "I appreciate that Jim. My advice to you is to continue to play as best as your aging body will allow. I'll play you in every game I can. You are not only a good hitter, but are one of the best pitchers I've seen. You're going to be my closer, and you are going to be so good that management will beg to have you in the majors."

That sounded like a good plan to Jim.

"Whatever you think is best for the team and my career is what I'll do. But it is also really important that I get to the majors. I need to do it for my father and my people. I have something to prove. I think my success will help the white man see the Indian is worth respecting."

Benson was quite impressed with Jim's ideals and goals for his life.

"Jim I'll do all I can to help you. But I want you to know that you have nothing to prove. It is clear that you have already shown you're an exemplary man regardless of your race. If you remember that fact, you will feel better about your life."

"Thanks, Coach, but I will make it to the majors. It is my destiny. I will make my father proud."

While Jim easily said these words, believing them was more difficult.

CHAPTER 59

The Spartans had a good season. They won the league championship for a second year in a row, with Jim once again being a major contributor to the victories. His batting average was down a few points primarily because of the focus on his pitching. Even with fewer plate appearances, Jim hit 15 homeruns and had an impressive batting average of .320. He won the 10 games in which he was the starting pitcher, but in his primary role as closer, he saved 30 games. Aside from his impressive stats, Jim was pleased that his teammates improved during the season and pulled together in a cohesiveness that the he had not previously seen.

But still at the end of the season, Jim didn't get the call up to the major league team in St. Louis or even the minor league team in Kansas City. Once again the only thing that changed was his salary. So Jim headed home to see Gabriela and Jake. This year he planned to spend even more time with his family. As the train came to a stop in Oklahoma City, he saw both Gabriela and Jake waiting for him. After hugs and kisses, Gabriela asked Jake, who was happily situated in Jim's arms, to say something to Pop Jim.

Jake looked a little confused, but got a little grin on his face and said, "Pop, Pop, Pop."

Jim was aghast at this miracle and amazed at how much Jake had grown. This little boy had a unique personality and most importantly, he knew Jim was his Pop.

Jim kept one of his bags tucked under his arm. Gabriela thought perhaps he had brought a gift to surprise her. Unfortunately, she found out later that the bag was full of whiskey bottles. It was off season and Jim brought a good supply of booze. He was drinking again and trying to keep his habit a secret. He had no control of his addiction and alcohol was unfortunately added to his list of constant companions. In spite of this, Gabriela was glad to have Jim home. With each baseball season, her loneliness was becoming more and more difficult to face

Once he was settled in his room, he gave Gabriela and Jake presents. Gabriela received a blanket that was woven by Abotoe's wife before her death and a small bottle of perfume, which Jim personally selected. He told her that the fragrance was much like that of a beautiful Desert Lavender with it blue flowers known for a rich and luxurious fragrance. For Jake, there was a baseball, a small bat carved by one of his Arizee friends and a miniature baseball glove that Jim had made specifically for Jake. Of course, he knew it was too early for Jake to play baseball. But when he was older, Jim would be his teacher and Jake would have everything he needed. Perhaps he would even grow up to accomplish what Jim had failed to do, play in the major league.

One evening after Jim had put Jake to bed, he and Gabriela took time to discuss their future. Gabriela started with the troubling issue of Jim's drinking.

"Jim, you know I want to marry you, but I must tell you that your drinking will prevent that. I know you have been drinking for years and still been able to play baseball, but as your addiction grows, it will ultimately end your career at a time earlier than you will want. I know family and baseball are the most important things in your life. Don't let alcohol destroy them."

Jim responded as a typical alcoholic, "Gabriela, you worry too much. I don't drink much more than I did five years ago. I've been able to continue to be one of the best players in the league, and I don't recall avoiding my duty to you and Jake. But because it is so important to you, I will stop drinking, if you will marry me."

Gabriela was surprised, but quickly responded, "Yes, yes, of course Jim I will marry you!" They embraced warmly as tears ran down Jim's face. Even though he had prayed for the day Gabriela would accept his proposal, he had no idea that he would be brought to tears when she finally said "Yes." Their lips met in anticipation of their marriage

"Jim let's get married very soon, in a small civil ceremony, perhaps before you leave for the reservation."

Jim quickly added, "The sooner the better for me! I am so in love with you that the days get longer and longer waiting for the time we can be together!"

After retiring for the evening, Jim lay in bed still astounded by the fact that he would finally marry Gabriela. He had dreamed often of their wedding day. Jim thought of the promise he had made to Gabriela—stop drinking alcohol. That would be an immense challenge; but with the help of his friends and family, he knew he could do it.

The next morning, they told Jake about their marriage. Even though Jake was really much too young to understand, he still seemed happy. So the entire family went to Gabriela's parents' home to tell them the good news.

The following Friday, Patrick and Kathleen once again attended the marriage of their daughter. They, like most of their friends, had grown to love Jim and were happy to have him as Gabriela's husband. It was on a mild, sunny Saturday afternoon that Gabriela and Jim were married in a simple civil ceremony.

With the O'Connor's babysitting, Gabriela and Jim honeymooned in Kansas City. Jim was well known there because of his performance in the championship game, so he had no difficulty reserving a hotel room at the prestigious Muehlebach Hotel. It was with great pride that Jim registered as Mr. and Mrs. Eagleson. For once, Jim didn't bring whiskey along.

The newlyweds and Jake spent a wonderful Christmas together. They invited her parents and Peter for Christmas dinner. Peter brought his fiancé, and they all celebrated by watching Jake rip open package after package.

Shortly after Christmas Jim told Gabriela that he wanted to visit Abotoe before the new baseball season. Parting was difficult for Jim and Gabriela, but he promised it would only be for a few weeks. This was Jim's first trip to the reservation since Mansolin's death. It was sad to return without seeing his friend, but he soon adjusted. Abotoe had rejuvenated the reservation baseball league, naming one of the teams The Eagles, after Jim. Abotoe asked Jim to help him with scheduling and umpiring as well as coaching.

Jim was very pleased with Abotoe's efforts. He gave him some money to purchase equipment and uniforms. To celebrate, Jim and Abotoe broke open a new batch of whiskey. He rationalized his drunkenness as just part of the celebration of the new Indian Baseball League. He tried to avoid further drinking like he promised Gabriela, but his addiction was too strong to resist. His stomach seemed to worsen with each drink, but Jim was still unwilling to give up the booze entirely.

A week after Jim arrived at the reservation he received a note from Gabriela that she and Jake along with her parents were visiting Phoenix in three days and wanted him to meet them. By the time Jim received the note, there was only one day left before the visit. He naturally wanted to see them; but that left him little time to sober up. He, liked many alcoholics, thought surely he could cover his addiction.

When Jim saw his wife, he thought that she had grown more beautiful in their time apart, even though he knew that was not possible. He took her in his arms and held her tight. He delighted in her smooth skin and soft kisses on his neck.

He tossed Jake into the air which caused the little boy to giggle. His hair was growing longer, just like a young Arizee boy.

Jake continually yelled, "Pop, Pop, Pop."

Jim once again had gifts for his family. Jake had to open his first. It was an authentic Arizee outfit for a very young warrior. Jake was thrilled with his gift. Jim explained that the Arizee outfit was befitting to a young boy destined to be chief. Gabriela opened her present and found an Arizee necklace.

Each piece of the necklace had significance which Jim explained. "The three most important beads are for love, hope and fertility, my personal favorites." It was Jim's first official hint, since their wedding, that he was hoping that he and Gabriela would have a child.

Jim successfully hid his drinking problem while with Gabriela. He didn't like to deceive her, but knew she would be furious if she knew he had been drinking. She had such faith in him. But his alcoholism, as well as his deception, was a central issue and fatal flaw that negatively affected Jim through out his life.

CHAPTER 60

Jim was still drinking when it came time to report to spring training. He arrived early so he would have some additional time to prepare for the season. He was not feeling his best and could tell his physical condition had deteriorated, no doubt attributed in part to his drinking problem. He knew he was not even close to the top of his game. Even with the extra workouts, he begged off participation in the first day of training, attributing his problems to his age and the hot weather. He also told Coach Benson he had picked up a stomach sickness from drinking the water on the reservation.

Coach saw right through Jim's lie and it finally came to a point where he confronted him. "Jim, no matter your excuses, you are drinking too much whiskey. You can't expect to booze it up and still be in shape to play professional baseball. Hell, young players can't even do that."

"That's not it coach, I'm having stomach problems from the water I drank."

"Let's cut that crap. You have reeked of whiskey since you arrived at camp. Don't lie to me and stop lying to yourself to protect a habit that will stop your career faster than your age or your race."

"You're not being fair."

"I am being more than fair. If you were anyone other than Jim Eagleson, I would kick your ass off the team right now! So don't lie to me or you will be out."

Out of desperation from his disappointments, Jim tucked his head and in language so unlike him said, "Coach, You don't have any damn idea what it is like to be stuck in the minors just because you are different!"

Coach threw his hat on the floor in frustration. "Maybe I don't know exactly what shit you have been through cause you're an Indian; but you're not alone when it comes to misery. I saw my father kill my mother and then blow his brains out. I lived in more orphanages than I care to count. Baseball became my savior. But to make it, I had to clean out spittoons and commodes, wash underwear and scrub floors. When I was 30 I finally got to play, but physical problems soon ended my career. Coach McCoy, bless his soul, became my mentor and taught me all he knew about coaching. I tried to work my way up to the majors, but never got there because management said I didn't know how to get along with the young stars of the game. If Kansas City had not won the championship last year, I'd been fired. And even though we did win, I was demoted here to Phoenix. And I been told if we don't win the championship this year, it will be my last. I too have had my hardships, but baseball is my life, the only family I have. So you see Jim, you ain't the only one around here who has been kicked in the teeth. So take ya whining elsewhere."

Jim sat frozen in his chair, like a statue. He was mute, not knowing what to say.

Coach pleaded with Jim once more. "I consider myself lucky just to be able to put on my uniform and be part of baseball. I know down deep you feel that way, too. And you're even luckier. You not only got baseball, but you got a great family—a beautiful wife and young son. Count your blessings; don't destroy them with whiskey."

Jim sat with his head in his hands, finally realizing that he could really lose everything he loved because of whiskey. He might not make it to the majors, but he did have a damn good life when he was sober.

Jim stood up, thinking more clearly than he had in a long time. "Coach, thank you. I often think more about the bad things than the good things in my life. I'll get some help with my drinking problem." Jim grinned at coach and continued, "Gabriela will be very happy. When she spoke with me about my drinking, I lied to her; the person I love the most." He hesitated for a moment, trying to control his emotions. "You're right; in the long run, whiskey has only made my life worse!"

As he left the room, Jim turned to Coach Benson, "Thanks for caring enough to be honest with me. And don't worry about being fired; we're gonna win the championship this year!"

Benson sure hoped Jim was right. The conversation had been a good one, and both men felt better after having this talk and unloading personal burdens, friend to friend.

Just as Jim predicted, Phoenix won the league championship, and Coach Benson remained with the team. And just as in the past, Benson recommended Jim for promotion to the majors with the same disappointing result. In fact for the next two years Benson made the same recommendation with no success. By now Jim lost hope and knew that his age, race and his growing stomach problems, would probably keep him right here in Phoenix. But Jim did not let his disappointment keep him from trying to improve his performance, especially in relief pitching. He compensated for any deficits attributed to age by using his experience and intelligence to continue to save games for the Spartans.

Gabriela, Jake and her parents attended games whenever the team was near Oklahoma City. Jake always wore a Spartans cap and cheered for his Pop. He loved watching fans scramble to get an autograph from his father, who was now team captain. This all made Jake very proud to be Jim's son.

Jim's family life was even better than he expected. He and Gabriela enjoyed watching Jake grow and flourish. He was already showing real baseball talent as he could run, throw and hit a ball better than his playmates. Just as Jim had hoped, the boy seemed like a natural. While his family brought him great happiness, Jim continued to struggle with the likelihood he would never become the man his father was. He was still resentful, which made his recovery from alcoholism very difficult. He occasionally "fell off the wagon," which caused Gabriela great concern. She knew that he would always remain troubled until he succeeded in what he called his destiny and worried that his life would be shortened by the alcohol.

CHAPTER 61

Jim was now in his early forties and been with Phoenix since he was released from prison. Last season his hitting suffered and his batting average was no where near its peak. But he still made hits in pressure situations and often ignited his team in a late inning rally. His most important role with the team was relief pitching, most often being the all important closer. Jim still had most of his pitches of old; but he also developed an amazing knuckle ball. Between his knuckle ball, slider, fastball and an occasional changeup, Jim could easily confuse the opposing batters, which continued to make him a critical part of the Spartan's success. Still though, his body and stomach problems were making it almost impossible to last out a whole baseball season.

In fact, before the start of the new season Jim asked to meet with Coach Benson to discuss his future. When Jim walked in with Gabriela, Benson knew Jim had something on his mind other than preseason plans. He had seriousness in his voice that immediately told Coach that Jim wanted to talk about something very important.

"Coach, this has been a very difficult decision for me; but I have decided this will be my last season. I need to; I guess the word is retire. I want to step down while I'm still an asset to this team, you know finish on a high. I don't want to be that old fart you keep around just because you feel sorry for him."

Benson, not entirely surprised, replied, "I knew something was amiss when you showed up with your wife. You know 'm a sucker for a beautiful face. Madam, I assume you agree with this decision?"

"Yes sir, I do. Jim is having more health problem, particularly with his stomach. I know he has talked with you about his drinking; and even though he is controlling it much better than in the past, he realizes that he has done a good deal to damage to his body. Realizing that, we want to have more time together with our son."

Sadly, but also truthfully, Coach Benson understood. Jim was obviously playing ball way beyond the age when most players retire.

"Jim you will be impossible to replace and not just for your ability on the field. You are an inspiration to all of us. We didn't win the championships just because of your hitting and pitching, even though they were important. We also won because of your leadership. As to retirement, given your health and your wonderful family, I understand. It's a wise decision. I've seen too many players and coaches try to extend their careers only to retire embarrassed. I only hope that I'm as sensible as you when my time comes. But then baseball is the love of my life. I'm not fortunate to have a family like you. I know how much baseball means to you. You've given it your all for many years, and I know I can count on you for your last season. Toward the end of the season, I'll talk with management about keeping you on as an assistant coach. Now understand, I can't guarantee anything; but I will do my best to keep you in the Spartan family."

Once again, he cautioned Jim that there were no Indians on the coaching staff, and there may be a problem with him becoming an assistant coach.

"But if there was anybody the Spartans would be willing to take a chance on, it would be you. So I'll do my best, and see what happens."

"Thank you, Coach. That's a good plan. Once again, you revive my soul just as you did when we first met. You gave me the strength to stay with the game."

Even though Jim left the meeting confident in his decision to retire, he still felt melancholy.

The Phoenix Spartans had a good year and won yet another championship as Jim again predicted. Jim saved 35 games, which was a career and league high. With such a successful season, Jim felt pressure from his teammates and even local baseball fans to stay on, but he was unwavering in his decision, particularly with the relentless pain in his stomach. At Gabriela's insistence he finally saw a doctor. The doctor told Jim that his years of drinking had damaged his stomach, but there were no signs of any life threatening illness. The doctor prescribed pain medication and told him he would need to retire as soon as possible for the sake of his health. Gabriela was relieved with the diagnosis. She feared Jim had some terrible illness like Jacob. The doctor's diagnosis just confirmed what he already knew. The time had come to say goodbye to the game he loved so much.

On his last day with the team, Coach Benson told Jim that the team had been sold and there was a letter for him from the new owner. Jim opened the envelope, thinking that perhaps it was a letter congratulating him on a job well done and wishing him well in his retirement. But what he read in the letter was far from that.

Jim turned to Benson. "Coach, they want me to play in the majors for the rest of their season. And they want me in St. Louis in three days. My dream; this is my dream come true!"

Benson couldn't believe what Jim was saying. He had touted Jim's abilities and pleaded with the owners for years, but to no avail. Now within days of purchasing the team, the new owner called Jim up to play for the St. Louis Spartans.

"I can't believe this is happening. Thanks coach; how did you do it? I've got to tell Gabriela!"

"As much as I'd like to take the credit for this, I had little to do with it. We have a new owner and seems he is open to new ideas. He called me and asked about you. I gave him the complete low down. I told him that Jim Eagleson was the man he needed." Then Coach yelled, "Jim, you are going to the big show!"

Jim was overwhelmed with excitement. His long, difficult struggle to make it to the majors was over. The brave warrior had won his battle. He immediately called Gabriela saying, "I'm going to the big league. Meet me in St. Louis!"

CHAPTER 62

Jim was on the next train to St. Louis. Even though his stomach troubled him, he was not going to let that dampen his celebration or his shot at the major league.

The train was behind schedule, and he was worried he would be late for his appointment with the new owner. He went straight to the St. Regis Hotel and met Gabriela, who accompanied him to the meeting. On the way to the meeting, Gabriela tried desperately to talk to Jim about whether he should play particularly after just finishing a long season and his worsening stomach pain. But the few times she started that discussion, Jim changed the subject by asking about Jake and her parents.

She finally conceded to Jim's elation and joined the celebration. "Jim, I am so happy for you. This is the opportunity you have waited for."

"I know, Gabriela. I've waited so long for this day."

"Who are we meeting with, the owner or the coach?"

"The new owner, but I was so excited I don't even remember his name." Looking in his pants pockets, he said, "I have it somewhere."

Jim was still looking for his letter as they approached the stadium. A security guard stopped them and directed them to an entrance one block east.

He was emphatic. "This entrance is for whites only."

While Jim was accustomed to such discrimination, Gabriela was not. As she and the guard exchanged angry words not befitting the lady she was, Jim interrupted and gave the guard the letter he finally found in his back pocket. It stated that he was a member of the team and had an appointment with the owner.

The guard quickly offered an apology. "Mrs. & Mrs. Eagleson, I must apologize for my rudeness. Please let me show you to Mr. Thompson's office."

Even though Gabriela was not yet finished with the guard, she knew it was time to be silent. Jim reached for her hand and smiled. When they walked into the large executive suite, Jim knew that he must be meeting with someone very important. The guard introduced them to the secretary, Madelyn Smith, who asked them to please call her Maddy. In contrast to the original disposition of the guard, she was pleasant and made them feel at ease by asking about their trip and offering refreshments. She also knew they had a son and asked about Jake. As she led them to Mr. Thompson's office she told them that he was the president and owner of the team. Maddy mentioned that he had been eagerly awaiting their arrival.

The office was an expansive room with large windows, elaborately adorned with velvet curtains. There was leather furniture and a big desk which sat on very plush carpet. When they entered the office Mr. Thompson was sitting with his back to the door.

Maddy spoke, "Mr. Thompson, Mr. & Mrs. Eagleson are here to see you."

As he turned and rose from his chair, he smiled broadly and said, "Well, Jim Eagleson, it is good to see you again. How are you, my friend?"

Jim looked at him with bewilderment.

"I gather you don't recognize me since it has been many years since you saw me."

Jim quickly tried to recollect his past and how he may have known Mr. Thompson.

Then with a big smile he rushed over to his friend saying, "You are little Joey, John Thompson's son!"

The two men hugged, remembering the great friendship they shared so many years ago.

Gabriela stood, clueless, watching in wonder. Suddenly realizing this, Jim made an introduction and reminded her of the story of John Thompson's kindness to him and his mother.

Gabriela extended her hand. "It's a real pleasure to meet you, Joey."

"The pleasure is mine, Gabriela. You know, it was Jim who taught me about baseball. I will always remember how brave he was. His family had been killed, his mother dying and yet he remained strong in spite of the hardships. Before my father passed away he asked me to try and find Jim. He thought Jim was one of the greatest young men he had ever met." My father said, "When you find him, help him in anyway you can. He deserves the best life has to offer.'"

Jim replied, "I am sorry to hear that you have lost your father. He was so good to me. But don't worry; he is with God."

"He died three months ago today. He had a weak heart that finally just stopped."

With memories of the pain he felt at the loss of his family and now with John Thompson's passing, tears came to Jim's eyes.

"Your father was my friend. He was a great man, and he left this world a better place. I hope to see him again some day when we are both in the glory of God."

Joey changed the somber mood. "My father was a very successful lawyer and became a very successful investor later in his life. He had been trying to buy the St. Louis Spartans for years from Gen. White and his partner. When the General retired, his partner was ready to sell. My father bought the team just before he passed away."

Jim inquired. "Was this the same Gen. White who was commander of the fort?"

"Yes, the same one."

"Now I know why I was never called to the majors. Gen. White was an owner!"

"No doubt there is some truth to that; but he's gone. I am in charge now and when I found you playing ball in Phoenix, I knew I had a way to carry out my father's wishes. Finally finding you was one of God's miracles."

Jim and Gabriela agreed that it was truly a miracle that Jim now had the opportunity to realize his dream of playing in the major league. John Thompson was an honorable man and even in death he kept the promise he made to Jim so long ago in the army hospital.

Joey asked Jim and Gabriela to have a seat.

He looked solemnly at Jim and said, "On behalf of the entire Spartan organization I want to apologize to you. Gen. White was a bitter man, and he was not going to let an Indian play for his major league team, much less the Indian he sent to prison so many years ago. When my father was finally able to purchase the organization, I saw your name on the roster of our Phoenix team. I called Benson inquiring about you. He told me your pitching and hitting as well as your leadership is what allowed the team to win championships."

"Joey, thank you. It was an honor to have known your father, and I am fortunate to be with you again. I am so proud to be able to play for St. Louis."

"It is I who should be thanking you for being so patient with our organization. You waited for us to right the wrong."

Gabriela gave Joey a big hug. "You'll never know how much you have done for my husband. You have opened a door for him to live the dream that has eluded him for much too long. He now has a chance to be as his father wished."

CHAPTER 63

As joyful as their reunion was, Jim was there to play baseball.

Joey got down to business and asked, "Jim, are you ready to pitch today?"

Before Jim could respond, Gabriela spoke up. "I must tell you something about Jim because he never will." She paused a moment and avoided looking into Jim's eyes. "Jim's health is not all that good. The fact is that he was about to retire from baseball when you contacted Coach Benson. I worry about him very much."

Joey smiled and said he understood. He knew of Jim's health problem by way of Coach Benson.

"Our goal is to use Jim only as our closer—which is frankly where we need him the most. Hopefully that role will not be all that physically demanding. Be assured that the Spartans want Jim on our team in some capacity for years to come. We will do nothing to hurt him. But Jim, you will have to be honest with us. Tell us if your pain is too bad for you to play. As long as you are still standing, it will be your call."

Gabriela wasn't sure she was completely comfortable with this; but it was good to know that the Spartans were aware of her husband's condition and had called him up to the majors, hopefully, for only a limited role.

Joey told Jim that the Spartans were tied for first place with the Chicago Rangers in the race for the National League pennant.

"If we win tonight's playoff game with the Rangers, we'll make our first appearance in the World Series, and play against the New York Titans."

"Ok, tell me exactly what can I do you for?" Jim responded.

"I've talked with the coach. As I said, we want you to be available as a relief pitcher, probably as a closer. Our best reliever is out with a torn muscle in his shoulder. He's not expected to return to the line up anytime soon. Benson tells me that you are the best closer he has seen. I have a high regard for Coach Benson; and if he says you are the best, then that's good enough for me. So be ready to relieve tonight and if we win, be ready for the series. After that, we can talk about next season."

Jim responded, "Sounds good to me, Joey!"

Although Gabriela did not like the sound of "next season," she remained quiet trying not to spoil Jim's excitement.

Joey noted, "There are still a few introductions I want to make. One is Coach Henry Lassiter and the other is Spartan Stadium.

After a very brief introduction to Coach Lassiter and a quick tour of the stadium, Jim accompanied Gabriela to the train station for her return home to Jake. She wanted to stay and watch the game; but the physical frailty of her parents made it necessary for her to leave. In addition to that, she had another reason that required her to go back home.

Just before she boarded the train, Gabriela smiled at Jim saying, "Honey, I think I have some good news!"

Jim felt a little awkward in that he had no idea what she was talking about.

She continued, "You remember those times when I visited you in Phoenix?"

Of course he remembered; in fact, he would never forget. But was not aware of what she was trying to tell him—at least until she winked at him.

At the same time, they both said, "We're going to have a baby!"

"Well at least I think so. But before we celebrate too much, I have to see the doctor tomorrow."

Jim looked into her eyes, "My sweet Gabriela, what wonderful news!"

Jim still could not hold his excitement much to the surprise of the passengers who stared at him as he twirled Gabriela in circles. Gabriela was a little embarrassed by this, but she did not spoil the moment by complaining. She just smiled at those who stared at Jim as if he were just a tad unbalanced.

Jim could not believe his good fortunate. Both his dreams of having a child with Gabriela and playing in the majors were becoming realities. It looked to Jim like he had turned a corner and life was looking up. Other than the worrisome pain in his stomach, life was very good for Jim Eagleson.

CHAPTER 64

Before the game Jim met with Coach Lassiter or Coach L as he liked to be called. He talked with Jim about his role with the team, which was consistent with what Joey said.

"Jim, after talking in detail with Coach Benson, we'll use you as our closer. As I think you know, our regular closer is injured—so it's up to you! We need all the savvy you have because you are going to be facing some of the best hitters in the major league!"

"Coach, all I can tell you is I'll do my best. My father taught me how to handle pressure."

"So I've heard. I think we're lucky to have you playing for us."

Jim got to the stadium early so he could get acclimated to his surroundings before he met the players. "He prayed that today would be different from his first days with the other teams. He wanted so much to be liked and respected by his new teammates."

When Jim first put on his St. Louis uniform, he stood in front of the mirror admiring his imagine. He clearly was not the physical specimen he used to be, but that was okay with Jim. He had finally made it. This one game may be his entire career in the majors, so he was going to make the most of it. Whatever it took, he would give his all to be successful in his first major league game. This was his chance to show the country, or at least this city, that he was a great player worthy of respect and maybe even a chief. Even the pain in his stomach would not stop him; he would endure almost anything for this chance.

When his teammates arrived, Jim knew at once that God had answered his prayers. He was warmly accepted by all his teammates without having to prove himself. His old friend and catcher, Joe Dominic, was there offering Jim his support. It was good to see Joe healthy again after being hit so hard by the bat of the angry batter in that championship game in Kansas City. In fact, other than that brief altercation with the security guard, everyone welcomed him as part of the St. Louis family. Of course it didn't hurt that many of the players on the team had heard of Jim's legendary accomplishments in the minors. While Jim appreciated the recognition and respect, he did not crave the attention of his teammates. He was a simple, hardworking ballplayer who wanted to prove to his teammates and the rest of the world that he was able to play the game as well as anyone.

Coach L, who came to the locker room to check on his players, had a few words for Jim,

"Jim I want to tell you that it's likely you'll be called in to pitch in the late innings of today's game. Take the time to talk with Joe to learn more about the batters' weaknesses and strengths." Coach paused, then continued, "Jim, while you were welcomed by your teammates, you may not be so lucky with the fans. So try to ignore any derogatory remarks and just play like I know you can. You have the whole organization behind you. So just do your best."

Jim, with his usual confidence, promised Coach L and Joey Thompson would never regret promoting him to the majors.

When Jim entered the stadium for the game, he was astonished at what he saw. The seats were filled with more fans than he had seen at any of his other games. They waved flags, signs and red scarves, leaving not doubt for whom they were rooting. There were vendors selling hot dogs, peanuts, and popcorn. Men were dressed in suits and hats and some were smoking cigars. A few seemed to be sipping from small bottles discreetly hidden in their jackets. Women were dressed in what looked like their Sunday best. This was no ordinary place. It was major league baseball. It was his dream.

As Jim walked back to the dugout to talk with Joe Dominic, he had a sharp pain in his stomach that almost took his breath. He stopped and fell to one knee until he felt better. This was the worse pain he could ever remember. Nerves, that's what he thought. Jim slowly stood up, hoping his teammates would think he had offered a prayer for a Spartans win.

When the Spartans took the field, the fans welcomed them with a deafening roar. Jim stood outside the dugout and looked with amazement

The game went well for his team as the Spartans built up a five run lead going into the top of the ninth. Three more outs and they would be in the World Series. Initially Coach L. was going to let Paul Sistine, his starting pitcher, stay through the final inning. But then realizing Paul may be needed early on in the World Series, he decided to go with a reliever. Based on what the Coach had said, Jim thought surely he would be brought in, but that was not to be. Coach L called a young reliever, Chris Erickson to close the game and secure the win. Even though Jim was confused by that move, he was confident that his new Coach knew what he was doing. At least, he hoped he did.

The first Chicago batter hit a homerun over the centerfield fence. The second one walked and the third man up hit a single to left field. The Spartans' lead was down to four runs, and there were two base runners and no outs.

Coach L called a time out to talk with his young pitcher. "Son, if you don't get the next batter, I'm pulling you for that old man in the bullpen. You have one more chance."

Chris tried to compose himself and concentrate on striking out the next batter. His first pitch was hit over the right field wall. Homeroom, score Spartans 7, Chicago 6, and there still were no outs! Coach L took one step out of the dugout and called in the right hander, Jim Eagleson. Jim, ignoring the pain in his old legs and his stomach, jogged to the mound looking younger than his years. Nothing was going to spoil this day.

Since Jim was a newcomer, there was little reaction from the fans. There were, however, some disgusting remarks from the Chicago dugout that Jim chose to ignore, just as he always did.

Coach L handed the ball to Jim, "Just do what you did for Benson. Kick some butt for me!"

Jim had a short conversation with Joe, his catcher.

"Jim, I forgot to ask you, when you throw that damn knuckle ball which direction does it normally drift so I will know where to catch it."

"Damn if I know, Joe."

Joe looked worried. Then Jim laughed. "Just kidding; it usually drifts down toward the batter's feet."

Joe was greatly relieved, but surprised at Jim's humor in such a tense situation. "I like your style, Jim Eagleson. Let's get these suckers out. I wanna go to the World Series"

Jim's first major league pitch was a slider, a line drive hit to the pitcher. Jim snagged the ball for the first out. The next batter struck out on Jim's killer changeup. Two outs. Jim was fast becoming a hero to the hometown crowd. The hum of indifference from the crowd had been replaced with cheers of encouragement. The next batter was leading the league in hits. Joe wasn't sure Jim knew that, so he called time out to talk with Jim.

"This guy is a dynamite hitter. So pitch to him carefully. If you want we can walk the slob and deal with the next batter."

Jim rubbed the ball in his hand. "Let's see what he can do with my knuckleball. If he can't hit it, then I know I can get him out. If he hits it, he won't get past first base."

Joe was impressed with Jim's analytical abilities and said, "Why did it take so long to get you up here?"

"I don't know." Of course he knew why, but it didn't matter right now.

Jim's first pitch was his "circus pitch," better know as a side arm knuckle ball. The batter swung, but only nicked the ball resulting in a little dribble in front of the plate. Joe jumped from behind the plate and threw the runner out at first. The crowd and the dugout exploded. Once again Jim had proven to be the hero. With confidence and bravery, he faced a difficult situation and pulled his team to a victory. He knew his father was proud of him.

After the game, Jim heard from Coach L what he had heard before from his other coaches.

"That was possibly the best relief job I can recall." But he then added, "The New York team has the best batting average in baseball, so you gotta be even better to shut them down."

"Hey coach, the bigger they are, the harder they will fall! After today's game, I think our team will get them good; you can count on it."

Coach L smiled believing that the team and Jim could do just that.

The morning newspaper had a big article on the win even though Jim's performance was not acknowledged as being that critical to the victory. In fact, it was quite the opposite. Without naming anyone specific, the article said that the Spartan relievers had almost blown the game and the season. However, Jim was mentioned in the last sentence as the pitcher who finally shut Chicago down. As soon as Jim got his hands on a paper, he circled his name and mailed it to Gabriela.

As he was quietly reveling in the success of his first major league game, he noticed that his stomach was throbbing with pain. The trainer gave him some pills to help with indigestion, saying nervous stress was surely the cause. With this new medicine along with his pain pills, Jim found some relief, but he still felt a deep soreness in his stomach. But like with most problems in his life, Jim persevered.

CHAPTER 65

The time between the end of the playoffs and the beginning of the World Series was helpful to both teams, but particularly the Spartans. Whereas the Spartans won the National League pennant in a playoff game with Chicago, the New York Titans won the American League pennant outright. The Spartans definitely needed the rest.

The team's overall health was good, except for the injured closer Jim replaced and Jim, who did his best to conceal his stomach problem. His biggest concern was whether he could hide it if he had to work too many innings in the Series. Whatever the case, he would give all that it took for the Spartans to win the World Series because his father would expect nothing less.

Being anxious about Gabriela's doctor appointment, Jim decided to try a long distance call from the locker room. Long distance calls were in their infancy and often took up to 20 minutes to complete. Jim waited patiently as his call was relayed to Oklahoma. Finally the phone rang. He was about to hang up when Gabriela answered.

"Hello."

"Gabriela, I can't wait any longer. What did the doctor say? Is it true? Am I going to be a daddy?"

"Jim, I just walked in. Let me put my packages down. Okay. But first tell me how you are feeling."

"Me, I'm fine. I guess you know from the paper that we won the league championship, and will play in the World Series. I shut Chicago down in the ninth and saved the game. It was great. Just wish you had been there. Now tell me, I cannot wait any longer."

"Yes, I am so proud of you. The doctor said you will be a father. Jim, we are going to have our own baby!"

"Oh Gabriela, that's wonderful. I am so happy. I wish I could kiss you right now. I can't wait to come home. We'll have a huge celebration party."

"Yes, we will. But for now you concentrate on your game. You know the newspaper here had a big story about you. Said you were the reason that the

Spartans are in the World Series. I'll send it to you. Jim, I am so proud of you. I know this is your dream, but please take care of your health. Our family needs you more than baseball needs you."

"I'm fine. Really I am. Don't worry about me. Just take care of Jake, yourself and our baby. I'll see you very soon. I love you."

"I love you, too Jim."

Gabriela did not believe Jim's assessment of his health. She could not help but be concerned, particularly since she had already lost one husband. She did not want to lose Jim, too. She had to see him to know that he was as he said. That's the only way she would be satisfied.

Jim told everyone who would listen about the new baby. He continually had a smile on his face. But he knew that he had to concentrate on the upcoming game. When he was not meditating or praying, he occupied his time studying the New York players. He found they were good at hitting fastballs and hard sliders, especially on the inside corner of the plate. He remembered the words of Coach McCoy and Benson. "All players have strengths; but they all have their weaknesses, too."

So Jim discussed their weaknesses at length with Joe Dominic and decided some well placed changeups and knuckleballs would be problems for most of the Titan hitters.

On the morning of the first game of the Series, Jim went to the locker room very early to prepare himself both emotionally and physically for the game. There was a knock at the door. He thought it might be a reporter hoping to get an interview with a player. He was not in the mood for talking as he had been up for several hours during the night with stomach pain and it wasn't much better this morning. He almost yelled for the visitor to come back later, but decided that if someone wanted to talk, then he was available. When he opened the door, much to his surprise there was Joey Thompson with Abotoe and AJ, Coach Benson and most importantly Gabriela and Jake.

Joey joked, "Jim, the security guard called me to say there were several people outside yelling your name. When I went to investigate, I found your fan club."

"Well I don't know what to say. I am so happy to see everyone. Gabriela, you didn't tell me you were coming."

"I wanted it to be a surprise. And I can see it certainly is!"

Sensing that Gabriela and Jim needed some privacy, Joey took Jake by the hand and invited the others to accompany him on a tour of the facilities.

Jim first concern was whether Gabriela should be traveling and how she managed to come with her mother's illness.

"Once my mother found out that I would miss the Word Series because she was sick, she perked up pretty quickly and ordered me out of the house. Honestly, though, she did not have to twist my arm. Fortunately I was able to get word to Abotoe and Coach Benson and asked them to meet me at the stadium." She paused, then said, "And yes, the doctor said I can travel."

With all the excitement, Gabriela did not question Jim about his stomach problem. Seeing that he looked well was enough. So she did not say anything that may spoil the thrill of Jim's first World Series game.

Joey gave Jim's fan club box seats right next to the Spartans' dugout. Jake proudly wore the Spartan cap that Jim gave him and was so excited to be in a big league stadium, especially since his Pop was going to be playing.

CHAPTER 66

Game One of the World Series was about to get underway as the teams lined up on the foul lines; the Titans on third base side and Spartans on the first base line. He was surprised to see a small group of Army soldiers march on the field with several flags and musical instruments. Jim did not have good experiences with the army so their presence was of great concern for him. The band began to play the National Anthem. Players and fans removed their hats, saluted or put their hands over their hearts and began singing along with the band.

In the past, Jim had no desire to honor a country that killed or enslaved his people. But times were changing and so was Jim. He was an Indian in the World Series of the American game of baseball. So as Jim stood on the field, he, too, removed his hat and held it over his heart. Had he known the words he felt for sure he would also be singing. After the anthem was over, the crowd roared its approval. Jim then heard an announcement that John Parker, President of the United States would throw the first pitch. Jim watched as his President stood on the pitcher's mound and threw the ball to Joe Dominic.

As the President walked past Jim to his seat, he reached out and shook Jim's hand saying, "Jim Eagleson, I am a big fan. May God bless you!"

With pride in his heart, Jim said, "Thank you Sir and May God bless America!"

It was a long awaited recognition, and Jim was proud to call himself an American.

With the pre game ceremonies over, the umpire yelled, "Play Ball."

As the crowd roared, the Spartans took the field full of hope and excitement. However it was short lived. On the first pitch, the talented lead off man for the Titans hit the ball over the right field wall. The hometown fans, who had been cheering for their team, were quickly silenced. The Titans scored two more runs in the first inning, but the Spartan pitcher held them at three runs through the eighth inning. The Spartans, with clutch hitting, tied the score in the eighth inning. Going into the top of the ninth, the Spartans' starting pitcher was exhausted so Coach L pulled him and sent Jim in to close the game. Jim found that his homework on the batters paid off. He struck out the side with his assortment of pitches. The fans yelled their approval, but the game was far from over. The bottom of the Spartan batting order was up in the ninth.

Jim was scheduled to bat second in the ninth inning, but expected that Coach L would put in a pinch hitter. The coach called to Jim.

"Coach Benson said you're one hell of a hitter, particularly in the clutch. So I'm going to let you bat cause if we don't score I'll need you to pitch again."

With a smile of confidence, Jim replied, "You bet, Coach."

The first batter singled to center field. Jim was up in his first major league plate appearance. To say he was nervous was an understatement. He was batting against the best reliever in the league. Jim took a few practice swings and then walked to the batter's box. When he saw the sacrifice bunt signal, he set himself for the pitch. As the pitcher released the ball, the first and third basemen ran toward the plate in anticipation of a bunt. Jim squared away and bunted the ball in between the pitcher and first baseman. Each hesitated thinking the other would field the ball and the runner moved forward. Jim, who in his younger days would have beat the throw to first base, was thrown out. But Jim did what he was asked; he moved the runner to second. As he walked back to the dugout to the cheers of the crowd, he once again felt burning in his stomach, but he was determined not to show it. He managed to smile at his fan club behind the Spartan dugout, all of whom were standing and applauding him.

The next batter hit a line drive to right center field for a hit that sent the winning run home. The fans and players went wild. The Spartans lead in the Series 1-0.

Jim suddenly found himself surrounded by news reporters. One loud mouth reporter, Frankie Pierce, started asking Jim how he felt being an Indian playing a white man's game. In an effort to protect Jim from this obnoxious reporter, Coach L jumped in before Jim could speak.

"This here player, Jim Eagleson, is the best kept secret in the history of professional baseball. Ain't it hard to believe that prior to being called up by Joey Thompson that he had never been allowed to play in the majors? You know why? Well I'm sure I don't have to tell intelligent reporters like you why." Coach paused for an answer but received none. It seemed that reporters only know how to ask questions. So he continued, "Cause he ain't white! Well I'm here to tell ya color's got nothing to do with playing baseball. This man is close to 45 years old and he's going to prove to you that he is one of the greatest players in the history of major league baseball. And remember who told you that!"

Coach hurried Jim off the field.

"Thanks Coach. I wanted to say exactly what you said; but you did a better job."

Coach L suddenly appeared very serious. "Just do what I said you would. I don't like being a wrong!"

"I'll try my hardest to make you proud."

The St. Louis papers had Jim's picture along with a story about his impressive performance. Coach L's comments were included in the article. The New York papers ran an article about an old major league rookie who was making a name for himself in the majors after having played in the minors for years. The article said that Jim Eagleson, an Arizee Indian had been unjustly sent to prison and had his conviction overturned. Jim was an instant celebrity, but Coach L warned that such accolades could be short lived.

"You know, Jim, the press can turn on you as fast as they supported you."

Even though he was never one to blow his own horn, Jim took Coach's wise words to heart.

Before Game Two, Jim talked with the trainer about his indigestion and got some medicine. Used in conjunction with his pain pills, they gave him only short term relief. Even with the pain, Jim felt he had no choice but to tolerate it because this could be his only chance to reach his destiny; the one chance to be admired and respected by all people.

He was called on to relieve in the eighth inning of game two. The Spartans had a one run lead. He faced three batters in each inning, quickly retiring the side by striking out four batters and getting two on pop flies. Once again he did not let his pain get in the way of victory or celebration.

The headline in the sports section of the newspaper read "Another Classic Save on the Part of Jim Eagleson." Jim was keeping Coach L honest. Sports writers around the country had seen enough of Jim Eagleson to realize that he was a damn good player. They started calling him "The Chief," which gave Jim great satisfaction. He gave a few interviews to the St. Louis paper, and the reporters found him to be confident, yet humble. Jim was a star in St. Louis and enjoyed the long awaited recognition. He never failed to mention his heritage. The country was finally becoming acquainted with Jim Eagleson, the son of Lone Eagle, Chief of the Arizee Indians.

The Spartans, along with Jim's family fan club, left St. Louis for New York with a 2-0 lead in the series. Jim was looking forward to the travel days. He was exhausted, not so much from the game, but from the constant pain he endured. Even though he was concerned how he was going to continue to play ball and conceal his illness, he knew that somehow he must.

When the team arrived in New York, they checked into the Palmer Hotel. Jim was a welcomed guest at the hotel and enjoyed eating in the hotel dining room. Jim felt it was only because he was an outstanding baseball player, and not because opinions had changed about Indians. He marveled at how this culture accepted him for what he did and not who he was. Maybe that's what life is all about. If you do the best you can, and never give up, things have a way of working out.

Looking back at his life, he knew he had come a long way. Jim hoped that one day all American Indians would receive the same respect.

CHAPTER 67

The Spartans received a thrashing by the Titans in the next two games. The sports writers said the Spartans were intimidated by the big city and enormous stadium, which was filled to capacity for each game. The Spartans were embarrassed by the losses and appeared to be on the verge of collapsing under the pressure. In a team meeting after the second loss, Coach L tried to inspire the team before they fell behind in the Series.

"Listen up. You look like rookies, all of you. We're better than what we showed here in New York. We got the hitters and pitchers to win this Series. I have confidence in you. Now let's win this next game and go back to St. Louis as winners!"

In Game Five, the Spartans took an early lead and were ahead 7-4 going into the bottom of the ninth. Chris Erickson, who replaced the starting pitcher in the fifth inning, held the Titans scoreless, but he was struggling in the ninth. The first Titan batter was safe at first after hitting a line drive just out of reach of the shortstop. On a three-two pitch, Chris walked the next batter. The top of the order was up. After Chris got two quick strikes on the first batter, he slammed the ball into the left field corner for a triple. All of a sudden the score was 7-6 with the tying run on third and no outs. Without hesitation, Coach L called for Jim. He met Jim and Joe Dominic at the pitcher's mound.

"The Titans got some good hitters coming up, Jim. Any hit can bring the runner home. But if you strike 'em out, we don't have a damn thing to worry about, will we? Listen boys, we don't want to go back to St. Louis down three games to two. So get 'em out Chief!"

Jim and Joe were looking for the Titans to try a squeeze bunt to bring home the tying run. But the batter let the first pitch go by for strike one. The next pitch was swung on and hit foul. The third pitch was Jim's change-up which caught the batter off guard, and he swung before the ball was even at the plate. Strike three! Joe stepped in front of the plate holding up one finger, indicating one out.

The next batter, who was powerfully built, stepped to the plate. Jim threw him a slow slider and the batter took a full swing and missed. Jim swore he felt the wind from the swing at the pitcher's mound. Still holding the third base runner as close to the bag as possible, Jim went into a half wind-up and was about to release the ball when he saw the batter square around for a bunt. A squeeze play was about to happen, confirmed by the third base runner breaking for the home plate. Jim quickly rethought his pitch and threw high and outside. The batter determined to hit the ball still tried to make contact. The ball ended being hit as a little pop up about half way to the pitcher mound. Jim ran toward the plate, dove onto his stomach and caught the ball in a fly. Knowing that the runner on third had broken for home plate, he rolled over and threw the ball to the shortstop covering third base—a game ending double play. Game five was over. The Spartans won 7 to 6.

Once again Jim was the hero. But instead of getting up to celebrate the victory, he rolled over on the ground grabbing his stomach in pain. The excitement of the moment ceased as Jim lay on the field hoping that his pain would stop. The Spartans surrounded Jim as Coach L and the team doctor attended to him.

Gabriela, helplessly watching, pushed her way through the crowd in tears screaming, "Jim, Jim, my God what happened?"

The doctor called for a stretcher. As Jim left the field, he smiled and lifted his arm to indicate to everyone that he was okay. Even the New York fans stood and applauded the injured hero. With Gabriela holding his hand, Jim was taken to the hospital. She noticed a small streak of blood coming from the corner of his mouth.

CHAPTER 68

At the hospital Gabriela was joined by Joey Thompson, Coach L and Abotoe. While Jim was being treated in the emergency room, Joey called his personal physician, Dr. Samuel Freeman, and asked him to see Jim.

After a thorough examination, Dr. Freeman reported on Jim's condition. "Based on the results of the tests, I would say that Jim probably has either a bleeding ulcer or a stomach infection. But whatever the case, he needs several weeks of bed rest. Any exertion could cause his condition to worsen, including additional hemorrhaging, which could be fatal. I hate to use these scary words; but you need to realize that Jim is a very sick man." To offer some possible remedy, Dr. Freeman added, "I want to try a blood transfusion. They have become safer and more widely used in the last few years, and I think it would be helpful."

"Whatever you think will help my friend, doctor," replied Joey.

The doctor's words did little to assuage Gabriela's fears. "Dr. Freeman, you don't think it could be cancer, do you?"

"Mrs. Eagleson, I briefly considered cancer, but feel it is quite unlikely. A man with stomach cancer would have such pain and weakness that he would normally be bedridden, especially with hemorrhaging present."

Dr. Freeman did not realize that Jim was not just a normal man.

Joey took visibly upset Gabriela into a private waiting room where Coach L's wife, Martha was taking care of Jake and AJ. Martha held Gabriela hand telling her and Abotoe that she would be happy to care for the two boys as long as needed.

Gabriela took a deep breath and held Jake in her arms. With a stiff upper lip, she reassured her son that his Pop was okay, and he could see him soon. Gabriela needed some time to get her emotions under control. While Joey and Gabriela stayed with Jake and AJ, Coach L and Abotoe went in to see Jim who had only just arrived in his patient room.

Jim looked at Abotoe. "Ah, my big friend, how are you doing?"

"What's more important, my chief, is how you are doing?"

Jim smiled and shrugged off his problem saying that he had some stomach pain, but was better now. "I think I had some nervous, I think you say, butterflies, plus it was unusually hot today."

Abotoe then spoke to Jim in Arizee. Coach L noticed that Jim was no longer smiling. Then Abotoe spoke in English, "Eagleson, my chief, you are sick. You must rest now before the next…"

Coach L interrupted, "Jim, don't you worry about the next game. You need to rest. You're too sick to play."

"No, coach I must play. This is my chance to excel as my father would want. I must play; there is no other option."

Coach L, who learned from Coach Benson of Jim's intense commitment to his goal, was nonetheless startled by his insistence. "Don't worry now, Jim. We will talk about it later."

Just then Gabriela and Joey entered the room accompanied by Dr. Freeman.

Gabriela sat on the bed beside Jim. "How do you feel after being the hero of the game?"

"I have never felt better. Just a small stomach ache, but I am fine and ready to go back to St. Louis to win the series. Right doc?"

"Mr. Eagleson, you are too sick to play baseball or even leave this hospital. You need several weeks of rest. Playing another game could end your life!"

Raising his voice, Jim replied, "I must play ball. You don't understand."

Gabriela kissed Jim on his forehead and say, "Listen to the doctor. Think of me, Jake and our baby. Please don't play"

With the exception of Abotoe, Jim politely asked the others to leave the room so he could talk with his wife. With teary eyes, Jim explained his feelings about his destiny. "You both know how strongly I feel about this. Abotoe can verify what I must do as an Arizee to complete my journey, to become a chief. I was chosen to be a leader of people. My father set the standard and I am challenged to meet it."

Gabriela started to interrupt, but decided to let Jim continue.

"Many years ago my father told me that I will become a great chief, loved by my friends, feared by my enemies, and respected by all. I gave my word to him that I would follow in his footsteps. If the price I must pay for this is death, then so be it. To sacrifice myself for this objective is honorable." He paused, noticing Gabriela's tears. "Please don't worry about me. Take comfort in knowing that what ever happens to me is only temporary. We will be reunited in eternity."

Jim touched Gabriela's face and wiped her tears. She had not lived as an Arizee and such promises seemed foolish until she thought of her religion. The Bible is full of stories of sacrifice made for the love of others and the promise of eternity. The greatest was made by Jesus when he sacrificed his life for the sins of man. Jesus knew that his disciples would take care of his family, just as Jim knew his friends would care for Gabriela and their children. Even though Gabriela had a strong faith, it was still very difficult for her to hear of death as part of honor. She knew too that Jim not only talked of his Arizee faith, he actually lived it.

Even though it was heartbreaking, she took Jim's hand and whispered in his ear, "I will do what you wish, my love; but please tell me again that we will one day be in Heaven together."

Jim kissed her. "You are my wife and my love for eternity. We will always be together!"

Abotoe began chanting in Arizee as Gabriela hugged Jim, trying to understand what he must do.

In a later discussion, Dr. Freeman was again adamant that Jim not play. He told Jim repeatedly that he could make his condition worse or even die. Jim thanked him for his concern, but decided that he would play the remaining games of the World Series. Jim promised he would get treatment in St. Louis after the Series was over. Dr. Freeman thought Jim had an extremely dangerous plan, the outcome of which could be disastrous.

Newspapers all around the country reported about the phenomenal St. Louis player, Jim Eagleson, who was rushed to a New York hospital for an undisclosed illness. The papers said Jim was a 44 year old baseball player, the son of the famous Arizee chief, Lone Eagle. The chief was a man of peace and strongly believed that the Indian and the white man could live in harmony. To add spice to the story, it was reported that Lone Eagle was killed in an unprovoked attack by the army under the commanded of Gen. White, former owner of the Spartans. These stories were extremely accurate considering neither Jim, the Spartans, nor the hospital ever commented on the matter. A rumor spread that Jim's favorite public relations person, Abotoe, may have let a few of those facts slip out. This was no wonder since Abotoe was determined to do everything possible to have his Chief reach his destiny.

CHAPTER 69

Sports fans clamored for news about Jim's illness. They were determined to know about the Indian who exemplified the spirit of America. With Jim's insistence, the Spartans downplayed the morbid rumors that were circulating about the seriousness of his illness.

Jim left no doubt in both Joey Thompson and Coach L mind that he was going to be available to play ball in the next game, which was the sixth of the Series. Of course, Dr. Freeman continued to warn that any further aggravation of his condition could be fatal. Since the next game was in St. Louis, Dr. Freeman told Jim that he would contact Dr. Stanley Morgan, a trusted physician in St. Louis, and consult with him regarding Jim's medical condition and treatment. He said he felt certain that Dr. Morgan would be available to treat Jim when he arrived in St. Louis. Dr. Freeman insisted that Jim stay in the hospital until the evening he left for St. Louis.

While Jim was waiting to be discharged, he joked with the staff about his simple stomach ache and was congenial as ever, signing autographs for his admiring fans. "The Chief," as he now was called, had become a hero across the country. Both the fans and the reporters loved him. The New York and St. Louis newspapers along with others carried stories of his many trials and tribulations and how he had finally succeeded in his mid 40's in spite of almost impossible odds. Many stories reported that Jim was a role model for those who have been victims of discrimination touting the message that anyone can succeed in America with courage and determination. While Jim appreciated the accolades, he still felt that he had yet to prove to the American people and the President in Washington that Indians were equal to the white man.

Joey Thompson called a press conference in the lobby of the hospital and he, Coach L and Jim spoke briefly with reporters to assure the fans that he was ready to play in the remaining games of the Series. Even though Jim was still experiencing considerable pain, he stood up through the entire conference looking quite fit. After the press conference Joey, knowing full well about Jim's pain, told his star player that he had nothing else to prove.

"You are an exemplary human being and a hero to many, especially me. If you never play another game of baseball, you have served yourself and your people well."

Joey added, "Jim, if my father was alive today, he would advise you not play."

Jim replied, "Thanks Joey and I believe what you say about your father; but I still have more to do."

Even though Jim's pain was at times almost unbearable, he continued to ready himself to leave for St. Louis, and promised Gabriela he would check into the hospital as soon as the Series was over. In her heart she knew by then it may be too late, but nothing she said could change Jim's mind.

Jim's teammates heard the good news that Jim would return to finish out the Series. After the scary scene on the field in New York, the players were afraid that Jim would be out for the rest of the Series. The news that he would play was an energizer for players and fans alike.

When he arrived back in St. Louis, Jim insisted on going straight to Spartan Stadium, where he was met with a standing ovation from his teammates. Not since the day he left prison had Jim received such an outpouring of appreciation. What made this day so special was this appreciation came from white men.

In his humble way, he spoke to the players. "I must thank all of you in this room. It is my honor to know you and play ball with you. You have made me feel like an American, and I love each of you."

Abotoe, who had accompanied Jim to the stadium, helped him get dressed. He was weak and still in pain, but he never showed this to his teammates or the fans. When Jim joined the team for the pre game pep talk from Coach L, he stood straight as an arrow not giving any indication of physical pain or weakness. He did not want pity. He wanted and got their respect.

Game Six did not go as the Spartans had hoped. The Titans' domination started early. They scored six runs in the first three innings, hitting almost anything thrown by any pitcher. The Spartans' hitting was no better than their pitching. They managed to score only one run in nine innings. Final score 9-1, Titans. This tied the Series at three games apiece. Although Jim did not pitch, he did prove to be their best cheerleader, shouting encouragement from the dugout. After the game and a challenge to excellence by Coach L, Jim made sure each player knew that he had confidence in their ability to win Game Seven. Shortly after his effort to bolster the confidence of the team, Jim began to feel weaker. He tasted blood and wiped it from his lips. He quietly slipped out and went to the hospital out of view of the players, fans and reporters.

At the hospital Jim, pale and exhausted, was given more pain medicine and another blood transfusion by Dr. Morgan. Abotoe helped him get cleaned up for a visit from Gabriela. Jim did not want his wife to see the blood on his face.

Gabriela walked into the room and found Jim resting comfortably. She was surprised at how good he looked and had no idea of how much work had gone into this masquerade. She spent the night on a couch next to Jim while Abotoe, who knew much more than he told anyone, slept in a chair at the foot of the bed.

CHAPTER 70

The following morning, Jim woke prior to Gabriela. He slept well without needing any pain medication during the night. But when he tried to sit up, the pain once again ripped through his stomach. He also noticed blood around his mouth and on his shirt. He very quietly woke Abotoe who helped him change and wash his face and hands so Gabriela would not be frightened. Jim was determined to be brave in the presence of his wife. She deserved nothing less.

As Gabriela stirred, he said, "Hey beautiful! How is my wonderful wife this morning?"

She replied, "More importantly, how are you my brave husband? How did you sleep last night?"

"Very well, and I feel rested and ready to play ball."

Gabriela knew her husband too well. She did not for one minute believe Jim was telling her the whole story. He may have thought he was fooling her, but she could see the pain in his eyes and hear the strain in his voice.

When Dr. Morgan came in to check on his patient, Jim, anticipating warnings from the doctor, expressed his opinion on his own condition.

"Doc, don't give me that worried look. I can tell that you are a great medicine man, but you worry too much. I am as strong as the greatest grizzly bear and as sharp as the soaring hawk. I can feel my insides healing. I am ready for today's game. We will win and be the World Champion of baseball."

The doctor looked at both Jim and Gabriela. His tone was far too serious for Jim.

"I don't know you well but I can tell that you are courageous beyond description. Jim, your condition warrants rest. Too much exertion and you could begin to hemorrhage and even die. Why then do you want to risk all of that for a baseball game?"

Jim speaking in his strongest voice said, "I am honor bound to make sacrifices in order to be worthy of spending eternity with my father and mother. I have to prove that I can be a great leader among all men. Not to play would be considered cowardly by Arizee Indian standards, and I would leave this world in disgrace. I must do this so when my time comes I will be accepted in eternity as a great chief. I am not determined to die trying; but if it happens, then it is meant to be."

Dr. Morgan, seeing a strong mindset in Jim, then pleaded with Gabriela hoping she would convince Jim not to play. Gabriela spoke, but it was not what the doctor had hoped for.

"I understand your words of earthly wisdom, but Jim is no longer playing by earthly rules. I was born an Arizee, but only in recent years has my husband taught me what it means to be one. Jim feels it is his destiny to achieve personal honor and respect. And he feels that if he has to sacrifice himself, then so be it. In his mind, he now stands on that threshold, and I will not stand in his way. Therefore, I will let Jim make his own decision about his future including playing in the remaining World Series game."

Even though the doctor could see that Gabriela was a brave and intelligent woman, he did not understand her logic and told her so.

"I think you are both making a mistake, but I will heed your wishes and may God be with you in this troubling decision you have made!"

The doctor then left the room bewildered.

Jim smiled and said, "Gabriela, I love you and have never been more proud of you than I am today. Thank you for understanding and giving your blessing for me to pursue my destiny."

Abotoe walked over to Gabriela and held her hand and bowed in reverence for her words. He spoke, "Gabriela, I am honored to serve the wife of a great man. Like the glorious Arizee women of our nation, you're willing to sacrifice your most loved one for the sake of his noble destiny."

After bowing her head to Abotoe in appreciation of his words, she turned to Jim and said, "I love you too much to stand in your way. I spoke those words because I am praying that you will manage to get through this last game and then come back to the hospital for treatment. I still have hope for a long life with you. If not, you have promised we will spend eternity together."

Jim took her face in his hands and looked deeply into her teary eyes. "The doctor is just being cautious. I am not as sick as he thinks. But I promise you as God is my witness, should I not make it through the game, I will be waiting for you, and we will be together for all of eternity."

The time arrived for Jim and Abotoe to leave the hospital to get ready for the seventh and final game of the World Series. Jim knew this could very well be the most significant day of his life in pursuing his destiny. When they stepped into the busy dressing room, each player prepared for the day in his own way. They felt the pressure of a world watching to see which team was victorious.

As Jim greeted his teammates, he handed each one a small American flag, asking them to wave the flags after the National Anthem.

Speaking to his teammates, he said. "We are going to be America's team. We are good Americans, and we will play not only for our fans and ourselves, but most important our country." He paused and then continued, "Today we won't play baseball as an Indian or white man, but as Americans."

Even though this seemed a little corny had it come from any other player, coming from Jim, it was inspirational. Here was an Indian pledging to win for the country that had time and again tried to destroy him.

Coach L arrived to give his pre game pep talk and asked. "What's with the flags?"

Joe Dominic spoke up saying, "Jim gave them to us."

Coach, smiling with pride and admiration said, "This man never ceases to amaze and inspire me!" Then getting down to the business at hand, Coach said, "It has all come down to this last game, and each of you knows what it takes to win this game. You'll have to stay alert, try your hardest, and play your best. So let's go out their and kick some Titan butt!"

The team gave a loud "Hoorah" and left to face their destiny, chanting "Spartans, Spartans, Spartans!"

After the playing of the National Anthem, the Spartans waved their flags. The hometown crowd went wild. Even after their players had returned to the dugout, the fans remained standing, showing their appreciation to the team.

Jim looked in the box seats reserved for the families. He saw Gabriela who looked deeply worried. He knew that she, too, was feeling pain. He smiled and blew her a kiss.

CHAPTER 71

It was an unusually hot and humid afternoon in St. Louis as the final game of the Series got underway. Temperatures were in the 90's and the sun was directly overhead. Game Seven began much like Game One. Titan's took an early lead and going into the fifth inning had expanded the lead to 4-0. The Spartans were able to scrape out one run in the both the fifth and sixth innings. Then with one man on second base, Joe Dominic hit a seventh inning homerun to tie the score. Chris Erickson, the young reliever, had been pitching since the sixth inning and had successfully shutdown the powerful Titan batters. Chris looked at Jim as his mentor. So before each inning he reviewed the Titan batters with Jim and Joe Dominic to set a strategy for striking them out.

Before the last out of the eighth inning, Chris was hit in his leg with a hard line drive. He managed to finish the inning, but limped off the field with a badly bruised right thigh. Neither team had scored in the eighth inning, so going into the ninth the score remained tied. Coach L had to make a decision and make it fast. The crowd was now chanting "Chief, Chief" expecting the coach to put Jim in the game. Coach L looked at Jim who was doing his best to appear fit in spite of his pain. Considering Jim's poor health, his decision was obvious. He decided to see if Chris could squeak through the inning. Feeling that he owed Jim an explanation for not using him, he moved down the bench and explained his strategy.

"Let's see if Chris still has his stuff. If he doesn't, you get the call."

"I'm with you on whatever you decide to do. I'm ready to pitch when you need me!"

Coach then told Jim to warm up in case he was needed. Jim went to the bullpen and started throwing some warm-up pitches. The practice helped to loosen up his arm, but not without a struggle.

In the top of the ninth, the Titans' lead off hitter singled up the middle. The second batter walked on four straight pitches. Coach L called a time out to talk with his pitcher.

"Son, how do you feel? Do you think you can get these next guys out?"

Looking exhausted and favoring his painful right leg, he said, "Coach, I feel fine. I think I can get the next batter out to win the Series."

Coach knew Chris was in trouble. There were no outs, and he needed to get three batters out.

"Boy, you got three batters left—are you sure you are alright?"

Chris, no longer able to hide his exhaustion, said, "Coach I'm tired. My leg is aching, and I can't seem to focus on the signals from Joe!"

That was it. Chris was finished for the day. Coach L looked at his bullpen and saw Jim warming up. His natural instinct was to call Jim, but he hesitated knowing the state of his health. The umpire yelled, telling Coach to get on with the game. He waved for his right hander Jim Eagleson. As Chris left the field he received gracious applause from the hometown fans.

When he met Jim, who was on his way to the mound, Chris hugged him. "You are my inspiration and my hero."

Jim grabbed Chris' hand and raised it over his head signifying that he considered the young pitcher a hero. Chris in turn applauded Jim as did the Spartan fans that were now standing in recognition of Jim, chanting "Chief, Chief." Jim tipped his hat and stepped on the mound.

Joe Dominic and Coach L were there waiting for him.

Coach said, "Let me guess, Jim. You wanna pitch."

"You damn right; give me the ball. I'm gonna get these suckers out!"

Coach got up close to Jim and whispered. "If I see any sign that you are in pain, I'm gonna pull you. Understand?"

Jim nodded in agreement, as he vowed to himself that Coach would not see his pain and the only way he was leaving the game was horizontally.

With two runners already on base, Jim faced the third batter in the lineup. He hit a well placed bunt down the third base line that Jim retrieved and threw to first for an out, however, the runners moved up to second and third bases. A single would give the Titans a two run lead. The heat and humidity were intense. Jim wiped sweat from his face with a handkerchief. As he was putting it back in his pocket, he noticed blood on it. In spite of that, he retired the next batter on three straight strikes. Two Out! Next up was the league leading homerun hitter. He swung wildly at the first two knuckleballs, but made good contact on Jim's fastball. He hit a line drive directly to Jim who caught the ball for out number three. The crowd exploded chanting, "Chief, Chief, Chief!"

Unfortunately for Jim, the ball was hit so hard that its impact was felt through the glove and into his stomach. The pain was excruciating and Jim could taste the warm blood as it leaked from the corners of his mouth. He turned quickly away from the dugout and wiped his mouth clean. He discretely stuffed the bloodied handkerchief in his pocket, out of sight. With the side retired, Jim walked back to the dugout. On his way, he was congratulated by his teammates and received a standing ovation from the fans. He tried to avoid eye contact with Gabriela or Abotoe. He knew they would see his anguish and did not want them to worry. Coach L sat down next to Jim.

"How ya doing, Jim? I saw that line drive right to your stomach."

Jim said, "Just had a little of the wind knocked out of me—nothing that a win won't fix."

Jim was still able to conceal the bleeding from his mouth by sipping water and constantly wiping his sweaty face. His pain was intensifying, but he willed himself to go on. Jim was up fourth in the final inning. Even with his age, Coach L knew Jim was a damn good hitter, probably one of the best. But he wondered if his star reliever was in any condition to hit. Jim insisted he was, even as warm blood continued to pool in his mouth. He was masking his condition superbly. Taking Jim at his word, Coach decided to let him bat.

The Spartans' first hitter nailed a fastball down the third base line for a stand up double. The second batter dropped a sacrifice bunt in front of home plate. With no play at third, the pitcher threw the runner out at first. There was only one out and a runner on third. The next man hit a line drive that was snagged by the second baseman, stealing what would have been the hit to bring in the World Series winning run. With a runner on third and two outs, the Titans brought in their best reliever to pitch to Jim. As he slowly approached the batter's box, Jim repeated a phrase that gave him comfort. "When things are at their worst, I must be brave and at my very best." His father always said that there was none braver than an Arizee warrior.

He once again wiped the blood from his lips and readied himself for the pitch. The first pitch was low for ball one. Jim swung painfully on the next ball and hit it foul. The swing was such a strain on Jim that he stepped out of the batter's box and wiped the beads of sweat from his hot sticky face. The combination of the intense heat and pain were taking a toll on Jim. Coach L, sensing that Jim may be in trouble, called time out to talk with him.

Jim tried once more to mask his pain. "Coach, this heat is really something."

"It's not just the heat Jim. We both know it. I'm taking you out. You're too sick to be here. You need to leave the game. If not for the team, then do it for Gabriela."

Jim looked at his coach and pleaded. "I know I got it in me to win this game. Please let me finish. I won't let the team down. Then I will go back to the hospital for treatment. Just give me this chance."

Coach L mulled over this request until he was interrupted by the umpire's strong urging to start playing ball again. He was tired of this umpire telling him the obvious.

He yelled back, "Will you please give me a minute. This is the damn World Series!"

"No kidding. Hurry up or I will throw you and your batter out of the game!"

Coach L looked at Jim. "Okay Jim, I know you are bound and determined to be in that batter's box, so I'll let you stay in for just one more swing. After that, for your own good and that of your family, I am taking you out. We all love you too much—this World Series is not worth you life."

Jim smiled and nodded a thank you to his friend.

When he got back in his stance, the third base coach signaled for Jim to hit away. However, Jim noticed that all the infielders were deep in their respective positions, no doubt waiting for this old man to strike out. Confidence showed in the pitcher's posture as well. Although Jim's body was weak, his brain was just fine. He knew that a bunt down the third base line would catch the Titan's completely off guard. He stepped out of the batter's box and signaled his intentions to the third base coach who relayed it to the runner. Coach L saw the coach's signal, but it was too late for him to call a time out. Jim was back in the box waiting for the next pitch.

As expected the pitcher went into a short windup and released the ball. With the third base runner charging toward the plate, Jim dropped a perfectly executed bunt down the third base line. By the time the third baseman got to the ball, the runner on third had crossed home plate, but Jim was struggling to reach first base. The third baseman scooped up the ball and with his powerful throwing arm hurled it to the first baseman. The blood from his mouth splattered his jersey as he struggled to get to first base before the ball. His legs were giving way under him. He knew he could only reach first base if he dived head first. As he closed in on his target, with his last bit of energy, he hurled his body forward, slamming his stomach on first base only a split second before the ball was caught. The first base umpire signaled "safe!" The Spartans won the World Series! The hometown crowd, players and coaches roared with excitement. Fans spilled onto the field. Once again, Jim was the hero. The players ran from the dugout in celebration. But when the dust cleared, Jim was motionless on first base, his uniform covered with dirt and blood. An uneasy hush settled over the stadium as the team doctor and Coach L ran to first base. The blood that had accumulated in Jim's mouth made it almost impossible for him to talk. He was put on a stretcher to be taken to the hospital.

With sweat washing away the blood on his face, Jim barely whispered, "Who Won?"

Coach replied, "We won. And Chief Eagleson won, too!"

Jim smiled, "Then today is a good day."

Jim dug deep for the energy to wave at the crowd as players from both teams stood still and applauded him. As Gabriela reached him, she held his hand tightly and heard his whispering, "I did it father, I did it." Jim slipped into unconsciousness as the ambulance went screaming through the streets of St. Louis.

CHAPTER 72

When Jim regained consciousness several hours later in the hospital, it was dark outside, but his room was flooded with light. Nurses were busily attending to him. He thought he heard Dr. Morgan, but found it difficult to focus on what he was saying.

Gabriela was sitting next to him softly crying and calling his name. "Jim, Jim, this is Gabriela, I love you."

Jim was groggy and struggled to speak, "Even though you are a little fuzzy, you are still beautiful. Give me a little smile."

Through her tears, Gabriela managed to smile at her husband.

"How is our baby?"

"Our baby is just fine."

The nurse then advised Gabriela not to talk to Jim as he needed rest.

Jim looked at the nurse and said, "Please, let her talk. She's what I need right now."

Just then Jim was struck with excruciating pain in his stomach. Blood appeared on his lips and his coughing spewed blood over his sheets. The nurse elevated his head to prevent him from choking. Jim could barely catch his breath, and he struggled to maintain consciousness. The doctor ordered an injection for pain, and he began to breathe more slowly and fell into a deep sleep. Dr. Morgan addressed Gabriela telling her that Jim was in grave condition, but his vital signs remained stable.

While Jim slept, Dr. Morgan asked to speak with Gabriela in his office. She asked Abotoe to come with her. She feared that anything the doctor had to say would not be good, and felt she would need Abotoe's support. After all he was an Arizee spiritual man and Jim's close friend.

Before the doctor could speak, Gabriela bravely addressed him. "I want to thank you for everything you have done for Jim. I truly appreciate your concern. I want to hear that my husband will be okay with rest and treatment, but I fear he is most likely dying. I struggle to understand what I am going to tell you, but I must respect Jim's beliefs. His religious convictions are strong. Jim feels that

Abotoe has religious powers that can help him go to meet his father. He must be there when Jim dies to open the pathway to the spiritual world. My husband has spent much of his life preparing for this moment when his soul will pass into eternity. He is not afraid."

Dr. Morgan apologized for his inexperience in understanding their religious convictions. He told Gabriela that she was correct in her conclusion that Jim was dying saying that tests revealed he has advanced stomach cancer, which was aggravated by excessive alcohol consumption.

Gabriela closed her eyes and bit her bottom lip in an attempt to control her emotions. The terrible disease had struck again. Once again staking claim to her husband.

"Gabriela, I am so sorry. His heart is weakened and his overall health poor, no doubt from the many physical hardships he has experienced. Jim's body is worn out. The likelihood of his survival for more than a few days, or even hours, is slim. I will make him as comfortable as possible for as long as he has the strength to fight the disease. I want you to know that in my many years in medicine that I have never seen one as brave and reconciled to his fate as your husband. He has lived these past few months on borrowed time. How he survived and won a World Series defies all that I know about medicine and is frankly phenomenal. Jim is an extraordinary man. I know now why all those who love him including family, friends, fans call him Chief. I do hope he knows how special he is!"

Gabriela and Abotoe both remained stoic. Gabriela showed more bravery than she thought she had. But then, she had to be strong for Jim.

She thanked the doctor for his kind and true words about her husband.

Dr. Morgan offered her his sympathy and apologized for not being able to save Jim.

"You don't need to apologize, doctor. My husband is not an easy man to understand. His life has been shaped by his religious conviction and determination to achieve what he felt was his destiny. I very much believe that Jim has proven himself to be a chief. You have acknowledged such by your words of this greatness. His mother and father would be pleased and their approval is important to Jim. He will die in peace with Abotoe to guide his soul to reunite with his parents."

Dr. Morgan said he would cooperate in anyway possible so as not to interfere with the peaceful passing of such a great man. Abotoe left to be with Jim, and Gabriela stayed with the doctor. She closed the door as if she had another thought to pass on to Dr. Morgan. Before she could speak, she broke down in tears. While her heritage allowed her to understand Jim's spirituality, the reality of his passing deeply tore at her heart. Dr Morgan hugged Gabriela trying to comfort her.

As tears fell down her cheek, she whispered, "Our baby will never know his father. What am I to do?"

"Gabriela, you will be strong and brave just like this great chief. The child will know his father through your stories of him. You will talk of his bravery, strength and his honor. You will tell the child how Jim played America's game and how he defied the odds to become one of the best and most beloved players."

Dr. Morgan glanced out of his office window and saw Joey Thompson. Looking at the anguish in Gabriela's eyes, he said, "There is someone waiting at my door who loves Jim very much. I understand that Jim is his hero. He can help you."

Gabriela averted her eyes to the door and saw Joey with his head hung down to hide his teary eyes. She opened the door, then she and Joey left to be with Jim.

CHAPTER 73

Jim was still sleeping when Joey and Gabriela arrived. Gabriela left for a moment to check on Jake, who had been asking about his father. Jim woke while she was gone and immediately began asking about her.

"Is she ok? What about the baby?"

Joey explained that she had just stepped out to see Jake and that she would be back soon.

Jim sighed deeply and saw Abotoe praying as he held his hand. Jim spoke to him in Arizee. Abotoe paused for a moment, opened his eyes and looked at Jim. His reply in Arizee seemed to give Jim comfort.

When Gabriela walked back into Jim's room, she went to his bed and kissed him gently on his cheek. She motioned to Abotoe to continue his prayers as Jim slipped into a deep sleep once again. His conscious world was fading, and Jim seemed to be passing into another place.

Joey leaned toward Gabriela and asked her what Abotoe had said to Jim. "He told Jim that the baby and I were safe and that his father, Lone Eagle, was preparing for him. This pleased Jim, as he needs the spirit of his father to guide him to God."

All of this was so new to Joey. Gabriela had told him that she was part Arizee, but had not lived as an Arizee. He was amazed at Gabriela's understanding and respect for Arizee religion and afterlife. While Jim slept, Joey asked Gabriela about the religion of the Arizee Indians.

Gabriela held Jim's hand as she talked with Joey. "I don't remember much before I was adopted by my parents. It was Jim who reawakened the religion as taught to me by my mother. Though Indians in general are looked upon by many as savages, we are in most cases a deeply religious people. Religious education is taught at an early age so that the child can understand and begin to prepare for the life cycle."

He was amazed by this religious perspective. This was all so new to him.

Joey shook his head. "How ironic, the white man believes it is God's will that he should convert the Indian to Christianity so that his heathen soul will be saved."

Then with a little smile on his face he continued, "I think the white man will be surprised when he meets an Arizee already in Heaven!"

Gabriela returned the smile. Cradling Jim's hand in her lap she said, "Joey it is good that you consider Jim's religion. Like your father, who did so much for my people, you must take this message to the people of this country. Once the truth is accepted, this country will be a better place."

"Well maybe we can do that together, in honor of Jim."

Gabriela smiled saying, "Maybe so; yes, maybe so."

For the next two days, Jim woke intermittently, asking for Gabriela. As always she was at his side. Once his vision focused and he saw her, he would smile and slip back to sleep.

His sleep was peaceful and intermingled with his dream of long ago. He was on a donkey riding in a large field surrounded by many Indians to his right and white men to his left. Jim was in a baseball uniform riding on a small donkey in the middle of the field. This time they were not readying for battle. Both Indian and white man alike showed great respect for Jim and were chanting, "Chief, Chief, Chief." He turned to the Indians and saw his father leading many braves. On the other side were John Thompson and Jacob. A very young Joey walked from behind his father holding a ball and bat. Jim rode up to little Joey who handed him the ball and bat. His father and John Thompson met him in the middle of the field and said "Job well done."

Around ten in the morning of the third day, Jim awoke and asked Gabriela to come close so he could tell her something important. He was clearly in great pain and blood stained his lips.

His throat was sore and irritated from the cough and blood. He spoke barely above a whisper.

"My beautiful Gabriela, I have seen my father. I will die soon."

Overhearing this Joey rushed to get Dr. Morgan.

Gabriela spoke gently reassuring Jim. "Yes, Jim, your time is coming. I will be fine. You must go to your father."

Abotoe, sensing that Jim's body was about to release his soul, continued to pray as the doctor and nurse worked to stabilize him. Jim once again rested peacefully, but Abotoe knew it had nothing to do with the feverish work of the doctor. It was the sweet song that Gabriela was humming. It was the lullaby that Jim's mother sang to him as a small child.

Jim opened his eyes but could barely see.

He whispered to both Gabriela and Abotoe. "I have been with my father, and he is pleased with me. He told me that I had proven myself to be a chief among men. And my mother was there, too. Her smile radiated approval upon me." Jim struggled to continue. "Gabriela, tell our children of their father. Tell them I will always love them. Give Jake my father's pipe and tell him it belonged to Jim Eagleson, Son of Lone Eagle, and Chief of the Arizee Indians." Jim appeared to sleep once again, but opened his eyes and said, "Tell our little daughter of her father. She will be proud."

When Gabriela heard Jim speak of a daughter, she gasped and wondered if Jim had seen her little soul as well.

Abotoe stopped praying and reassured Jim.

"Go, go to them. God, too, is pleased with you. You body will release the soul from its earthly abode and will pass on to Heaven for eternity. I love you, my brother."

Gabriela kissed Jim's hand. "I love you, Jim. I will let you go to eternity"

Jim struggled to smile. "Gabriela, I love you, too. Please give my love to Jake and our baby. Don't be sad. I am entering paradise. I will wait for you until we can be together once again."

Abotoe spoke first in Arizee, then English, the words of passage for Jim Eagleson, Son of Lone Eagle; "As sure as the Arizona sun rises in the sky, so does this Arizona son rise to his father."

Surrounded by his friends, as Gabriela held his hand, Jim took a deep breath that was his last. His body was still, but his soul was dancing with Lone Eagle. God had rewarded this extraordinary man.

Jim had followed the request of Gabriela and turned the cheek to his many adversities all the time playing the game of life as he did the game of baseball; with determination, courage and honor.

EPILOGUE

Jim Eagleson was a chief among all men. He accomplished this through the great American game of baseball. Men like Jim helped pave the way for baseball to become an avenue to success for many Americans without regard to race, creed or color.

Jim's performance was so extraordinary that his fame was truly worldwide. No player in the minds of baseball fans had sacrificed as much just to play the game of baseball. But to Jim it was more than just playing the game. He was voted the Most Valuable Player of his one and only World Series and received a permanent plaque in the St. Louis stadium commemorating his contribution to baseball. He was later enshrined into the St Louis Baseball Hall of Fame even though he appeared in only five major league games. His contribution to those five games was equal to players whose careers were measured in decades. As a final tribute to their beloved Jim Eagleson, the St. Louis Spartans changed their name to the St. Louis Chiefs.

Just as Jim said, Gabriela had a beautiful baby girl she named Jamie, in honor of her father. As she and Jake grew to be adults, they joined Joey Thompson in the ownership and management of the St. Louis baseball organization.

Abotoe, Jim's big Arizee friend, mourned his death for many years. To honor his friend he and Gabriela formed baseball leagues for Indian children who, thanks to Jim Eagleson, might have an opportunity to one day play professional baseball.

Gabriela and Joey remained close friends and eventually married. They worked tirelessly on their crusade to better the understanding between the white man and the Indian.

Until her death at the age of 88 when Jim greeted her to eternity, Gabriela recounted the story of Jim Eagleson, the great Chief, who lived his life as he died, with pride and conviction. He was a proud, yet humble man, confident of his destiny. He played the game of life, with honor, and he earned respect from all who knew of him. Jim's legacy will live forever in the voices of those who speak his name; the people who knew him and those who hear his story. A flame as bright as Jim can never fade away.

Also available from PublishAmerica

THE MAGIC COTTAGE
by Hannah Greer

Eight-year-old twins Asa and Prentiss Fallmark are spending the summer with their grandparents. Grammy and Papa set a goal for the month-long vacation: the twins are to investigate and stretch their imaginations without the use of television, electronic gadgets, or radio. Each morning, the siblings board their "imagination transporter" at the top of a hill adjacent to their grandparents' home. The twins have remarkable adventures in the land they call Serendipity where they "build" the magic cottage and meet many new friends who provide them with mystical gifts. The children become integral parts of exciting experiences in which they must use their minds and imaginations to overcome conflict. Scientific studies they learned in school develop special meanings as they explore Serendipity. Hints occur throughout the story that the grandparents know more about Serendipity than the children realize. Could it be that Grammy and Papa have magical powers?

Paperback, 132 pages
5.5" x 8.5"
ISBN 1-60672-190-9

About the author:

Hannah Greer has embraced writing since she was a child. As an educator and founder of an experiential school, she guided underachievers to utilize their imaginations. Teaming up with her illustrator sister, Tica Greer, a new series of books based on exciting adventures, *The Velvet Bag Memoirs*, has been born.

Available to all bookstores nationwide.
www.publishamerica.com

Also available from PublishAmerica

HOTEL TRANSYLVANIA

by Michael T.G. Yepes

This is a novel about exiles, refugees and immigrants. The time is the early 18th century; the scene is Paris. The location is a gambling establishment of dubious reputation—the Hotel de Transylvania. Situated on the Seine embankment, across the Louvre, a group of Hungarian expatriates support themselves on their good looks, charm, guile and political connection. This establishment is run by the grey eminence of the Abbé Brenner, under the protection of the exiled Prince of Transylvania. This is the story of the denizens of that hotel from 1713 to 1717. It is about being a foreigner, yet crafty and adaptable; it is about entering a new social environment, and succeeding or failing in Europe's most glamorous and exciting city. And it is also a reflection on a society that was rapidly emerging from the rigid rule of Louis XIV to the expanding freedoms under the Orléans regency. In the background, there is the still-smouldering conflict between the Jesuits and Jansenists. The sacred and the profane, constantly juxtaposed and confronting each other, in an environment of fabulous wealth and painful poverty—and four young men absorbing it all.

Paperback, 210 pages
5.5" x 8.5"
ISBN 1-4241-5219-4

About the author:

Michael T.G. Yepes was born in Budapest, Hungary, and came to the U.S. in 1956, after the Hungarian Revolution. He had received his secondary and college education in Budapest, and graduated from Medical School in San Francisco. A life-long interest in history and literature lead him to the California Missions, and eventually to the Jesuits on the California Peninsula. M.T.G. Yepes is married and lives with his wife in West Los Angeles. They have three adult children and 7 grandchildren.

Available to all bookstores nationwide.
www.publishamerica.com